Glory Be

Glory Be

A GLORY BROUSSARD MYSTERY

DANIELLE ARCENEAUX

PEGASUS CRIME

NEW YORK LONDON

GLORY BE

Pegasus Crime is an imprint of
Pegasus Books, Ltd.
148 West 37th Street, 13th Floor
New York, NY 10018

Copyright © 2023 by Danielle Arceneaux

First Pegasus Books cloth edition October 2023

Library of Congress Cataloging-in-Publication Data is available.

ISBN: 978-1-63936-483-1

10 9 8 7 6 5 4 3 2 1

Printed in the United States of America
Distributed by Simon & Schuster
www.pegasusbooks.com

For Barbara Arceneaux

Glory Broussard was tired of waiting. She figured this barista was new, and she would know since she was a regular at CC's Coffee House. With each drink order, he nodded and flipped through the pages of a thick manual, going back and forth between the espresso machine and the book.

It didn't help that he was grinning like a goddamn fool at that white woman. She was wearing a pink ribbed tank top, and as far as Glory could tell, no bra. Her jean shorts were so scant that you could see the bottom curve of her ass. Glory had seen enough of this recently at the Acadiana Mall to know it was not an accident but a trend, and a disgraceful one at that. Wet hair crept down to her waist, making her look like a creature that had crawled out of the Atchafalaya swamp.

Glory edged up to the counter, closely behind the braless woman. "Excuse me," she said to the barista. "Are you the only one working behind the counter? Y'all should be better staffed for the after-church crowd."

"I'm not sure. I'm new here."

"Clearly." She wiped the sweat from her forehead, a useless gesture in Louisiana this time of year.

"Be with you as soon as I can," he said, knocking a quart of milk onto the floor.

Glory squinted at the man, but since it was Sunday, she decided to summon her inner reserves of charity and bite her lip. The woman with the exposed derriere turned around. She scanned Glory's red dress, red shoes, and red hat with a jaunty, dyed-to-match ostrich plume, covered her mouth, and snickered. Earlier that morning, Glory had attended a breakfast with the Acadiana Red Hat Society, a group of pious, black Catholic women. Most of them had stayed for the group's special benediction with Father Romero after regular mass. Now that he was practically famous, those women flapped around him like a bunch of flightless birds. But Glory didn't have time for that. Sundays were when she made her money, and she had to get to work.

Maybe that derisive little laugh wasn't aimed at her all-red ensemble but at the essence of Glory herself. If she fluffed her hair just right and her makeup was squared away, she could still see herself as Miss Lafayette, colored division winner. But nowadays most people could only see the old. Melanin had been a barrier against the worst ravages of time, but black does eventually crack. The lines around her face and mouth had finally settled in, as lines do. And since the contentious divorce, the expanse of her hips had widened thanks to too many plate dinners. The hot plates at Dwight's Family Restaurant were cold comfort for the humiliation.

The barista working Glory's last nerve wasn't the only thing that was new at CC's Coffee House that morning. She eyed a slew of changes that had somehow been made since last Sunday. New uniforms. Merchandise for sale. For Christ's sake, what the heck was going on? Why can't folks leave good enough alone? Glory walked up to the counter, just beside the woman, to get a closer look at the sales display. She inspected the new navy mugs with puffy gold letters and shook her head. With one hand she opened her purse, and with the other she slowly lowered the mug inside, letting it fall to the bottom with her lip gloss and losing scratch-offs.

The woman who had been flirting with the new barista tossed her head back in laughter. Her wet hair slapped Glory's face, clinging to her left cheek like plastic wrap.

"Excuse me," Glory yelled, scraping the hair off her face in disgust.

"Sorry . . . didn't see you there." Given Glory's size, it was uncanny how many people chose not to see her.

Noah Singleton, the owner of CC's Coffee House, swung open the kitchen door and walked into the cafe. Glory had known him since he was a teenager with an Afro, but now he looked like the disciplined Marine he once was: squared-off hairstyle, thick neck, and efficient movement.

"Miss Glory, go ahead and take a seat while my new employee prepares your usual. Cappuccino." He nodded to the man behind the counter. He walked her to her usual spot, a simple wooden table and chair in the back corner of the coffee shop, which she liked because it gave her a clear view of the front door. Someone in her chosen profession never wanted to be startled from behind.

"Thank you," Glory said as she sat down on the pine chair. "Honestly, you have to train these people before you put them on the floor. On a Sunday, no less."

"I'm working on it. Not a lot of time to work with this one—just got him on a work release program a few days ago."

3

Her eyes widened. "You and your felons. I swear, Noah Singleton, I will never get how your brain operates. You're one of the few black business owners in all of Lafayette, and you go and hire a jailbird. Makes no sense, if you ask me."

"Ain't no one asking you," he said, wiping her table with a damp cloth.

"I know you have a soft spot for these hard cases, especially after everything with your daughter." She sighed. "But you ought to have more sense than to have some jailbird behind your cash register. You're letting a fox run wild in the henhouse."

"I've had no problems with the man—whose name is Gus, by the way," he said. "And besides, everyone deserves a second chance. Even you."

"*Me?* I have no idea what you're referring to. I am a proper Catholic woman in good standing at St. Agnes of Lafayette, located at the corner of love and mercy. And the Vatican, for that matter."

His eyes narrowed, and a powerful laugh rose from his belly. "Glory, I done seen you steal my mug," he said, gesturing to her bulging handbag and collecting his breath. "The only thief around here is you. But you know what? Keep it. Because that's how real Christian charity works. And you of all people, judging this man, with the dirty you bring here every Sunday."

Glory reached inside her purse, pulled out the mug, and pushed it across the table. "Here. Keep your damn ticky tacky." She leaned toward him. "You should be grateful this coffee shop is my office. Most of your Sunday clientele is here for *me*—not your watery coffee."

Noah slung the dish towel over his shoulder and shook his head. "You're insulting my coffee now?"

"I don't know why you need new mugs, anyway. Ain't nothing wrong with the old ones."

Noah shrugged. "Millennials love branding. Gotta stay relevant." He turned around to greet the Sunday crowd that was now trickling in—shaking hands and fist-bumping with a few kids—before disappearing to the kitchen.

A tall slender man dressed in dark dress pants and a long-sleeved polo, despite the late-summer humidity, strolled toward Glory's table. "You're that Broussard lady, right? The bookie that everyone at the casino recommended?" Crinkles from his eyes fanned over his face, which was leathered by the sun. His hair was carefully styled like one of those gay men on that makeover show she watched, but even Glory knew you couldn't make those kinds of assumptions anymore.

"I *might* know someone who can help you out, but I don't reckon knowing your name, son. I need to do a proper vetting with anyone I do business with."

"I'm a Benoit."

"There's about a million Benoits in Louisiana. You're going to have to be a little more specific."

"Oh, come on." He laughed. "Don't act like you don't know my family."

She was coy but knew full well which family he meant. There was the Benoit Medical Center of Lafayette and Benoit Stadium, not to mention Benoit Construction & Chemical Company. Everyone in town knew the Benoits whether they wanted to or not.

"My name is Keller Benoit," he said. He sat down across from Glory and extended his hand. "What's the money line on Tulane?"

It's not like Glory wanted to shake the man's hand, but what else was she supposed to do? Despite his questionable vibes, she'd had better home training than that. "I might know someone who will take that bet for you," said Glory, in a voice dripping with honey and sarcasm. "Minus 120."

He reached into his back pocket, pulled out his wallet, and started flipping through bills. "I'll take a dime." He plunked down ten crisp hundred-dollar bills on the table.

Glory smiled, then turned her head to one side and then the other. She took her purse off her lap and set it on top of the money. Smile intact, she said, "Child, that is not how business is done around here, you hear me?" She took a sip of her cappuccino, then whispered, "Next time, the money goes in an envelope. Don't put my name on it and don't seal it, so I can count it."

She pulled her purse, and the money beneath it, closer to her and let them both fall on her lap. She pulled out a royal-blue leather journal and scribbled in it.

"We good?" he asked, looking at the door and itching to go.

"We good." As he stood up, Glory grabbed his sweater sleeve. "And next time, I would appreciate it if you made some chitchat. Buy some coffee. Support a local small business. I know your mama taught you better."

She released her grip on his shirt, and he walked out, but not before running straight into Beau Landry. Even though Lieutenant Landry was in uniform, Keller Benoit barely acknowledged him or the collision. He stormed toward his flashy sports car, shooing away two kids leaning on the hood of his banana-yellow convertible and snapping selfies with their cell phones.

Like everyone that day, Lieutenant Landry got his coffee after Gus consulted his training manual. Landry's silvery hair was cropped short, and his pastel-blue eyes jumped out against his swarthy skin. He was white the way a lot of people in Louisiana were white, with a drop of something wicked from generations ago.

With a paper coffee cup in hand—emblazoned with the new logo—he walked over to Glory's table and sat down.

"What's going on with all the new stuff inside here today? I see Noah did some spiffing up." He crinkled the cellophane of an individually wrapped piece of praline candy. Tiny crumbs of browned butter and pecans fell onto the table as he bit into the sugary confection.

"Something about marketing," she said, waving her hand toward the merchandise.

"Funny seeing you here. I was just thinking about your mama the other day."

Glory's mother, Viola Williams Broussard, was the grand dame of Carencro, Louisiana. For nearly forty years, she worked as the help for several families and raised generations of children, including Lieutenant Landry. She didn't suffer, not with that big old stroke. When her funeral came around, more than twenty of the kids she'd raised, grown-ups by then, came and showed their respect at Blessed Sacrament for mass. Sister Amity Gay, who was as much a daughter to her as Glory was, led a rosary in Creole at the wake. Even Cardinal Johnson was dispatched for the service.

"They don't make them like that anymore," he said, recoiling when his lips grazed the scalding coffee. He lowered the volume on his police radio, which was more active than usual that morning. "I hate to say it, but she was more of a mother figure than my own mama."

Glory tapped his hand. "Remember when I'd babysit you and put curlers in your hair? You sure did howl."

"I wish I had enough hair to put in curlers now," he said, raking his hand through his hair from back to front. "Sure do miss that woman. And I know how much you miss her, how hard it's been on you with everything else."

She nodded, then stared out the window to try to suppress the flow of tears that came whenever someone brought up her mother. As it turns out, tears aren't just a physical reaction, but a feeling. Lieutenant Landry's radio continued to squawk.

Requesting available units near Bonaire and Highland to respond to a 911 call about a deceased woman at 361 Bonaire, apartment 6J. Possible suicide. Any nearby units, please respond.

"Sure was good to see you, Glory, but I . . ."

Glory stood up. "Amity."

"Glory, I don't know what you're . . ."

"That address on the radio. That's my friend. That can't be . . ." She took a step but went woozy, gripping the table for support. The blue mug with gold lettering crashed to the floor, smattering into chunks and shards. Noah Singleton raced over, and both men grabbed an arm to help her back into the chair.

"I'm going. I *need* to go. That's my best friend."

"It must be someone else. Anyways, you can't drive in this condition, Miss Glory," said Lieutenant Landry. "You just about fainted."

"I know the address. You can't stop me."

Repeat, request available units near Bonaire and Highland . . .

Lieutenant Landry grabbed his radio. "Lieutenant Landry here, car 12. I'm in the vicinity." He looked at Noah. "Take her."

Glory gripped the straps of her handbag as tight as a jockey holding a horse's reins, but no matter. Her hands shook with anticipatory grief. She thought about everything they shared as girls, from dances down at the church fair to that time Principal Thibideaux slapped both their hands with rulers for passing notes during class.

And then she thought about everything they had shared as women, from Glory's surprise pregnancy and unwanted husband to Amity's college graduation, her novitiate training at St. Agnes, and then a different kind of vow, one to God. At first, Glory's jealousy had boiled over as she saw her friend achieve so many of the things she wanted for herself but were out of reach. But eventually, the anger and resentment boiled down to its purest, strongest form, until all that remained was love.

First-responder vehicles congested the parking lot of Amity's redbrick apartment building. Without thinking, Glory flung open the door of Noah's Honda Civic and ran to the scene. She dodged through the police cars and ambulances and eventually made her way to the yellow crime scene tape, breathless.

"No, ma'am, not beyond the tape," said the young police officer.

She caught the eye of Lieutenant Landry, who was already huddling with a pack of cops at the landing of the metal stairs.

Glory grabbed his attention. "Let me in, Landry."

"I'm sorry. Only next of kin."

"I am next of kin. I'm the only family she has left."

He walked up to the police tape. "I want you to think real hard about this, Miss Glory. If you see this, you can't unsee it. This will be the last memory you have of your friend. Is this what you want?"

"I need to see her. I need to see it with my own eyes."

Lieutenant Landry nodded at the young officer, who lifted the tape to let her pass. Glory lumbered up the stairway, each step feeling heavier than the last. Another group of police were smoking outside the door to Amity's apartment, which was open. He steered her through the tidy living room. Religious texts and romance paperbacks packed her bookshelf, and the afghan Glory crocheted for her as a college graduation gift covered the back of her worn sofa. As they approached the bedroom, Lieutenant Landry paused again.

"You really want to do this?"

She nodded.

When Lieutenant Landry opened the door, she saw Amity Gay's body on the floor. One leg was straight in front of her, and the other was bent at the knee. The torso was held upright by the nun's habit, one end knotted around her neck, the other end tied to the closet doorknob. Burst capillaries dotted the whites of her eyes. A thick dark liquid oozed from the corner of her mouth and puddled onto her faded blue jeans.

Glory clutched the doorframe. Lieutenant Landry tried his best to hold her up, but the weight of deep grief is too much for any one man to hold. Glory slid down the door onto her knees and wailed.

2

St. Martin de Porres wasn't as grand as St. Agnes, Glory's church in neighboring Lafayette. It was built in 1942 as the black church, back when the South was divided into two: black and white.

Glory didn't truly understand what this meant in real terms until she was seven years old, when a brick shattered her church's simple glass window and a fire devoured the rest of it. For six months, while the church was rebuilt, the congregation was permitted to attend the white church a few blocks away. Her tiny eyes had widened to take in the glittering chandelier dangling from the church's vestibule, and her white patent-leather church shoes looked dingy on the crimson carpet nestled between the wooden pews. Her own church had simple metal chairs, requiring them to kneel on the tiled floor instead of padded kneelers. After months of Sundays in the white church, little Glory was sure God loved the people in that church more. She understood at last what the adults in the room already knew—that *black* was just another word for *inferior*.

It made perfect sense that Sister Amity chose a church like St. Martin de Porres down the road in the town of Scott. St. Martin de Porres is the patron saint of mixed-race people and hardworking folks, just like everyone who prayed there. It had no stained glass. No organ. No incense. In its blandness, it felt more like the local Elks Lodge than a typical Catholic church. That was why Sister Amity made it her home base. It was for the people. *Her people.*

Glory's thick-soled, lace-up shoes suctioned against the linoleum as she walked toward the altar, which was upholstered in a nubby brown carpeting. Glory had worn her good black dress for the event, with a Swarovski crystal brooch in the shape of a heart. Even if she could have afforded diamonds, which she could not, she would have opted for Swarovski because it was shinier than the real thing. A blue cross was nailed against the wood veneer that paneled the walls. Her walk was as solemn as the occasion—the funeral of Sister Amity Gay.

Glory gritted her teeth as she saw the state of her best friend. Sister Amity was dressed in a beige silk nightgown and tucked into a casket lined with baby-blue satin. On one side, a thin strap had shaken loose, exposing her bare shoulder. Delicate lace framed her décolleté, with the garment skimming her knees. How dare they do this. How dare they leave her so exposed. She tried to cast her anger aside, to not let it spoil this final moment with her beloved friend.

Glory shook her head and scanned the room, wondering if there was any way she could shield Amity from the masses in that condition. As she looked around, she saw the other sisters hurrying parishioners to their seats and, judging by the placement of Father Romero near the altar, guessed service was about to start. Later she would have to figure out who was responsible for this travesty and voice her strong displeasure. For now, she'd have to say goodbye and take a seat so that service could begin.

The community knew her as Sister Amity, but to Glory, the word *sister* wasn't a title. Amity and Glory were real sisters, lowercase kind of sisters, if not by blood then by divine happenstance. The two had shared an unbreakable bond, even as their lives took divergent paths. Amity had always been there to offer a hand to hold, or a shoulder to cry on, or a shot of whiskey when nothing else worked. Knowing that this would be the last time she'd ever see Amity, Glory took in her face. Her large almond eyes were closed, thank goodness, but Glory would never forget the terror she saw in her friend's eyes that day at the apartment, in that brief moment when Amity must have known her life was leaving her.

Glory caressed Amity's cheek and, after taking another quick glance around her, let her hand slide to her neck. The skin was smooth, her neck waxy and unstable. She lifted the fallen strap of her nightgown, tucking the extra length tightly behind her back.

She took a seat among the mourners as the rosary began.

Je vous salue, Marie, pleine de grâces;
Le Seigneur est avec vous.
Vous êtes bénie entre toutes les femmes,
Et Jésus, le fruit de vos entrailles, est béni.
Sainte Marie, Mère de Dieu,
Priez pour nous, pauvres pécheurs,
maintenant, et à l'heure de notre mort.
Amen.

It was a special rosary, led by nuns and another group of women just as revered. This ensemble of women, all elderly, traveled throughout the parish to lead a full rosary in Creole French. Trancelike, they chanted the Our Father and Hail Mary with acetate beads laced around their swollen, arthritic hands. They were the keepers of the language, and a holy tradition. It was more than a rosary. It was a vigil.

Glory tried to follow along. Her lips mouthed the words, but her mind kept flashing back to Amity's apartment. The habit tied around her neck like a garrote, the blood pooling on her faded jeans. She kept focusing and refocusing until there was a clamor at the church door, temporarily disturbing the rhythm of the rosary. Who would have the temerity to come late to the funeral of a nun? Glory swiveled in her seat, ready to pin that person to the wall with a withering gaze, but her anger dissipated when she saw her daughter, Delphine.

The mourners couldn't help but steal a quick glance at Delphine, either. Her clothes, on the surface, were plain—black trousers and a white blouse—but she looked more elegant than anyone there. Even in the most minimal outfit, she looked expensive. And she was. What the parishioners couldn't articulate were that her pants were wool gabardine, her blouse made of silk charmeuse, the woven leather sandals an indulgence from Italy. Her lips were painted red, and her curly black hair was tamed in a no-nonsense bun—each strand was on its best behavior, understanding that now was not the time to act up. Tall and lithe, with what folks down here called that "good" hair and fair black skin, she looked more like her father than she did her mother.

Delphine walked down the aisle, searching up and down until she found Glory and slid her way into the pew.

"I didn't think you'd make it," whispered Glory, her thick hand reaching for Delphine's slender fingers.

"I didn't either, but I was able to convince my client to settle instead of going to court, which he should have done months ago."

A fellow sister reprimanded Delphine with her face alone, in the way only a nun can do.

Delphine slid into her seat, knowing that a nun's glare must never be challenged, even if you're a grown woman with a condo in Manhattan. Delphine craned her neck and was quiet until the rosary was finished. She leaned in toward Glory and asked, "Mama, why is Amity wearing a negligee?"

Glory sighed and shook her head. "Don't even get me started. Stupid old Creole custom. You know, putting the dead to sleep forever in pajamas. I can't believe those crusty old sisters did that. Just because you're holy doesn't mean you have any class."

Father Romero had taken his prepared remarks out of his vest again, studying them before his eulogy.

"Is that the famous priest?" Delphine asked. She pulled a cashmere scarf from her bag and wrapped it around her shoulders.

"Winning that big old grant done gone to his head. I forget what it's called. And what are you doing with a wooly scarf in Louisiana in August?"

"The Lewiston Grant. And you know how cold I get on airplanes, not to mention all this Southern air conditioning."

"Me and the Red Hat ladies practically have to beg to get on his calendar since he got that grant. One million dollars to do whatever he wants, or nothing at all. I ain't ever heard of nothing like that before."

"He's *much* more handsome in person," said Delphine. His priest uniform aside, he was one of those older guys that could have pulled a woman twenty years younger. His gray hair was full, and his broad chest signaled that he hadn't been slacking at the gym. In the spectrum of older black men, he skewed more Denzel Washington than Morgan Freeman.

"Father Romero is a man of God. I can't even believe you would say that—and at a *funeral*!"

"Think of all that money, Mama. All you have to do is dust off those old beauty queen moves and . . ."

"Delphine!"

A smacking of the teeth from the left and a *shhhh* hissed from the right told the two women they needed to save this conversation for later. The church had been full already for the rosary service, yet the crowd had somehow doubled in size by the beginning of the funeral mass. The pews were stuffed shoulder to shoulder as latecomers insisted there was more room, and when there was not, they stood at the back. With the small church jammed with people, the service finally began.

The eulogies had this in common: stories of Sister Amity's generosity to those in need, mostly by the people who benefitted from her help. There was the new mother with the drinking problem that Amity helped to get sober. The child she tutored in elementary school who was now on scholarship at an Ivy League university. A family of four sat in the front pew, retelling the story that had elevated Amity from unknown nun to local legend.

When the Fontenot family house burned down in Opelousas, Amity somehow convinced Benoit Construction & Chemical Company to donate their time and resources to rebuild it. As the parents told the remarkable story, their children faced the congregation. The eldest held a framed portrait of Sister Amity leaning over a pool table, cue in hand, about to bank a shot in their new game room. The youngest grasped a picture of Amity alongside the construction workers, putting in a day's labor like the rest of the sunburned crew.

After these personal testimonies, Sister Jocelyn Cormier picked up her guitar, ready to lead the mass in song. Father Romero readied a wooden stool below the altar in front of Glory's coffin. She slung the woven guitar strap over her shoulder and began to sing Williard Jubusch's "Whatsoever You Do."

Whatsoever you do
to the least of my people,
That you do unto me.

Her crystalline voice punctured what little composure was left in the room, which was taken over by sobbing. But it doesn't matter how torn up a Catholic is. They know when it's their time to answer a song, and they did so, dutifully, when it was their turn.

When I was hungry, you gave me to eat;
When I was thirsty, you gave me to drink.
Now enter into the home of my Father

Father Romero rose to the altar. "I'd like to first thank Father Andrew for letting me preside over mass today for my beloved friend and colleague Sister Amity Gay, who passed away last week under tragic and senseless circumstances. As many of you know, the Sisters of the Holy Family was founded by freed slaves, for women of color, to minister to their own. This was Sister Amity's lifelong calling. What you may not know, however, is that when I started the Equality Project eight years ago, I didn't do it alone. It was a beautiful collaboration between me and Sister Amity. Though, when the time came, she didn't want any of the credit. She never wanted attention. She did not seek your adoration. Instead, all she wanted was to continue to minister to people in need and create a world that was more equal and just for everyone.

"Without her at my side . . ." He paused, his lip quivering. "She was the oxygen of my movement, the heart of Scott, and the better angel inside all of us. Her death is a tragedy, a sad and elusive mystery, but let us all take solace in her many good deeds. May her journey be peaceful, and may the Lord have mercy on her soul." He put one hand on the altar and covered his face with the other as tears gripped the entire church.

These were new details even for Glory, who knew everything about her friend. At least she thought she did. Glory clenched her fists to avoid crying, because she knew that once she started, the tears would flow with the volume of a fire hose. Amity spent her entire life helping everyone else, yet died in that brutal way, alone, in that drab apartment. Glory ran through all the good she had done and how devoted she had been. It would never feel right.

Once he collected his composure, Father Romero stood at the middle of the altar to prepare the Eucharist.

When mass was over, mourners lingered outside the church for hours. It was not only the funeral of a beloved pillar of the community, but as can only happen in Louisiana, it strangely turned out to be the event of the season. Getting an invitation to this particular funeral, with the famous priest and the death of a nun, was not an everyday occurrence. But even though the sun shone brightly, the mood was gray. Everyone's faces were frozen in despair, as if captured by daguerreotype. Delphine was searching through her handbag to find her sunglasses when Lieutenant Landry approached her.

"Well . . . will you look at this? Delphine Broussard. Wait, what do you call yourself these days?"

"Murphy."

"That's right," he said, averting his eyes. "I didn't know you were coming down for Sister Amity's funeral."

"Amity was like a second mother to me," she said, making eye contact with Landry and then staring into the distance. "I wish I had known she was suffering so much."

"We're all in shock, especially your mama. I told her not to come down to the scene, but she doesn't listen to anyone."

"What?"

"She didn't tell you? She and I were having a catch-up at CC's Coffee House when we heard it over the radio. She insisted on seeing the body. I warned her not to, but you know how pigheaded your mama can be."

"Huh. Well, yeah, she has a mind of her own." She glanced over at her mother, who was in charge of the table with coffee and donuts. It might have been a funeral, but in Louisiana there was always plenty of food, no matter what. Folks stay hungry whatever the occasion.

"Last time I was out here in Scott was for your grandmother's funeral," he said, stopping as fast as he started, as if he regretted it. "Anyways, you and that husband should see about having a little one. It would be nice to have a baptism or something happy to celebrate at this church. It's been a while."

Irritation flickered across her face. "Yes, we'll think about that, Landry," she said. "I guess people around here call you Lieutenant Landry now. Anyway . . . I'm gonna check on my mama."

The catering table was mobbed with people hovering for coffee and donuts. "Here, let me help you guys out," Delphine said.

Noah Singleton had donated all the food, which Glory had to concede was generous, even if the coffee was too thin. Delphine grabbed a pot and filled Styrofoam cups, while Glory hustled to replace the donuts, which disappeared almost as fast as she could bring more. After tending to the crowd's appetite, Glory could finally rest for a bit.

"People act like they ain't ever had a donut before," griped Glory.

"Why don't you sit down for a minute?" Delphine suggested.

"If I sit down, I won't ever be able to get back up." A cluster of women at the other end of the church parking lot erupted in laughter. Delphine shielded her eyes from the bright sun and squinted to catch a closer look.

"You didn't tell me Aunt Shirley was coming," said Delphine.

"Don't worry. We're not talking to her," Glory said, biting into an apple fritter.

Delphine raised her eyebrows and cocked her head. "And why is that?"

"She'll deny it, but I'm pretty sure she's been stealing from my house." She wiped glaze off the corner of her mouth and took a sip of coffee before continuing. "I gave her a set of keys for emergencies, and soon after, my collection of brooches started dwindling—and then I seen her with an angel pin on her coat, just like mine. And my orange Dutch oven has gone missing, my good one from Guy Fieri, and I know she took that too."

"Mom, Aunt Shirley is a lot of things, but I don't think she's a thief. Why would she steal from you?"

"Because she's jealous, that's why. She's jealous that *Maman* left the house to me. And she's always been jealous of you and your success. Meanwhile her children ain't amounted to nothing at all."

"That's not very charitable."

"I never said I was charitable." She ate the last piece of her donut, and was fixing to get another, when Sister Jocelyn walked up to the table.

"Is this your pretty daughter I've heard so much about?" asked Sister Jocelyn.

"Yes, all the way from New York," beamed Glory.

"I was so moved by your singing," said Delphine. "Your voice is stunning."

"You really think so? I haven't sung in a very long time."

Glory fought the urge to roll her eyes. Everyone knew Jocelyn Cormier could sing. Especially Jocelyn Cormier.

Jocelyn continued. "I haven't sung publicly in a very long time, but I wanted to make sure that the service was as beautiful as possible. And I thought the body looked great, considering everything. Mother Superior has been too sick to oversee things like she normally would, so I stepped in."

Glory walked closer to Sister Jocelyn, until her red face was just centimeters away from Jocelyn's. "Shame on you," yelled Glory.

"I'm sorry, I—"

"Shame on you for dressing Amity like that. A woman of God, no less, looking like a tramp in her very own church. It was a downright disgrace."

"You of all people have the nerve to criticize me?" she asked, disgusted. "You look here, this suicide has terrified all the sisters. Everyone is shaken to their core, and the old-timers like Mother Louisa think it's a grave sin against God. Didn't want to even view the body, let alone dress her, because she doesn't want to be contaminated by that sin. So criticize me all you want. I've done my best to make her acceptable to the Lord after that unnatural thing she wrought upon herself."

The parishioners watched as if it were a pay-per-view match on cable TV. Father Romero excused himself from a conversation with the cardinal and sped over.

"Let me tell you, you're not half the woman as Amity was, with your fake smile and that stupid guitar of yours, not to mention . . ."

"Sister Jocelyn, can you get some water for Sister Eleanor? She's feeling unwell, as you might imagine," said Father Romero, shooting a disapproving glance at Glory. Sister Eleanor was propped up against a garden retainer wall, her hand pressed against her forehead.

"Yes, of course, I'd be happy to," said Sister Jocelyn, walking over to help. But before she reached her colleague, she spun around and screamed, "She started it!"

Glory took a few determined steps, like she was ready to wallop her.

"Sweet Jesus," said Delphine, grabbing her mother by the arm. "Let's go before you start more trouble."

Moments later, when the crowd's excitement had been reduced to just a few murmurs, the church emptied and the sisters started to walk over to the adjoining cemetery. Nearly everyone had left except a couple of men sent from the diocese to make sure the day went smoothly.

Glory and Delphine were walking toward their car when Glory stopped. "I have an idea. We will not stand idly by and let Amity go into the afterlife looking like a brazen hussy thirsty for the Lord's salvation."

They reconvened and walked toward the church, knowing that they didn't have much time. Delphine tugged her mother's hand to get Glory to move quicker, but it was useless. Fast was a speed that Glory didn't do. Once inside the church, Delphine did a quick lap to see if anyone was inside. Once she she'd made sure they were alone, she reached back into her handbag and pulled out her scarf.

Delphine nudged the stiffened body to one side and then the other, while Glory wrapped her torso in the feathery cashmere scarf. Once Glory was satisfied that her friend was appropriately covered, she removed the angel brooch from her dress, pinned the scarf securely into place, and shut the coffin.

Delphine was behind the wheel of Glory's SUV as they drove back home. To their left and right, and even below them, were cypress-tupelo swamplands. Moss stretched across the tops of trees like a canopy, swaying in the sticky late-summer air. Angry clouds of mosquitoes were no doubt blowing on the waters, even in the cooler temperatures, and crickets chirped their nightly chorus.

"Mom, what was Sister Jocelyn saying to you? Something about 'you of all people'?"

"I have no idea. You know how people are down here, always trying to start some mess."

"Landry told me you were at the apartment . . . with the police. Is that true?"

"Good timing, I suppose. Or bad timing. But you know what . . . I don't believe it."

"Don't believe what?"

"That Amity committed suicide. It makes no sense."

"Mom, the police have investigated. And didn't you see it with your own eyes? That she hanged herself?"

"I saw it all right. But it was a crime scene, not a suicide."

"What makes you say that?"

"I just have a feeling."

They rode back to Lafayette in silence, past the junkyards, the Acadiana Mall and miles of big-box stores that all looked the same, and eventually made their way back to the old house on Viator Drive. As the house came into view, Delphine started to make a mental checklist of all the things that needed to get done before she went back to New York: mow the lawn, or even better, hire a landscaper. When was the last time Glory's chimney was cleaned? Maybe it was time for a new paint job. Without a doubt the gutters needed to be cleaned, she realized as she parked in the carport.

Delphine was six steps ahead as Glory slid her way out the passenger side. A bright orange envelope was trapped behind the glass storm door. Delphine grabbed the envelope and opened it.

"What's that?" asked Glory.

Delphine's arms went limp beside her. "It's from the city of Lafayette. They want to condemn your house."

3

Glory Broussard
3763 Viator Avenue
Lafayette, Louisiana 70596
Dear Ms. Glory Broussard:

You are hereby notified that a complaint in condemnation has
heretofore been filed in the office of the City of Lafayette, due to
the dangerous condition of the domicile located at 3763 Viator
Drive.

The domicile has been deemed as an immediate risk to inhab-
itants due to the poor condition of the home. The conditions of
concern may include a proliferation of items that block exits,
unsanitary conditions in the kitchen and/or bathrooms, and
general squalor.

As such, you have been ordered to answer this complaint at the
Superior Court of Acadiana Parish within thirty days.

Regards,
Javiera Garcia
Lafayette Parish Clerk of the Court

Delphine pushed the storm door open and unlocked the front door. The scent of mothballs was so overwhelming that Delphine couldn't help but twist her face. Then there were the stacks. The stacks of newspapers that lined the entryway. The stacks of cookbooks with stained covers and oily pages piled on what looked like a sofa. Across from a large TV that was always on sat a hutch that was overflowing with crystal punch bowls, cake stands, and a silver tea service, which was laughable, as there were definitely no tea parties or social gatherings hosted at this house. In the corner was a stack of mismatched chintz plates that tinkled with each step she took. A pile of shopping bags stuffed full of clothing with tags still attached took up the corner behind a tattered plaid armchair.

Glory had followed behind her, reading and rereading the letter from the city. "What does this even mean? It doesn't make any kind of sense."

"I'll tell you what it means. It means they think you're going to get suffocated by a stack of *Good Housekeeping* magazines from 1986 or impaled by an imitation silver teapot."

"You take that back," Glory fumed. "That is real sterling silver."

"I knew I should have come down here more often, especially after Grandma died," Delphine said, gripping her forehead with the palm of her hand. "I always knew you were not the tidiest person, but now you've veered into full-blown hoarding territory. When did this happen?"

"Hoarder? I'm no hoarder," Glory said, her face buckling as if she had just swallowed something bitter. "Oh, I see, you want to diagnose me because you saw this on some reality show. Those people are disgusting. I am not a hoarder. I am a *collector.*"

Delphine was unmoved. "Tell that to the City of Lafayette when they condemn your house and board your windows with plywood," she said, searching for a place to sit. Finding nowhere other than her mother's tattered chair and a sofa scattered with Easter decorations in the dog days of August, she stomped into the kitchen. She placed her leather purse on the laminate countertop and started typing on her cell phone.

"What are you doing?" demanded Glory.

"I'm emailing my paralegal to get a court date for my mother, who is sick in the head and can't stop shopping at estate sales and needs a firm hand to restore order in her home."

"You are doing no such thing," Glory said, sinking into her armchair and hoisting her feet onto an equally worn ottoman. "I'll deal with the city myself. I just wonder why I got this letter. What exactly are they doing? Sending folks to peep inside my windows? Going through my trash? I'm going to ask Beau Landry how that works."

"Stop," said Delphine, exasperated. "Do you realize how serious this is? They're trying to condemn your house. Are you not at all concerned?"

"Yes, Delphine. I am. My mind just operates different than yours. First, I need to know who's responsible for this, so I can plot out my revenge. And second," she said, looking around at the cluttered house, "I suppose my collections have gotten a little bit unwieldy."

"Maybe I can file an appeal or an extension . . . something to buy us some time," Delphine said. "Regardless, tomorrow morning, eight A.M., we start cleaning up this mess."

The ancient alarm clock glowed 6:31 A.M. when Glory was awakened by the ruckus outside. She had been fast asleep in her pink nightgown, her hair swaddled in a silk bonnet. She may not have been a beauty queen anymore, but she still abided by this beauty queen law: thou must not let a cotton pillowcase rob your hair of moisture like a thief in the night. She tugged at the underwire of her Maidenform bra, which dug into her ample flesh. It didn't feel right to have her bosom flapping in the breeze, even if no one else knew. She always wondered how people could sleep in the nude. She had tried it once and feared her organs would fall out of her body.

She leaned over in her bed to investigate the noise, opening the curtain a smidge and squinting in the sunlight. The ruckus was Delphine, who had already emptied what looked like an entire house worth of contents into the backyard. Glory moaned and swung her legs over the side of the bed. She flexed her ankles a few times before standing up, part of her daily warmup routine for stiff joints.

Until a year ago, Glory had gone to her mother's one-bedroom apartment every day, washing and ironing her clothes, cooking meals, and smudging Merle Norman lipstick onto her wrinkled mouth with the tips of her fingers. Now that she was gone, there was no reason to get up at all, except for Sundays.

She placed her hands on her knees and lifted herself up. Eventually momentum took over and carried her down the hallway. A dozen bones crackled at once, and a burning sensation lit the heel of her foot aflame, causing a temporary morning limp. Lately, it had felt like her body came apart overnight and had to snap together again in the morning. She was nearly warmed up as she made her way to the veranda that led to the backyard.

"Thought I'd get a jump start on things," said Delphine, who was dressed in jeans and a tee shirt from NYU. Glory recognized it instantly as the one she'd bought for her when she dropped Delphine off for college all those years ago, right as she was becoming another person.

"Girl, what are you doing up at the crack of dawn, flinging all my worldly possessions around for the entire neighborhood to see?" A dozen U-Haul boxes filled with what Glory considered to be important paperwork took up one corner of the yard. Various estate sale finds—chipped china, oil paintings, weathered books, and assorted tchotchkes—filled the other. Glory's lips flattened when she saw that her daughter had unearthed her entire stash of holiday decorations.

"There's not enough room in the house to work," Delphine said, struggling to drag an artificial Christmas tree across the lawn. "We need a staging area."

"Girl, don't drag my good tree across the lawn like that. You'll strip off all the needles."

"Looks like you better get out here and help me out, doesn't it?"

Glory took in the mess. It wasn't as if she didn't know things had gotten out of hand. She did. But the chaos had taken root a while ago, like the wet rot that invaded her old magnolia tree. It was silent at first, and by the time anyone noticed the swollen trunk, the tree was too far gone. All that remained was a smooth stump in the yard.

"Fine. Lemme go get dressed right quick."

More than an hour later, Glory shuffled into the backyard wearing her elastic-waist jeans and matching chambray shirt. In one hand she clutched a paper coffee cup with the new branding from CC's and in the other a plastic bag from Piggly Wiggly.

"Jeez, Mom, I thought you were getting dressed, and you went to the grocery store?" Delphine smacked her arm, aiming for a mosquito, which became a part of the air's molecular formula in the summertime.

"I need coffee to start my day, and that Noah Singleton was out of half-and-half. I hope he was a better Marine than he is a coffee shop owner. So I just ran to the store real quick because I'm not putting that watery skim milk in my coffee. And don't even get me started about that oatmeal milk he started carrying."

"Oat milk," Delphine corrected.

"Whatever." Glory set the coffee down, opened a pint of cream on her patio table, and walked into the yard. "Okay, what are we doing here?"

"I cleared out most of your living room. I've put all like items together. All the china in one spot, all books together, all your papers together. We'll go through each pile and decide what stays, gets trashed, or goes down to the Goodwill."

"I guess we can do that," said Glory, a hint of surrender in her voice.

"Let's start with the holiday stuff and these blue-and-white candles. I say trash."

"Trash? Those are perfectly good candles. We are not throwing those away."

"They're Hanukkah candles, Mom. Are we Jewish now?" Delphine had tied a thick black garbage bag onto the top of the chain link fence. She threw the candles into the bag, which was brimming with receipts from Dillard's and Chico's, decades-old gas bills, and a case of Ritz crackers that were four years beyond the expiration date. She walked back to the pile in the yard that she had deemed as miscellaneous items, picked up a red cardboard box, and was headed toward the trash when Glory stopped her. Glory's head stretched out like a turtle emerging from its shell.

"Oh, bring that box over here," Glory said, taking a seat at her patio table.

"Mom, we can't go through everything with a fine-tooth comb. This isn't an archeological dig."

"You told me we were sorting, right? Then let me sort."

Delphine huffed and walked over with the musty box with the banged-up corners. Glory lifted its lid, revealing a bunch of loose photographs sliding around inside. On top was a photograph of newborn Delphine taken in the maternity ward, with her eyes swollen shut like a prizefighter, her curly hair combed into a dollop atop her head.

"I've never seen this picture before," Delphine said. She leaned in and took a thick stack of pictures to flip through. "Who's this woman?" she said, holding out a stiff photograph with yellowed Polaroid borders. A black woman with a midriff-baring macramé halter-top and bell-bottom jeans sat on the back of a red Harley Davidson. Her arms were raised above her, victorious. Her companion on the bike looked over his shoulder, his eyes smiling in her direction.

"That's Amity."

Delphine covered her mouth in surprise.

"She wasn't always a nun, you know. She used to be wild back in the day. Tequila. Bad men. Worse decisions."

"Who's the guy on the Harley?"

"One of those bad decisions."

"She stayed straight all these years?" asked Delphine.

"She changed her life. Once she made the decision to become a nun, she stayed on the straight and narrow."

Delphine sat down. "Are you sure? I mean, how do you know that's true?"

"Let me tell you, I seen her when she was strung out, all those years ago. There was nothing subtle about it."

"How does being a nun work?" asked Delphine. "I mean, it's not exactly a nine-to-five job, and Amity was so active in the community. Did she have to report into anyone . . . let anyone know where she was and what she was doing?"

"I think Mother Superior supervises everyone's work, but I've been hearing that Mother Louisa has been checked out lately. Some kind of health issue, I think. Next in line is Jocelyn Cormier."

"You know, I can't stop thinking about what you said yesterday in the car, when we were coming home from the funeral," said Delphine, sitting down near her mother. "What did you mean when you said it wasn't a suicide? Based on what?"

"Based on common sense," Glory said. "Let me tell you, Amity had a full schedule for the fall, and I mean full. She was organizing more protest rallies against that chemical plant in Mosstown. They were even saying that she and Father Romero might testify in Baton Rouge about that plant. Maybe even Congress. This was not a woman about to end her life."

Delphine touched her mother's shoulder. "I know how upsetting this has been for you. But the police investigated, even Landry was on the scene, and the autopsy report ruled it a suicide."

"The police don't get everything right, Delphine. Not around here. Not even Landry."

"I guess so." The conversation was interrupted by a buzzing. Delphine retrieved the vibrating phone in the back pocket of her jeans. "I'll be back. Let me take this call from Chad." Delphine walked back into the house, shutting the door behind her.

Delphine had arrived at the Lafayette Regional Airport two days ago. It was about time her good-for-nothing husband checked in on her, Glory thought. Delphine always had an excuse for him. "He's a surgical resident. He's busy," she'd say. Just one excuse after the other.

But Glory never liked the way she pined over him, and she certainly knew what Chad's white family thought of her. It did not go unnoticed when Chad's mother placed Glory at a corner table at the wedding at the Essex House, tucked far away from their fancy friends. Or how quickly his mother sprang into action at their sprawling apartment the time Glory tried to sit in an antique armchair. As if she would sully it. As if she was unworthy. It had made her feel like she had all those years ago when she went to that white church.

Out of the corner of her eye, Glory saw an ebony cat step from the never-used garden beds filled with weeds and saunter across the lawn. Glory had seen this cat before. Sometimes it staggered into the yard with a puffy face lined with scratches. Today it was free of scratches, if skinny.

"Go on, get out of here," she said to the feline trespasser. "Get."

The cat stood its ground, looked Glory squarely in the eyes, and meowed.

"I told you, I ain't got nothing for your raggedy ass."

Unmoved, the cat licked its paw and wiped its face clean. It strolled onto the patio and jumped onto the chair Delphine had been sitting in.

Glory sighed, exasperated, then confronted the cat again. "I told you I ain't got nothing for you. *Go away.*" The cat lay down on the cushion of the chair, squinting smugly.

"Good lord." Glory stood up, taking her coffee and cream with her. "A woman can't even have coffee in her own yard without some creature interrupting the peace." She dumped the remaining coffee into the yard and was about to head inside when the cat stood up and vocalized in her direction again. She got a better look at the animal, who had a knowing look in its eyes and whose sharp ribs jutted out against its taut skin.

She tore the paper cup in half, setting the smaller, narrow part on the table, and filled it with cream. The cat leapt onto the table and lapped it up. After the last few days, Glory had had her fill of suffering.

She walked back into the house, but not before pointing at the cat and warning, "Don't get used to this." The blinds swayed as she slammed the door.

"Chad, that's not what we agreed to." Delphine had raised her voice, which carried from her bedroom to the living room just as Glory walked in. "Are you kidding me? I'm going to fight this."

Glory stopped, afraid any movement would tip her daughter off that she was eavesdropping.

"No, I'm not having this conversation. Our lawyers will have this conversation." Delphine stormed out of the bedroom, muttering to herself, but stopped when she saw her mother in the living room.

"Oh, hey," she said, surprised. "Taking a break?"

"That sun is merciless today," Glory said. "Everything all right with Chad?"

"Yeah, just some family business," she said, scratching the back of her neck. "His family is doing some estate planning, and you know how they are. They make everything as difficult as possible." She walked into the kitchen and pulled out a plastic cup from Evangeline Downs racetrack from a cupboard where about forty other plastic tumblers were all tucked into each other like Russian nesting dolls. She filled the cup with water and sat at the kitchen table.

"I've been thinking," Glory said, joining her. "Whenever something happens to a black woman around here, the police don't do nothing. They ain't ever found out who murdered that woman in Grand Coteau last year, or that little girl down in Opelousas. But when that white woman was hit by that truck and kidnapped, they found that man and locked him up in Angola. Even made the national news."

"I'm sure you're right," Delphine said. "But I don't see how those cases are connected to Amity."

"I'll tell you how they're connected. They're connected because when it comes to black women getting hurt or disappearing, folks look the other way. No one is working overtime for us. Damn, they ain't even doing their jobs at a basic level. And I'm tired of it. No one is coming to save us. If we want the truth, we're going to have to go out and find it."

"So what's your plan?"

"I don't know, but I intend to get one. But . . ." She hesitated. "I sure do think it would be helpful to have a lawyer on my side."

"You want me to help?" Delphine asked. "No. Absolutely not."

Glory searched for the words that might win her over. She made her final argument. "Justice has been in short supply down here. It don't just roll up on the front porch for women like us. Isn't that what you do for a living, get justice?"

The hard edges of Delphine's face softened, and Glory hoped that her words had had an effect. At the very least, Delphine would probably enjoy bossing her mom around and running her affairs, something she'd tried to do many times before.

"You probably do need a lawyer with the trouble you're bound to get into, nosing around this town like some kind of black *Murder, She Wrote*. And my jury trial just got settled . . ." she said, exhaling and rolling her eyes. "Okay, here are my terms. I'll call the office and see how much time I can take off. We spend the mornings pulling this house together. In the afternoons, you do your sleuthing, and I'll try my best to keep you out of jail. Deal?"

Glory suppressed a smile.

4

Glory whacked her shoulder against the door of Amity's apartment, hoping it would give way.

"Mom, you can't just knock the door down," Delphine said. "Besides, maybe it's already cleared out."

"There's got to be a way," Glory said. She lifted a woven doormat, then stood on her toes and ran her fingers along the top of the craggy doorway. When that uncovered nothing, she dragged a potted plant across the apartment landing, revealing a ring of soil and a key.

An older white man clanged his way up the metal stairway, unintentionally announcing his presence. His face was red and bulbous from what must have been a skin condition, and his stomach paunch was wrapped tightly by a red tee shirt. His knee-high socks were as white as his sneakers.

"Excuse me, ladies, I'm the manager of this apartment complex," he said. "You can't go in there. The owner . . . she ain't here right now."

"I can explain," Delphine said with all the confidence of a New York City trial attorney. "We're friends of . . ."

"We're with Acadiana Aftermath Cleaning," interrupted Glory. "We specialize in the cleaning up after difficult situations like these." Lowering her voice to a conspiratorial whisper, she said, "You know, suicides and such. Just here so we can get this apartment cleared out. For the church." Glory waved the key in front of him, as if it were a credential.

The apartment manager's face became redder, which didn't seem possible. After stammering for a few seconds, he managed to sputter out, "I'll let you ladies get to work, then." He raced down the stairs without looking back.

Delphine looked at her mother, astonished. "The speed at which you invent the most elaborate lies is impressive and horrifying."

"If you're gonna lie, you gotta go big or go home," said Glory. She slid the key in the lock and opened the door.

"Do you just go about lying like this all the time?"

"Look, he saw two black women and wanted to believe that we were the help. It's not my fault the man has no imagination."

Glory drew the curtains and opened the window. The drapes fluttered in the breeze.

"Don't touch anything you don't have to," warned Delphine.

"It's an old Louisiana custom. You have to open the windows to let her spirit soar free."

Delphine's confused face did not escape her.

"Just let me do my thing." This custom made more sense to her, anyway, than that awful negligee, Glory thought.

The apartment air was still and stale. The place looked exactly like it did when Glory visited Amity for coffee and to catch up on the gossip. Amity may have been a nun, but she still liked to be in the know, especially when it came to who was stepping out of their marriage and other sordid matters.

"So what are we looking for?" Delphine asked, snapping photographs of the apartment with her cell phone. "I'm not accustomed to breaking into people's homes to investigate a possible murder, so you're going to have to point me in the right direction."

"Anything unusual, or something that might belong to someone else. Anything that looks . . . weird." The two women got to work, sorting through a stack of mail on the kitchen counter, searching behind the sofa cushions, and examining the bookcase.

"Amity sure did like romance novels," said Delphine, running her index finger across a bookshelf full of them. "She lived alone, right? Don't you find it odd that she'd have an extra key under the plant? Who was she leaving a key out for?"

"Ohh, that's a good point," Glory said, scrawling in her notebook as she walked into the bedroom. She stopped cold as she crossed the threshold into the room. The hairs on her arms remembered what they'd witnessed that day. So did the pit in her stomach. This was the spot where life had left her friend. Or more likely, where her life was taken, thought Glory.

She scoped out the bedroom, as orderly as the rest of the house. "Delphine, come here."

Delphine walked into the bedroom.

"Take a look at this," Glory said, sweeping her arm across the spotless room. A simple gray bedspread was tucked tightly into the sides of the bed. Neat file folders were arranged on a small writing desk in the corner. In the sparse closet were stiff skirts and starched blouses that still smelled of detergent.

"What am I looking at?" Delphine asked.

"Precisely. Here is a room that the police have barely touched. An entire apartment that they didn't even bother to search. If this was a suicide, did they even bother to look for a note? Did they open a single drawer? Did they attempt to find a single shred of evidence? I'll tell you what they did in here—they put her body in a bag, typed up a report, and went home."

Glory placed her large purse on the bed and rummaged through its contents. She pulled out a fanlike brush and a pot filled with black powder, which she dusted onto the doorknob.

"You brought fingerprint powder?" asked Delphine, incredulous. "Where on earth did you get that from?"

"I found it when we were cleaning out the house. Bought it on Amazon," Glory replied. "I told you your Aunt Shirley has been stealing things out of my house. I've been trying to catch her red-handed."

". . . or you could just get an internet camera?"

"Ohhh, that's an excellent idea. They teach you that in law school? You've got to hook one of those up while you're here," said Glory. "Don't just stand there. Start looking around."

The powdery knob began to reveal its secrets. Swirls and eddies of lines contrasted against the powder. Glory pulled out a roll of clear packing tape from the depths of her purse. Carefully, she situated the tape over the knob and folded it back onto itself.

"What do you intend to do with those fingerprints?" asked Delphine. "You can't just walk into the police station and have them run it through the database like some episode of *Law & Order*."

"Girl, I don't know, but I'll figure something out."

Delphine looked under the bed, where hardly a speck of dust could be found. She fingered the files on the desk. Newspaper clippings about Mosstown. Studies from the Environmental Protection Agency. Printed-out bios of the board of directors.

"I'm taking Amity's research on Mosstown to do some research of my own. I'm sure they didn't appreciate a nosy church woman speaking out publicly about the plant."

"That's my girl," said Glory. "See, I knew you'd get into this."

Delphine dragged the desk chair over to the closet and stood on it so she could examine the top shelves. There she found half a dozen boxes, each stuffed with files. "Maybe I won't have to do much research. Looks like Amity did it already."

"Let's take it all."

Delphine hauled the boxes from the closet shelves down to the floor. They were all lined neatly on the uppermost shelf, except for one, which stuck out a few inches beyond the shelf's edge. She moved the box to the side, finding a smaller shoebox stuffed with lollipops. Delphine climbed down from the chair and showed the box to Glory.

"She always did have a sweet tooth," Glory said.

Delphine unwrapped a lollipop and examined it. It was tiny and rectangular, with the edges rounded off. A purple wrapper with a small bar code ran down one side of the cardboard stick.

"Those are some funny-looking lollipops," said Glory.

"These aren't regular lollipops. I think this is fentanyl."

"Fentanyl? Isn't that the drug killing off all those hillbillies?"

"It's not just hillbillies, Mom. And that's a very prejudiced thing to say."

Glory rolled her eyes. "It's mostly hillbillies. You don't see black people hooked on that stuff."

"That's changing," Delphine scolded. "I worked a big case last year where this respected cancer doctor was writing prescriptions for these lollipops as part of an illegal drug operation. My firm was hired by the pharmaceutical company to make sure the case didn't affect their reputation."

She explained further. The fentanyl lollipops were prescribed to patients in extraordinary pain, usually cancer patients at the end of their lives. The doctor wrote prescriptions in large quantities to a Manhattan hospice because it made sense to have them on hand in an environment where people were facing end-of-life pain. At least on the surface. But the doctor was really in cahoots with a notable Bronx drug dealer. His guy on the inside of the hospice would scan the lollipops to real patients, as if they were being prescribed, then take the whole box to be sold on the streets of the city for twenty dollars apiece.

"I have three questions," said Delphine. "How did Amity get her hands on this fentanyl? Why did she have it? And why does she have so much?"

"I don't know, but I know someone who might."

5

The ceiling fans inside CC's Coffee House struggled to keep pace with the heat and humidity. Presently, the fans were losing. The Saturday afternoon crowd was thinner than the Sunday crowd, just a few people sprinkled about and focused on their phones. It was remarkable that anyone was there at all, given the temperature inside. Glory took a seat at her usual table while Delphine walked to the counter to place her order.

"Iced coffee with light ice. And a splash of almond milk," Delphine ordered, looking down at her wallet. When she finally looked up to hand the cashier her money, a quizzical expression traveled across her face. "Do I know you?"

"I'm . . . uh, I'm not sure," said Gus, in his typical nervous way, as if he had been caught doing something illicit. He looked over his shoulder and shrugged.

"Wait a minute. I've got it. Third grade. Mrs. Buck."

"Oh wow, yeah," he said, taking Delphine's money and making change. "I'm afraid my memory's not as good as yours."

"Delphine Broussard. I was class president."

"Oh yeah," he said, smiling. "Prairie Elementary. Home of the Pandas."

"*Ici on parle Français!*" they both said in unison, recalling the sign in front of the school that heralded its French-speaking teachers. Glory, displeased, strained her neck to hear what they were saying. She remembered him from last time, smiling all goofy at that immodest white woman, not to mention that work release program he was enrolled in.

"But did anyone really speak French there?" Delphine laughed.

"Never heard a lick of French." He poured the coffee and topped it off with a bit of ice. "You with her?" he asked, nodding toward Glory.

"Yes, that's my mother. Do you know her?"

"A little. She doesn't seem to like me, though. Always complaining about how slow I am."

"Don't take it personally. She doesn't like most people." Delphine sipped her coffee. "She was born with a side-eye and a scowl across her face."

"But she's real popular here on Sundays."

"*Is* she?"

Glory coughed loudly, feigning the international sign for choking at her throat. She had the dramatic instincts and believability of a Juilliard acting student on the verge of flunking out.

"Looks like I'm being summoned," said Delphine. "Good to see you, Gus." Delphine sat down near her mother. "What was that all about? Did you swallow an elephant?"

"No, I was trying to save you."

"From who? My third-grade classmate?"

"No, a convicted *felon*," spat Glory. "You know how Noah Singleton's daughter got caught up in those streets? Well, his heart never recovered, so now he hires these jailbirds to work here in some work release situation."

"We don't call them felons anymore, Mama. They're called people with prior justice system involvement. You lead with the person first. And I'm sorry to hear his life took a turn. He was a quiet kid who never got into trouble," said Delphine, fiddling with her straw. "But God bless Noah for hiring him. It's not easy for these guys to get back on their feet."

"I would just like to enjoy my coffee without worrying about a hostage situation."

"That's a little dramatic, don't you think?" Delphine said. "Do you know what he was in for?"

"Does it matter?"

The squeaking of Noah's wheeled bucket interrupted them. He was pushing a mop, his shirt drenched from the labor and the soupy air. Glory waved him over.

"Now listen here, Glory. Nobody has time for your complaining today. Yes, the air conditioning is broke. And yes, someone is on the way to fix it, after they fix the other three hundred units across Greater Lafayette that are broken today. If you don't like it, you can head to one of those senior citizen cooling centers."

"Believe it or not, I had no intention of complaining."

"I don't believe it."

"And let the record show that I am not yet collecting social security and, until such time, do not consider myself a senior citizen. I have my own air conditioning at home, which is functioning at the strength of the Arctic Circle."

"Even the Arctic Circle is experiencing record heat, on account of global warming," said Delphine. Noah held back a laugh.

"Come see. I need to show you something," urged Glory. He exhaled, pushed his mop and bucket to the side, and joined the two women at the table.

"What is this about?" he asked. It was clear from his slumped shoulders and the sweat on his brow that he was in a mood.

"I have formally opened an investigation into the murder of Amity Gay."

"*Murder?*" said Noah. "No, ma'am. I want no part of this. None. You already got me complicit with that other mess."

Delphine opened her mouth, and Glory knew the look well. She was about to launch into a line of questioning that Glory did not want to be on the other side of. She needed to act fast. She pulled one of the lollipops out of her purse and slammed it on the wooden table.

"Do you happen to know anything about this?"

Noah froze. Even though he and Glory were regular sparring partners, the gentleness in his eyes never extinguished. But his demeanor changed when he saw that evil on the table. His face went hard, his eyes cold.

"It's fentanyl," said Glory, pleased at herself for sounding like a vice detective.

"I know what it is," he said, raising his voice. "Where did you get that?"

"It was in Amity's apartment," whispered Delphine, hoping Noah would take her cue and lower his voice, too.

He unwrapped it, stretching its wrapper until it was taut between his fingers. In this position, a picture of a snake emerged, its forked tongue flickering. "Please tell me Amity wasn't caught up in this. Please," he pleaded.

"We're not sure," said Delphine. "But we could use your help. What do you know about this?"

"You know what this snake is? It's branding," said Noah. "He puts a snake on it because he wants people to know he's got the strongest stuff in Lafayette. It's what killed my Sarah. No, *he's* what killed my Sarah."

The darkness that resided in Noah opened up for everyone to see. He knew far too well what it was like to have a loved one caught up in drugs. He had watched his daughter go from being a dean's list nursing student at LSU to comatose with a needle in her arm within just a couple of years. That was one of the dangers of raising a child in Louisiana, Glory knew. Too many distractions, not enough opportunity. Maybe it would have happened no matter what, but in hindsight, Glory was relieved that Delphine saw another slice of life in New York. Maybe what happened to Sarah could have happened to Delphine.

"Who is this person?" asked Delphine.

"Milton Knowles."

"Dear God," said Glory, touching her cheeks with her palms and shaking her head. She had always thought of Milton as a cancer in remission, knowing that he could pop up at any time and destroy things all over again. His depravity may have been subdued for twenty years, but Glory never believed he was ever truly gone.

"Who's Milton Knowles?" asked Delphine. Judging by the bitter looks on the faces of Glory and Noah, he was not one of Lafayette's finer citizens.

Glory's erect posture and the final traces of her self-righteousness had vanished. She couldn't stop shaking her head in disbelief, as if she had woken up from a nightmare. "Remember that picture you found back at the house? The one with Amity on the back of the motorcycle? The man in that picture, on that bike, is Milton Knowles." She went on to tell Delphine about Milton, Amity's former boyfriend and now, it seemed, her drug dealer. It was a tumultuous love affair. One minute they were making plans and talking about houses and babies. Not long after, the back of his hand was imprinted on Amity's face. Somehow, after all the crying and making up was done, they'd seal the deal with a glug of this, a sniff of that. Glory always thought joining the Church was, at least in part, a way for Amity to stay away from substances. But it was really a way to make sure she never ended up with Milton ever again.

"This has got his name all over it," Noah said, balling up the wrapper in his fist and throwing it onto the floor. "And you found this in her apartment?"

"Not just one," said Delphine. "An entire shoe box filled with them."

The three of them sat silently, each fuming, each grappling with the weight of the discovery. Glory hadn't thought of the man in years. She knew he had done some time. She knew he was up to no good. But she didn't know much beyond that. Amity had been done with him for eons, or so Glory thought. Apparently he wasn't done with her.

6

Glory lay in her queen bed, which really was only a twin bed if you factored in usable space for sleeping. The rest was piled high with clothing, shopping bags, old picture frames and vintage cookbooks, and inexplicably, a bocce ball set, all procured from various estate sales. Delphine wanted to tackle this room next, but Glory was adamant. It was off-limits. Her daughter had backed down for now, not wanting to upend the good progress she had made in the rest of the house, but it was a hollow victory. Glory knew the time would come.

What Delphine didn't know was that Glory seldom left the bedroom on most days. Her bedside table was overflowing with hand lotion and sweets, stacked with unopened mail, and lined with bottles of translucent orange pill bottles. There were pills for lowering cholesterol and blood pressure, and also for the thyroid problem, all of which she took as prescribed.

And then there were pills for the unshakeable sadness which had dogged her since the divorce. That emotion had surprised her. She had been reveling in her newfound freedom, in having the house to herself. And yet somehow it still managed to be harder than she expected. The doctor had also prescribed something else for when the walls were closing in on her, which was how she had felt ever since her mother died. Wasn't sadness a necessary and inescapable part of life? she wondered. She did not take those pills because she did not deserve any shortcuts. She was no one special. At least that's what she told herself.

But every Sunday, Glory woke up at four in the morning to get ready for seven A.M. mass. That was how long it took her to get ready. Not because she had an elaborate beauty ritual but because her body ached with each movement. Mornings were the worst, especially the moment when her feet hit the ground. There was no amount of stretching, physical therapy, or Advil that could make it go away, and she had tried them all.

Everyone likes to talk about how strong black women are, but no one ever talks about how painful the feet become. Perhaps it was the steel-toed shoes she wore at the grocery store all those years that mangled her feet. Or maybe it was the weight of having to do it all. All the working, parenting, cooking, and worrying had always fallen on her. Her feet had paid the price.

Glory winced at the first footfall and then limped to the bathroom. A few steps warmed up the tendons, and she settled into a slow but normal gait. Hot water would make the rest of her body serviceable. She turned the shower valve left as far as it could go. When the temperature was near scalding and steam fogged the bathroom mirror, it was ready. Holding onto the wall rail she'd had installed, she carefully lifted one leg over the side of the tub, then the other. Her shoulders relaxed as the hot water warmed her like an embrace. She bowed her head and stood still under the pummeling hot water for several minutes.

Afterward, she wrapped herself in a yellow terry-cloth robe she'd bought on discount at Dillard's and thumbed through her closet. She landed on a floral top and a pair of loose black pants. The shoes were almost always black, sturdy and slip-ons. She preferred not to bend down unless absolutely necessary. The look was topped off with a pair of sparkling diamond studs.

The bedroom clock blazed 7:10, making her late for service before she even left the bedroom. She double-checked her handbag to make sure her ledger was inside, grabbed her keys, and squeezed behind the wheel of her Honda CR-V. Maybe one of these days she could convince Delphine to join her, she thought, but the only time Delphine willingly went to church these days was for funerals or weddings.

Glory sped into the St. Agnes parking lot, reaching into the cupholder and hooking a handicapped placard onto her rearview mirror. It was something she'd found in her mother's house, from back when she used to clean for other people. Glory snuck into the church just as communion was finishing. After mass, she joined the Red Hat book group and waited for the right moment to approach Constance Wheeler.

"Constance, how lovely to see you here today," said Glory. "I was just thinking about you the other day and how much I need to renew my license."

Constance grew up a mile from Glory but acted like she was Michelle Obama instead of the regional manager of the DMV. She had assumed these airs when she married Clarence Wheeler and his accounting degree from Xavier University. He worked at one of the oil companies, and maybe he was good at his job. Glory knew he wasn't so discerning when it came to other fiduciary matters.

"Hello, Glory." She smiled, looking around the room for an exit. "How are you holding up? I meant to reach out to you after Amity's funeral. I know how close you were."

Glory knew this shallow sympathy was utter bullshit but stayed focused. She slipped her hand into her purse and kept it there. "Thank you. Devastated, of course, but moving forward. You know, I wanted to ask a favor of you."

Constance's fake smile teetered. "Anything for a fellow member." She looked around the room, where everyone else was engaged in conversation or lined up at the table for Meche's donuts. There was no escape to be found.

"I don't know who would do such a thing, but someone has been coming into my backyard and messing with my garden. You see, I've gotten very into cultivating the soil these days. And I always close the side gate, except one day I came home, and my garden was all dug up. Those thieves ran off with all my tomatoes and radishes."

"How dreadful, but I don't see how I can be of assistance to you," said Constance. "Maybe you should get a lock."

"I thought the same thing, so I went to Guidry's Hardware. You know, the one down on Jefferson? Anyways, can you believe they sawed it off and then stole my okra!"

"Again, I'm really sorry, but I don't see what I can do," said Constance, eyeing a group of women by the coffee thermos. "Have a good day."

Glory stepped in front of her, blocking her path with her body. "I'd love it if you could help me run these fingerprints. I heard once how the DMV is connected to all sorts of government databases and I found these smudges on my fence post," said Glory, pulling her hand out of her purse and offering the fingerprint she'd captured on packing tape back at Amity's house.

"I'm afraid I can't do that. That would be against regulations."

"I see," said Glory. "I just thought you might be a little flexible, seeing that your husband made an ill-advised wager with me a month ago. I've tried to be accommodating, but I'm sorry to say he hasn't exactly kept up with our payment schedule."

The weather around Constance shifted like a hailstorm on a summer day. "What are you going to do?" Constance seethed. "Go to the police to complain that someone is late in making a payment to your illegal gambling operation? Tell me how that works, Glory." Constance was triumphant. Checkmate.

"This is what confuses me about that husband of yours. Such a smart man, but he bets with his heart instead of his head. That's why I always ask for a bit of collateral when I know he's about to do something stupid," said Glory, smoothing the side of her hair down with one hand, stopping at the diamond earrings. "These came in a real pretty burgundy box from some store in New York. I think it was called . . . Carter?"

"*Cartier*," Constance corrected, appalled. "How did you get those? Those were an anniversary present!"

"Like I said, nice guy, bad bets. At any rate, I'm keeping them safe until he settles up," said Glory. "Or maybe we could work out a little debt-forgiveness program?"

A group of Red Hat members had noticed the prolonged conversation between Glory and Constance. Memories of last year's Mardi Gras mishap would not be easily erased. When Constance caught them watching her with Glory, they all turned away.

Constance snatched the prints. "Fine, but I want my earrings back first."

"Nice try." Glory walked away and took a seat for the monthly book club. She had not read the book.

✳

After the Red Hat meeting, Glory walked into CC's Coffee House, ready for a full day's work. Gus was still behind the counter, slow as ever, but the instruction manual was gone. Glory walked up to the counter.

"Cappuccino," she ordered.

"Yes, ma'am." He pressed the espresso grounds against the machine, then frothed the milk and poured it into a glossy blue mug.

"Well, looks like you're finally picking up a few things around here."

He nodded and pushed the cup her way.

Glory sat down at the table and tended to her regulars. The interactions were brief and friendly. Her clients knew the drill—money in a plain envelope, and buy a little something to support a black-owned business.

"What are the odds for LSU?" asked a man whose shirt buttons were struggling to contain his belly.

"Minus five," said Glory.

"Why you gotta tax LSU like that? I can get better odds online."

"You know better than to question my lines, Wilson. And if you prefer the odds somewhere else, then you are welcome to take your business elsewhere. That's how it works."

The man huffed and put down forty dollars despite himself.

Glory recorded the wager in her blue book. Her eyes hardened when she saw her daughter stride into the coffee shop in cuffed jeans and a crisp white shirt, her curls piled onto her head. Glory's first thought was that she wished she was young and beautiful and could look like that in mere minutes again. Her second thought was how was she going to hide her occupation, such as it was, from Delphine. She slammed her ledger shut and put it on her lap.

Delphine waved at Gus and sat down at Glory's table. "I heard you were popular on Sundays. Thought I'd stop by and see what all the fuss is about."

"Well, I just like to unwind after church. And the coffee," said Glory, sipping her coffee. "Yes, I need coffee after waking up so early to get to that seven A.M. mass."

"So, tell me, what's the spread on LSU today?" Both women were fluent in the patois of gambling.

Glory racked her brain for a response, but she knew she had been found out. "Okay, fine, so you caught me red-handed. And you know what? I'm not ashamed."

"So all those years protesting against Daddy being a high roller, and now you're one? And just wait until he finds out you're competing with him for clients . . ."

"Child, settle down. He already knows. This was part of our agreement."

"Agreement?"

"Yes, our agreement," said Glory. "You've never had to do backbreaking labor like the work I did in that grocery store, and that's the way I wanted it. But when your Daddy and I divorced, I thought, why shouldn't I get to sit down for a change? I was the one who kept the wagers straight and worked out all the betting lines. So part of our unofficial divorce settlement was that I get his clients, and he'd start new. So that's what he did. New wife. New town. New book. And this is my fresh start."

Gus fired up the steamer of the espresso machine. Glory shot him an annoyed look, and he turned away.

"Mom, running a criminal enterprise is not exactly a fresh start."

"This ain't no criminal enterprise. I am a small-business owner. A risk-management consultant. Or . . . what is it you millennials call it these days?" asked Glory, searching for the words and pouring more creamer into her mug. "Girl boss. Yes, I'm a girl boss. All about that hustle."

"So you just break the law, in plain view? In a public space?"

"I am an entrepreneur working in a collaborative workspace," said Glory, before shifting gears. "Come on. I'm an old, fat, black woman. Nobody pays me any mind. In fact, most people don't even think I have a mind of my own, let alone that I'm someone who's capable of thinking and doing for herself."

Delphine's shoulders softened. "I know things have not been easy for you, especially over the past few years. But this is too dangerous. You could get into legal trouble, and I don't want to even think about what one of these lunatics on the bad end of a wager might do if they can't pay you."

"Look, things are different nowadays," Glory explained. "There's online gambling. My customers like a personal touch. They can't work a computer. Or don't have the minimums they make you put up on the internet. Or they don't want a paper trail. I'm proud to report the local bookie has not been outsourced to the internet."

"And what happens when someone can't pay up?"

"That is rare, and when it does happen, I tap into my freelance network."

"You mean freelance muscle?"

"I'm not big enough to employ someone full-time, so yes, free-lance. They get a cut of what they bring in."

Delphine looked at her mother as if she had two heads. "If you needed money, you should have just asked me."

"I'm fine, and I like having money of my own," Glory reassured her. "I done spent my whole life working for other people. Now, I get to have something of my own."

Delphine sighed. "I just never thought I'd see the day when my mother was the mastermind of an urban gambling operation headquartered in a coffee shop."

"Pretty cool, isn't it?" said Glory, sipping her coffee. "I'm surprised to see you up. If you're up this early, you might as well come to church with me."

"I'm not letting you off the hook. We'll continue this conversation later," Delphine said, yawning. "I was up late last night sorting through a mountain of paperwork."

"And?"

"Well, there's reams of Mosstown research. I've barely made a dent," said Delphine. She reached into a tote bag and flipped through a stack of dog-eared papers. "Have you ever heard of Oleander Industries, LLC?"

Glory cocked her head to the side, intrigued. "No, what's that?"

"It's a shell corporation in Breaux Bridge. Its holdings include three warehouses, five storage units, an apartment building, and two single-family homes. Both homes and four of the apartments are leased to one Milton Knowles."

"Hot damn," said Glory, slapping the table. "Where'd you get that info?"

"My paralegal did some digging back in the office."

"But how do we pinpoint which house or apartment he lives in?"

"I already have a pretty good idea."

7

It was dark as Glory and Delphine drove toward Jennings. Yet despite the darkness, the inky silhouettes of old cypress trees were still visible. It was like daylight, when you look at something in daylight and then close your eyes, the form lingering inside the eyelids.

"It's too quiet in here," said Glory, turning on the radio. A bright pop song with a peppy syncopated beat pulsed through the speakers. "This is my song. The Pointer Sisters!" she said, turning the volume up and shimmying her shoulders to the electronic beat. "If you want to take my kisses in the ninth inning . . . jump! Jump!"

"Those aren't the lyrics," Delphine corrected. "The lyrics are, 'If you want to take my kisses in the night then . . .'"

"See, that's the difference between you and me. You sing the song as it's written. I sing the words that should be there," said Glory, turning the volume even louder. "Leave me alone and let me enjoy my music."

The Pointer Sisters. Luther Vandross. Anita Baker. Maze. Bobby Womack. Curtis Mayfield. Al Green. Chaka Khan. This was Glory's milieu. She was bumping to her favorite music for nearly the entire ride. It was too bad music was so terrible today, she thought. These poor kids will have nothing but vulgar lyrics and electronic singing to remember as the soundtrack of their youth. But as they got closer to Jennings, Glory's dancing behind the steering wheel became less exuberant, until she was no longer moving at all. She lowered the volume until the chirping of cicadas blended with the music on the radio.

Delphine was absorbed in her phone, and from the sporadic grimaces that came across her face, Glory guessed she was dealing with Chad-related matters. She had warned her not to marry him, though maybe leading with "white boys are trouble" was not the best way to dissuade her. Delphine looked up from her phone, catching Glory's eyes observing her. She put the phone on her lap.

"So what was Milton like before he started selling drugs?" asked Delphine.

"I don't recall knowing him before he got wrapped up in that life," said Glory. "Seems like he was born wicked." Glory's body stiffened at the mention of his name. Her arms had been waving and grooving with the music just a minute ago. Now they were locked in position as she stared at the interstate ahead. "How did you even figure out that he lived at this address?"

"I'm not entirely sure he does, actually."

"What?" asked Glory. "I thought you said you knew he lived here? Don't tell me we're driving an hour outside Lafayette for some fool's errand . . ."

"I said I'm pretty sure he lives here." She lifted the phone from her lap, gave it a few taps, and showed Glory the screen.

"What's that?"

"I did an online search of each of the properties registered to Oleander Industries. They were all in Lafayette, but one was suspiciously located in Jennings. I was able to zoom into the satellite images online and found pictures of people in the backyard. When I zoomed in on the others, nothing. I can't say for sure this is where he lives, but it seems to me if you're going to have one of the largest drug dealing operations in southwestern Louisiana, you'd want to do that outside city limits." Silence filled the car. Delphine reached into her *New Yorker* tote bag and pulled out a tube of shimmering, clear lip gloss.

"So . . . what's our game plan?" asked Delphine.

"Not sure."

Glory drove another thirty minutes until it was time to pull off the expressway. She weaved the car in and around small residential streets, and eventually, down a long road without any other homes and no streetlights. The darkness in the country is a different kind of darkness. These country roads always made Glory nervous, on account that it seemed almost anything could happen and there'd be no witnesses. No help.

Glory pulled over to one side of the road, slowing down on the gravel and eventually stopping the car.

"What are you doing?"

"You asked me what the plan was. Well, I might have a plan. Just need a moment to think about it," said Glory, reaching into the cupholder and popping a butterscotch candy into her mouth. "We can't just go knocking on the man's door. He's liable to shoot us both if we do that. Let's just confirm that he lives here for now."

"Okay, sounds good," said Delphine, opening the passenger door. She slid down a slanted gravel ditch briefly, before catching herself and walking to the other side of the car, over to her mother. Glory, like any black woman over fifty, had stored her purse in the backseat of the car and was bent over rummaging through it. She emerged with a pair of binoculars around her neck and a stun gun in one hand.

"Where on earth did you get all this?" asked Delphine, shocked.

"Girl, quit acting like I'm some criminal. Got it at Walmart. This ain't New York. Folks are looser down here. And the binoculars were from my brief foray into birding. The people at the Audubon Society said we had to get these binoculars, but I found my own eye to be more precise in most settings." Glory adjusted the lenses and caught Delphine's astonished face. "You don't know everything about my life."

They walked silently along the side of the dark road. The air was putrid with the spray of skunks and roadkill. Was it a raccoon or an armadillo? wondered Glory. It really didn't matter, because whatever it was, it was deader than dead.

The house itself was a Louisiana McMansion, as big as it was dumb. Corinthian pillars stretched from the garden to just the first floor, stopping at the fake terraces on the second floor. It was topped with a red-shingled roof that looked like a Pizza Hut franchise. The driveway was flanked with at least a dozen cars—mostly SUVs, and mostly European. Ornate rims twinkled under the moonlight, and nearly all the windows were blacked out.

They walked closer to the long paved driveway. Without warning, what seemed like a dozen lights flickered on simultaneously, flooding the driveway and the nearby areas. Delphine grabbed Glory's arm, yanking her out of the light's path. But whereas Delphine was able to start and stop on a dime, Glory wasn't as agile. Momentum carried her body forward until her chin was headed straight toward the darkened soil. Her face skidded across the dirt, and the rest of her body followed.

Delphine scurried over. "Are you okay?"

Glory lay on the ground, inhaling the dampness of the wet soil. Delphine straddled over her and tugged upward on her shoulders.

"Stop pulling on me," said Glory, bracing her hands under her face. "I can get up by myself." Glory lifted her torso off the ground and then swung her legs around.

Delphine extended her hand, which Glory was ready to take. Delphine bent her knees deeply and flexed her biceps to help her up.

"Can't believe you pushed me down like that," said Glory.

"I didn't push you! I wanted to get you out of the light. We have to be careful. Look around," said Delphine, pointing to cameras aimed at the driveway turned drug-dealer parking lot. "Motion detection lights, video cameras. They're everywhere. Let's hope he didn't see us."

Glory clutched at the searing sensation in her chest. The binoculars hanging off her neck had pressed against her during the fall. She dusted off her clothing and limped over a few feet to pick up her purse. She doused herself with hand sanitizer, wringing her hands together until they were slippery.

Glory took a few moments to evaluate the damage. She wiped the grime off her face and dusted her hands against her jeans, which were smeared with dirt and ripped in two spots. Beneath the tear was a crimson streak of blood trickling down her knee. Her ankle socks left the bottom of her legs exposed. Grated flesh was hanging off the knobby ankle bone.

Delphine swiveled her body around suddenly. "Do you hear that?"

Glory squinted, as if that would improve her hearing. In the distance was a muddled growl, and then, the vicious howling of a pack of dogs.

"Lord have mercy, they're sending the dogs for us," said Glory, limping as fast as she could to the car and opening the door. The howling of the dogs became more primal and painful to listen to. A chorus of men erupted in raucous cheers, which was punctuated by a loud gunshot that pierced the air.

"What the hell is going on back there?" asked Delphine.

Just as Glory was about to step into her car, she stopped cold and shook her head. "I should have known. Milton always did like to have more than one hustle."

"What are you talking about?" asked Delphine.

"Dog fighting. That's what's going on back there, and that's why that dog was crying out like it was being ripped apart, because it probably was." Glory shut the car door, making it clear that her investigation was not over. "Looks like this is the right house after all. Come on."

The women avoided the bright driveway and moved furtively along the shrubs that lined the house, outside of the zone of the floodlights. They froze as they saw a gate in the chain link fence on the side of the house open. Two men emerged. One man, made entirely of muscles and gold necklaces, was talking and cursing fast. The other man carried a lifeless dog in his arms like a bride over a threshold. His white tank top was drenched in blood. The men laid the dog in the back of their SUV and drove off into the countryside.

Glory scrutinized the scene in the backyard as best she could through the rubbery eyecups of her binoculars. Blood soaked through the cement patio. Men with diamond crosses in their ears mingled, laughing with one another. The aroma of smoked meat filled the air, along with the sound of the Isley Brothers. It almost had the vibe of a cookout, except for the dogs howling from a row of steel cages and the spatter of blood seemingly everywhere.

"Well, goddamn," said a towering man, startling them. From afar he might have looked like an old man with a balding head and a graying muzzle, trying to relive his glory days. His paunch was covered by a gray sweatshirt, and baggy basketball shorts nearly fell off his skinny legs. A closer look revealed something more sinister. Rudimentary tattoos, like the kind a person gets in prison, were carved in his neck. The ink was not much darker than his ebony skin, but if you stared enough, the shapes became clear. The king of spades. A fat dollar sign. And then Glory saw the snake, the same branding found on the drugs inside Amity's apartment.

"I never thought I'd live long enough to receive a social visit from Glory Broussard."

Delphine's eyes shot toward Glory, as if she was looking to her mother to know how to handle him. Glory's heartbeat became irregular. Water was trickling down her scalp, but she somehow rustled up some composure.

"This ain't no social visit, Milton."

"I suppose not. Most of my guests have manners and knock on the front door. They don't go skulking around my house and diving into the bushes," he said, pointing upward and swirling his finger around in a circle. "Got cameras all up in this joint. A bird can't build a nest on my property without me knowing about it."

"I came to talk about Amity."

"Now hold up," said Milton, turning his attention toward Delphine. Vulgar rap lyrics from the back patio filled the silence. His eyes inspected the entirety of her body, making their way from her stylish sneakers to her tiny waist and finally up to the curls which had frizzed out in the humidity. "This your daughter? She grew up real good. *Real* good."

Glory noticed Delphine slump a little under his gaze. Delphine looked as if she was trying to find the perfect retort, but Glory jumped in. "After Amity died, I found your drugs in her apartment, in a box hidden in the closet." She pulled the purple wrapper with the snake out of her pocket and thrust it in front of him, like a trial attorney introducing evidence in a courtroom.

"You always was one nosy bitch," he said. A cacophony of dogs yelped from the yard.

"And I guess your little logo is spot-on, because you always were a snake, Milton Knowles. You sold her those drugs, didn't you?"

He snickered. "No, I didn't sell her the drugs. I gave them to her. So what?"

Glory winced. She had already suspected it was true, but she didn't want to believe it. Amity had worked so hard to get clean of substances, including scrubbing her life of this godawful man. The vision of her cavorting with him—at this place, in her final days—made her stomach lurch.

"So"—Glory paused—"she was back on drugs?"

He shrugged. "I don't ask personal questions of my clientele. She asked, and I gave them to her, for old time's sake."

The men in the backyard laughed. Delphine turned her head reflexively.

Milton gave her a lascivious smile. "You want to join us back there?"

"The way you treat those animals is disgusting," Delphine fired back.

His face went cold and expressionless. "You two have worn out your welcome. Don't let me catch you this way again, or else I won't be so nice." He turned around and disappeared into the backyard.

Glory and Delphine walked away, this time on the brightly lit pavement, down the same bloody driveway as the men with the dog carcass.

"Jesus Christ, Mom. That is one terrible human being. Can you please walk faster so we can get the hell out of here?"

"I'm walking as fast as I can," said Glory, annoyed.

They didn't notice the footfalls of padded steps until it was too late. By the time Glory turned around, the pit bull had already made its move. All four legs were in flight, tucked into themselves, before it sank its incisors into Glory's leg.

8

Glory's legs dangled off the hospital bed inside Benoit Medical Center of Lafayette. Behind their curtained partition, Delphine watched the nurse as she removed her mother's shoe, then her sock. The wound was surprisingly shallow, all things considered. The dog hadn't torn the flesh but punctured it. The nurse irrigated the wound. A metal pan collected the runoff—blood, dirt, and rock fragments embedded in Glory's ankle.

"So you zapped that dog with a stun gun?" asked the nurse.

"I wasn't about to go down without a fight," said Glory, rather satisfied with herself for bringing along the right tools for the job.

"And let me get this straight," the nurse continued, dabbing the wound with sterile gauze. "You don't know the owner of the dog and have no history with the particular dog that bit you. Is that right?"

Glory could tell Delphine was about to open her mouth, which might have been the way a corporate attorney handled business. It was not the way to handle business with Milton Knowles. Glory responded, "No, ma'am, just went out for a walk with my daughter here, and that mean old dog came out of nowhere."

"Hon, I hate to tell you, but you're going to need some shots. Rabies. Tetanus. Not to mention stitches. You're lucky you tased that dog when you did, before he did any more damage. Anyways, let me get the resident on call and some supplies—be right back."

Delphine sat next to her mom on the bed. "Why did you lie about who owned the dog?"

"Tell me what good reporting Milton to the police is gonna do." She peeked at her calf and scrunched her face when she saw the condition of her leg. Chewed-up flesh surrounded an open wound, with pink-and-white tendon peeking through. "Besides, Glory Broussard ain't no snitch."

The doctor and nurse returned and silently arranged their supplies. The nurse ripped apart packages of tweezers, needles, and scissors, lining them up on a gauze-covered tray. Delphine shuddered when the doctor stabbed a needle into a small vial of clear liquid, then squirted a few drops into the air.

First up was a shot of local anesthetic, but there's no numbing shot for that first shot. Glory balled the sheets beneath her as the long, thin needle plunged into her calf muscle. The second shot hurt only a tiny bit less. The local anesthetic marinated in her bloodstream and calf muscles for fifteen minutes before the doctor continued. He threaded a needle with the skill of a cotillion dressmaker and stitched the wound.

Glory looked down, glimpsing the needle weaving in and out of her skin. The ragged pieces of flesh were pulled taut and smooth by the needle. Finally, the doctor gave the thread a good tug, knotted it up, and snipped off the long ends with a pair of scissors.

"We need you to stay here for a bit longer, to make sure you're stable," said the nurse. "You'll get one rabies shot tonight and then a series over the next couple of weeks. And we're going to send you home with some antibiotics—and crutches. Try to take it easy for a bit, okay?" She walked out of the room.

At last, Glory could relax. She propped her legs up on the bed and leaned into the incline of the upright hospital bed.

"Don't you worry," said Glory, "I'm going to get my revenge on that Milton. I just have to figure out how."

"Maybe we should just put this whole thing on pause for a bit," said Delphine. "We investigated one lead, and now you're in the hospital getting rabies shots."

Glory propped her hands behind her neck and knitted her fingers together. "You do what you want."

Delphine sighed. "I see there's no point trying to talk any sense into you," she said, standing up from a chair in the corner. "I'm going to the cafeteria. You want anything?"

"Ohhh, see if they have anything sweet for me, will you? Sometimes they have those popcorn balls with that cane syrup."

Delphine left Glory alone in her emergency room nook, nestled within three curtained walls. Glory thought about the night and smiled. She was the one who had confronted Milton and taken that big old dog down. If only those dull Red Hat ladies could see her now. She replayed the thrilling events in her head until she heard a mellifluous sound drifting over the curtain. Glory could pick out that voice anywhere. Jocelyn Cormier.

She swung her legs over the side of the bed again and gingerly placed her full weight down on her gnawed-upon calf. With each step, she grimaced with pain. She hobbled the distance of three beds and was confronted not only with Sister Jocelyn Cormier, whom she expected, but also Father Romero and Mother Superior.

"Glory, how did you know we were here?" asked Father Romero, surprised. "I didn't know word had gotten out."

Mother Superior lay in bed in front of her, sleeping. Wires snaked from her chest to equipment measuring the beating of her heart, the pumping of her lungs. Jocelyn Cormier's eyes were dry, even though the rest of her face was red. Father Romero stood steadfast, as always, over the two women.

Not expecting company and at a loss for an elaborate story to tell, Glory relented and told the truth. "I was bit by a dog. I'm fine, just got a few stitches."

Father Romero sighed. "It feels like the entire congregation is falling apart tonight."

"I had heard that Mother Superior was ill. I didn't know things had reached this point."

"Stage four stomach cancer," said Sister Jocelyn Cormier. "The sisters all know, but please don't spread it any further. I know you love to gossip, but this is not the time."

Father Romero's face tensed at the tone.

"I would never gossip about Mother Superior," said Glory. "Is it happening . . . now?"

"No, no. At least we don't think so," Father Romero reassured her. "She's having a pain episode. It was well managed for a good while, but now it's become unbearable. And the doctors don't seem to have any answers. I'm afraid we'll have to ride down to Tulane again for another round of tests. And you . . . you got bit by a dog? How did that happen?"

"I was just taking a walk with my daughter, and some big old dog just came out of nowhere. I'm fine. Just waiting for some shots, that's all."

"I've been meaning to come around and pay you a visit," he added. "How have you been since Amity's passing?"

Passing. Such a pleasant word, yet what a strange way to convey that her best friend was buried in a hole, like a turnip seed.

"I will never, ever believe that Amity did such a thing," she said before shifting gears. "And how are *you*? I know how closely the two of you worked."

"Honestly? It's been a real struggle without her," he said, dismayed. "We were supposed to testify in Baton Rouge against that chemical plant, and she did a lot of work on the Equality Project. I'm afraid I'm drowning."

"You know, I helped Amity with a lot of the research on that chemical plant. We pored over those files together," Glory lied. "I could help prepare you for that testimony to the State House."

"You?" snickered Sister Jocelyn Cormier. "A researcher?" Still asleep, Mother Superior shifted in her bed.

"Now is not the time for this petty infighting or whatever it is that's simmering between the two of you," Father Romero whispered to Sister Jocelyn. He turned his attention back to Glory. "I wasn't aware you were working with Amity on that research. How familiar are you with the water quality reports?"

"Very familiar with the water quality reports. As well as the . . . geological reports and topography surveys," she added, thinking it made her sound smart, like something Delphine might say. Sometimes what came out of her mouth surprised even her. "I have all the duplicate files at home. Boxes and boxes of them."

"I'm absolutely certain I could help," chirped Sister Jocelyn. "I'm a quick study. Took a semester of earth science in high school."

It took all the determination in Glory's body not to pop that woman upside the head.

"I'd love your help, Glory."

In the hospital cafeteria, Delphine sorted the items on her tray for the cashier: one slice of to-go cherry pie for her mother, some sort of granola bar with seeds for her. Two coffees and bottles of water, for whomever needed it most. She paid the cashier and slid into the cafeteria banquette. Under the glare of the fluorescent lights, she propped her elbows on the table and let her face collapse in her hands.

Lieutenant Landry was at the other end of the cafeteria dining room, pouring himself a coffee, when he spotted Delphine. He instantly went red, even though no one had said anything or was looking at him. After gathering the empty saltine wrappers on his tray, he placed it on the conveyer belt and walked her way.

"Delphine. How are you?"

Startled, she wiped her eyes with her hands and patted down her face. "Well, Landry, today has been a day."

He slid next to her on the banquette and placed his arm around her. "Aww, come on. It can't be that bad."

"It is," she said, her voice becoming stronger and picking up steam. "And to make matters worse, my mother is in the emergency room getting stitches because some vicious pit bull took a chunk out of her calf."

"Oh, that's Miss Glory?" We got a call about a suspicious or falsified report concerning a dog bite from the ER doctors. That's your mama?"

"Yes, but it's not falsified. It's real."

"Well, I'm going to have to talk with your mama about it."

"Be my guest. She seems delighted with herself for fending off this dog. I'm sure she'd love to tell you all about it." She wiped the last of her tears away with her shirt sleeve.

Lieutenant Landry removed his arm and with both hands fiddled with his coffee cup. "So that's why you were crying?" he asked shyly.

"Things have been hard lately," she said, resigned.

"I can't even imagine how hard Amity's death has been on you and your mama. I know we haven't seen each other in a minute." He paused and looked straight into her almond eyes. The lines in her face looked more pronounced in the harsh lighting, but they didn't detract from her beauty. The imperfections made her more earthly, accessible. "But you can always talk to me."

She gave his hand a squeeze. "Thank you."

The two had been so engaged in their conversation that they failed to notice when an older woman approached them both. "Hi, sorry to bother you two lovebirds," she said. "Delphine Murphy, right? From New York?"

"We're not together," Delphine corrected. "I'm sorry, this has been a terrible week. How do we know each other?"

The woman flicked her wrist. A manila envelope landed with a thud on the table. "You've been served. That's how I know you."

9

The worst part of being back in Lafayette, Delphine decided, was sleeping in her childhood room. The shelves were still lined with trophies and ribbons. Spelling bee. Volleyball. Speech and debate. On the bedside table was a framed picture of the sixteen-year-old version of herself, with her hair straightened and her slender frame drowning in a puffy pink dress for her Jack & Jill debutante ball, a kind of social group for well-to-do black children. Her membership had been sponsored by one of her father's gambling clients. His ne'er-do-well instincts gained her admission to the elite group of Lafayette's finest black families even though they were anything but.

It was one of her earliest attempts at social climbing, though to be fair, it wasn't her idea. It was Glory's. Nonetheless, she had enjoyed the glazed teriyaki meatballs and dancing with boys in tuxedos. The Jack & Jill ball was the first time her eyes were opened to a bigger world, which was followed by NYU, and eventually marrying into Chad's family. But here she was, back in her childhood room splayed out on a pink chenille bedspread, about to join a video call that could ruin everything she had worked so hard for.

She set her laptop on her white rolltop desk, where she had once studied for her SATs. Now, divorce papers sat on the same desk where she once did algebra. She replaced the ribbons and trophies on the shelf with a few books to ready the background for the call. When she clicked into the disciplinary hearing, two squares were already populated. Leo Swenson, senior partner, and Elizabeth Buck, HR manager.

"Good morning, Delphine. How's Louisiana treating you?" Leo asked, as if he was nervous to dive into the unfortunate agenda.

"It's good. Well, I actually came down for a funeral."

"I'm sorry to hear that," he said. "In that case, I suppose let's not drag this out any further. The firm has finished an investigation into your conduct over the past few months."

Exactly what *conduct* was investigated? she wondered. Was it the late nights that had started off in a totally professional way with another attorney while working the firm's biggest case of the year? That is, until it became slightly flirty and eventually sexual (even if legal and totally consensual on both sides). If that was the conduct he was referring to, Delphine had wanted to remind them that the firm had won, the client was happy, and they had billed a shit ton of hours.

Both attorneys had vowed to handle it like proper adults. No tears, no meltdowns at work, no tantrums. They were sophisticated people who could work together, enjoy sex with each other, and keep their mouths shut.

At least that was how the relationship had functioned until the night of the summer party. Maybe it was all the champagne or the mounting seasickness Delphine felt on the boat in New York Harbor. The details were still hazy, although she remembered the moment when the palm of her coworker's wife struck her across the cheek. As a final indignity, she threw up overboard. This was probably the conduct under investigation. She could still picture Chad's face that evening, which was as bitter as the acid that had burned her throat. She could still remember the sour smell of vomit that got tangled in her hair and the cab ride to the hotel where she'd spent the night. The driver had rolled down his window and snuck pitying glances through the rearview mirror.

"There is no doubt you are a fine lawyer. One of our best," said Leo, talking through the screen. "While there are some partners that think you should take your skills elsewhere, I have somehow managed to save your hide, for the time being. Between your billable hours and your talent bringing in new clients, it makes more financial sense to keep you. That said, you are being placed on a three-month probation without pay, which our HR lead will explain in further detail."

Delphine's face was flushed with shame. This bedroom had been her sanctuary when she was grounded as a teenager, and here she was once again, punished and banished to her room.

"I'll leave you two to discuss the details, but let me say this before I go. Please clean up your act and settle your personal affairs before you come back. Don't make me regret fighting for you."

And with that, he dissolved from the screen.

Bobby Womack was playing on the radio when Delphine turned into the parking lot of the Lafayette Parish Court. Glory instinctively reached for her handicapped parking placard and dangled it on her rearview mirror.

"Put that away," snapped Delphine. "You're not handicapped."

"I'm on crutches," said Glory, triumphant.

"That's not handicapped." Delphine turned the ignition off, removed the sign, and stuffed it in the cupholder. "You're going to let me do the talking," Delphine commanded. "Now is not the time to go running your mouth. Not today."

"You tell that judge that my house is fine. And that the city needs to find something else to do other than snoop in people's windows," said Glory, pointing to the street. "They can start with those potholes on West Congress if they need something to occupy themselves."

"That's exactly what we're *not* going to do in there," said Delphine. "We are going to explain to the court that you've made considerable progress on the house and beg their forgiveness and mercy. Let's go."

The combination of the crutches and the humidity activated every pore on Glory's body. By the time she'd walked the three minutes into the courthouse, her hair was frizzing at the edges and her white polyester blouse was damp where her crutches connected with her armpits.

Delphine's heels clicked against the chipped courthouse tiles, while Glory's crutches—courtesy of the dog bite—made a heavy thud. They fed their bags into the security X-ray machines, and Delphine breezed through the metal detector.

"Crutches in the machine," barked the police officer.

Glory smirked and placed them on the machine. She hobbled through, gingerly putting weight on her wounded leg. The machine screeched as she passed through.

"Over here," said the police officer, pointing, in a tone Glory found disrespectful.

Ordinarily, Glory would have served this man a piece of her mind, had her daughter not warned her against it. She knew Delphine was not happy about all this house business, but Glory had noted the irritation in her voice, bordering on anger.

The police officer waved a wand over Glory's body, starting at her feet and working his way up. She huffed when the wand creeped between her legs, and then across her torso.

"Is this necessary?" Glory complained.

The police officer pulled the wand away and shot her a brief but menacing glance. "You're free to go."

Delphine handed the crutches back to Glory, and they went up in the elevator to the appointed room. The palmetto ceiling fan provided only the smallest grace for those lucky enough to be seated directly beneath its wide blades. Glory and Delphine made their way down the black-and-white checkered tile and sat in the front row of the church-like wooden pews.

An old white judge with disheveled hair and a wrinkled robe took a seat behind an elevated desk. The wood-paneled room fell to a hush.

"The people of Lafayette versus Glory Broussard," the judge declared.

Glory and Delphine rose and walked behind a podium that was directly in front of the judge.

"Am I to understand," the judge continued, scratching his head with a pencil, "that the domicile of the complainant violates city ordinances and presents a danger to the defendant and others?"

"That's what you wrote on that note, the one you left on my door. But those are outright lies," Glory answered.

Delphine aimed a furious look at Glory and jumped in quickly. "The defendant understands and appreciates the city's perspective on this matter and as a result has made a good-faith attempt to ensure her home meets the standards of local laws. May I approach the bench?"

The judge nodded. When she approached the judge's bench, she reached up to hand him a large envelope filled with photographs of Glory's tidied-up home.

The judge slid his eyeglasses to the tip of his nose and rifled through the pictures, occasionally nodding. He jotted a few notes onto a pad of paper before speaking. "According to the file before me, the complaints against the home of Glory Broussard were confirmed by the city, but the pictures here do show significant progress, which should be commended."

"I move for the complaint to be dismissed without prejudice," Delphine pleaded. Glory folded her arms and nodded along.

"Hold on. Not so fast. While I am glad to see Ms. Broussard taking this matter seriously, the court does not yet have faith that she can maintain this progress," he said. Glory smirked. "That said, I do prefer to move these matters out of the court system and into the hands of our trained community team. Ms. Broussard will be assigned a court-appointed community advocate. There will be an in-home visit scheduled for next week, another in three months, and a final visit at six months. The advocate will share her findings, and the complaint may be dropped if Ms. Broussard complies. Is that agreeable to you?" asked the judge, looking at Delphine.

"I'd like to confer with my attorney first," said Glory, agitated and leaning on a single crutch.

The judge raised an eyebrow. "Go on."

Delphine walked back to Glory, her eyes shooting fire. "What is wrong with you? I told you not to say anything."

"You mean to tell me I have to open my doors to some stranger off the street for an inspection? I won't do it. I will not."

"Okay, then the alternative is the condemnation of your home and a fine of up to ten thousand dollars. Is that what you prefer?"

Glory pouted, knowing she was out of options. "No."

Delphine swiveled to face the judge. "Community intervention is agreeable to my client, Your Honor."

"If there are no further questions, I will see you here in six months," said the judge.

"Actually, I do have one question," said Glory.

Delphine massaged her temples, resigned.

"How did my house end up on your radar in the first place? How did I get in the system?"

"It appears that an anonymous caller tipped off the city," said the judge. "Someone apparently very concerned with your welfare."

Glory nodded, as if she had a sudden revelation. "Thank you, Your Honor."

"I can't believe you did that in there. You're lucky we've resolved this so quickly," said Delphine, unleashing on Glory inside the car.

"I can't believe I caught charges in the first place," said Glory, her back as straight as a rod. "It's a travesty of justice, that's what it is. And who the hell are they sending to my house?"

"The person coming to your house is whoever they send. Look for a letter in the mail," Delphine said. "And while we're on the topic of mail, that's something that you need to do. You need to start checking your mail. You know, opening the letters and *reading* them, not just tossing them on the bench by the front door."

Glory was silent. It seemed the more she talked, the angrier Delphine became. Ever since she had arrived in Lafayette, Glory had sensed that something was off with her daughter but had kept mum. She didn't want to make her any angrier. On top of that, she couldn't refute what Delphine was saying. Yes, there was a mountain of mail by the door, but that didn't mean she wasn't paying her bills. She made her monthly rounds in person to the electric and gas company to write a check, and if she was a few days late, she could smooth things over with folks in person. Everything else the mailman dumped in her mailbox was just noise.

"You missed the turnoff," Glory said.

"No I didn't. We're going somewhere else."

Glory protested. "I don't have time for any detours today. I'm all adventured out. My leg hurts, and you done worn me out with this court and this stranger doing home inspections. Just take me home."

"You're on my clock now."

10

They drove wordlessly for more than an hour. First down the highway, then down lonesome rural roads where kids played in the streets with stray dogs and the crickets buzzed in a way that sounded like electricity.

Judging by the set-in-stone look on her face, Glory figured that Delphine had decided upon something and Glory suspected that any amount of objecting would only strengthen her resolve. And given that Delphine had more or less taken care of her legal problem, Glory figured she should keep her mouth shut, at least for a moment.

Delphine drove down one dusty road until it didn't seem possible to turn down another one. At last, she drove up to a plot of land with about a dozen shabby trailer homes. They were scattered about like they'd been picked up by a hurricane and spat back out.

"You tell me right now what we're doing here," Glory demanded.

"So there's a woman we use sometimes for legal cases," Delphine said, searching the backseat for sneakers to change into. "Well, the entire firm doesn't use her, just our founding partner who's into chakras and energy and some unorthodox solutions. I talked to her once, and she seemed pleasant and smart."

"You're here doing research on a case?" asked Glory. "Who is she?"

"Felice Phelps. Spiritual intuitive," said Delphine, lacing up a pair of black running shoes. "And yes, it's research for a case. The case of Amity Gay."

"Oh no, I am not participating in any kind of sacrilegious activity."

"According to the *Daily Advertiser*, the Lafayette Police Department used her to find that woman who disappeared near Vermilionville. They consult with her all the time. I thought she could help us with our investigation, or at least tell us whether Amity was on drugs or not."

"Let's go before Jesus strikes us down and swallows us up in this sinkhole trailer park, on account of placing another god before him."

"Hold on, don't you have an app on your phone for horoscopes?" countered Delphine. "Isn't that the same thing?"

"That is for entertainment purposes only!" explained Glory, reaching for the car keys. "I'm warning you, I will not worship at the altar of false gods."

"Come on, we're here already," Delphine said, snatching the keys from the ignition before Glory could claim them. "We might as well see what the woman has to say. You don't have to do anything. You can just watch."

"I'll stay here inside this here car."

"Fine, suit yourself," said Delphine. She gathered up her purse and got out of the car.

Glory fumed. The only thing that was worse than being in this godforsaken trailer park was being left alone in said godforsaken trailer park. Against her better judgment, Glory exited the car. The slow shuffle of crutches and all-day-comfort orthopedic shoes slowly caught up with Delphine.

"I refuse to partake in this foolishness," Glory reaffirmed. "I just can't have my only child descending into the mouth of hell without a witness. You need a godly woman in the room so you don't get seduced by this black magic."

"Thanks, Mom, appreciate your vigilance."

They walked further into the trailer park, which was really more like a junkyard. A swinging garden seat on a rusted frame housed a litter of flea-bitten kittens with distended stomachs. Glory's crutches sank with each step into the rain-soaked mud. Delphine gazed back and forth between a slip of paper and the trailers until she found the right one.

"This must be the place," Delphine said, bounding up a couple of cinder blocks that doubled as stairs and knocking on the door.

The woman that answered gave off a chic but mystical air, a cross between Stevie Nicks and Eileen Fisher. She wore a black button-down shirt tucked neatly into the elastic of a long, tiered skirt. A chunky turquoise-and-silver ring was perched on a slender finger. A single braided ponytail stretched down the length of her entire back.

"Good afternoon. I'm Delphine Murphy. I believe we're scheduled for a two P.M. session."

Felice motioned for the women to enter. Delphine waved at her mother to follow and walked inside the trailer. Glory moved more cautiously, looking right and left and up and down before swinging her crutches over the threshold.

Butterfly wallpaper bubbled off the walls. The green linoleum flooring was outdated but otherwise clean. One end of the rectangular room was a kitchen with a sparkling hot plate lit up red under a steaming kettle. A damp towel dangled off a dish rack, where a single plate and coffee cup continued drying. Patchouli and lilacs fragranced the room.

"Please, take a seat," said the woman, gesturing toward an old plaid sofa. "Would you like a cup of tea?"

"That would be nice, thank you," said Delphine.

"No thanks," said Glory, looking away and clutching her purse on her lap.

Felice dunked a tea bag into a mug, which she set upon a saucer. She reached into a ziplock bag and loaded the saucer with three tiny cookies. She placed it on a tray on the coffee table before them.

Felice looked Glory squarely in the eye. "I can see by the way you're clutching that bag that you're either afraid, or you think my floor is too dirty for your purse. My home may not be grand, but it's very clean. You know what they say . . . cleanliness is next to godliness."

Glory felt pretty certain that this heathen knew nothing about godliness but placed her bag on the floor anyway. At the very least, she could see that this pagan was trying to be hospitable.

"Why have you sought me out today?" asked Felice, lowering herself down on a simple wooden chair.

"A family friend of ours . . . died. The police say it's suicide, but we have reason to believe that foul play was involved," said Delphine. "I guess we're looking for answers or validation or clues. Just anything."

"She was murdered," said Glory, who was fed up with the speculation and pussyfooting around.

Felice leaned in toward the coffee table and lit a tall purple candle. With her arms outreached and her palms up, she began to chant. It was guttural and rough. The lights flickered with uncertainty. If earlier in the day Delphine was the one with the dirty looks, now it was Glory. Delphine raised an eyebrow toward her mother, shrugged slightly, and took a sip of her tea.

The chanting abruptly stopped. Felice's eyes snapped open, as if she had been startled awake.

"The energy in the room is very dank, specifically around you," she said, pointing at Glory.

"Me?" asked Glory, wide-eyed. "Oh no, I don't want none of this demon voodoo talk."

"Protest all you want, but dark forces surround you. A curse from the depths of the underworld was affixed to you many years ago. It is an incredibly unfortunate affliction. As I see it, a jealous woman close to you is rooting for your demise."

Glory clapped her hands and then smacked Delphine on the shoulder. "The only jealous woman I know is Aunt Shirley. I told you she has it out for me. I knew it!" She looked at Felice. "How do I break the curse?"

"I cannot confirm the origins of the curse. Unfortunately, it can never be removed."

Glory looked disgusted. "What kind of bullshit operation is this? You just take people's money, give them bad news, and leave them high and dry? If you tell someone that they've been cursed, I think the least you can do is give them some practical solutions."

"This is not voodoo, and I am no priestess," said Felice, whose face could no longer hide her annoyance. "The curse cannot be removed, but it does not mean there is no remedy," she said. "You must pray for a symbol of protection to be visited upon you, and even then, you must be wise and brave enough to accept this pro-tection into your life. But I can see that you are very hardheaded, and this has made your lot in life more difficult." Felice's face disappeared into a mug of tea.

Delphine placed her hand on Glory's knee, as if holding her back from a fight. "Do you have any information about our friend's death?" asked Delphine in an attempt to prevent her mother from throttling the woman.

"I can see beyond the dimension that your friend has found peace, but she had found peace a long time ago, after many troubles, yes?" Out of the corner of their eyes, Glory and Delphine gave each other knowing looks to each other. "I have two things to say about your friend. As you suspect, she was murdered. And as is the case with most things in life, the answers are right in front of you."

"That's it?" asked Glory.

"That is all."

Glory stood up. "I've had enough of this voodoo gobbledygook. Let's go."

Delphine set her mug on the table, readying to go.

"Before you leave, dear, let me offer you some advice," she said, grasping Delphine's hand. "Unlike your mother, I see you are a more willing and open-hearted receptacle for wisdom." She shot a withering look at Glory. "For you, I see you have many large debts. You must free yourself from these dreary obligations so you can move on."

Glory guffawed. "Shows what you know. She married into money. Big-time money. Doesn't owe a thing, right, Delphine?"

Delphine looked away, embarrassed. "How can we compensate you for your time?" Delphine asked, smiling at the woman.

"You can Venmo me," she said. "CreoleIntuit52."

Glory was hopped up on the car ride home. "I still can't believe you made me go to a trailer park of all places. Talking about how I have *dank* energy. You know what's dank is that trailer park of hers. But I just knew your Aunt Shirley done put a curse on me. Symbol of protection? I'll have to keep my eyes open for that. Do you think that's real?"

Delphine steered back up the roads they had twisted down on the way. They passed the old Piggly Wiggly where Glory had been produce manager. Then the old Rexall Drugs in Scott, where Delphine had snuck a couple of scented candles into the pockets of her overall dress when she was small. Eventually Glory had found the candles and dragged Delphine back to the store to apologize, even though Delphine had not been sorry for wanting nice things.

"And the way she was talking about some kind of debt you owe."

Delphine swallowed hard and began to talk. "I suppose now is as good a time as any to tell you . . . Chad and I are getting a divorce. And he's demanding alimony."

"What . . . How is that possible?" asked Glory, confused. "He's the one with all the money."

"No, his *parents* are the ones with the money. They always insisted Chad and I make our own way. They gave us reduced rent to live in their apartment, which I've been paying while he finished up medical school. He's claiming that I . . ." She could barely finish. "He is asserting that I have been the primary breadwinner in the family and, as such, that he is entitled to support."

"You've been paying the rent? To his parents?" asked Glory.

"The idea was he'd eventually become a doctor, and then one day, he'd get an inheritance. Of course, what I didn't count on is that he would just . . ." She stopped. This time, she couldn't finish.

Glory shook her head. "I told you not to marry that white boy," she said, pointing a finger in her direction. "I should have known he would run off with a white woman. One of *his* kind."

"There is no other woman," Delphine said. "He just . . . wants out." She couldn't bring herself to reveal the real reason why.

Glory couldn't wrap her head around this. She slumped back into the passenger seat and didn't say a word for the rest of the ride home.

11

The sky was barely blueing when Glory awoke. She had found that it was a little easier to get out of bed these days, if only because she had a purpose.

Even the staff at CC's Coffee House had taken note of Glory's new routine. Everyone had grown accustomed to her Sunday office hours, but the staff did a double take when Glory started making six A.M. appearances at the drive-through. On weekdays. "Look here, my Morning Glory is the first customer of the day," Noah snickered.

"I do not need your color commentary this early in the morning, Noah Singleton. And please tell that boy not to put so much milk in my coffee," she pleaded, gesturing toward Gus, who was still slow and clumsy and, as far as Glory could tell, was not improving no matter how many shifts he worked.

"Now listen here. You got my employee to be such a wreck that he's started to measure your milk, Glory. The man literally *measures* two tablespoons of milk," he said, pointing to Gus, who was grasping a plastic measuring spoon with one shaky hand, and with the other pouring from a cardboard carton. "The milk in your coffee is the same every day, Glory, just like your complaining."

Glory rummaged through the compartments of her car for money. "Here," she said, leaning out of her window and shoving a couple of crumpled dollars and a fistful of change his way. "And don't forget to stamp my card."

"Download our app and you don't have to be scrounging for change every day," he reminded her, handing over the coffee and her freshly stamped rewards card.

"Absolutely not, I do not need the Chinese government hacking my phone and stealing my information," she said, balancing her cup in the half-full cupholder. "Have a good day." Glory raised the window of the passenger side and drove home.

Glory was awake particularly early today because later that morning, the court-appointed community advocate would be arriving for the first inspection of her home. She wasn't going to take any chances. She had been up late wiping down counters, dusting, and giving her wall-to-wall carpeting a final vacuum. If she was being forced into this arrangement, she wanted it to be over as soon as legally possible.

The commotion in the house had woken Delphine up early too. She had offered to be there when the advocate arrived, but Glory wanted her out of the house. Part of her was growing tired of Delphine bossing her around, and she'd be heading back to New York soon enough. Glory might as well deal with it herself.

Instead, Delphine made plans to meet up with Landry, who claimed to need help reviewing some real estate contract, something about a hunting cabin in Catahoula Parish. Delphine had made it seem like it was a burden, but Glory could smell the fancy perfume on her as she left.

Glory parked her car and entered her kitchen through her garage. She knew that Delphine thought the kitchen was still too cluttered. Each shelf of the antique mahogany hutch was stuffed from top to bottom with china, earthenware bowls, cookie molds, and teapots, but eventually Delphine conceded that they had purged enough. Glory was not going to allow Delphine to discard all of her treasures in a thrift store bin. Her daughter may have been smart, but she didn't appreciate fine things like Glory did. Sure, Delphine liked expensive things, but without the label or the price tag, would she have appreciated them as much?

Glory headed toward the sink and lifted the lid of her coffee for an inspection. She shook her head in disapproval. That boy doesn't even know how to measure correctly, she fumed. She grabbed a carton of milk and poured in more. Never one for silence, she turned the dials of the radio on the kitchen windowsill.

"That's my song," she said to absolutely no one when she heard Luther Vandross. She turned up the volume louder and sang along. She was swaying to the music when she heard rustling in the yard. This time she knew exactly what it was. The same raggedy cat that had been begging around the neighborhood was back.

The cat was too skinny for its own good, but its black fur somehow managed to have a sheen anyway. The beast sat still on the patio table, noble and silent, staring directly at Glory. It reminded her of those Egyptian cat statues she saw in that museum in New York that Delphine had dragged her to. She couldn't remember the name of the museum, but she remembered all that walking she did that day and that crinkly scarf she bought in the gift shop.

Without knowing what came over her, she extracted a delicate bone china saucer decorated with yellow daisies from her hutch. She carried the saucer, brimming with milk, outside and eased it onto the patio table. The cat meowed and brushed its head against her wrist. "Can't even be nice," she snapped, yanking her hand back. The cat meowed again, then lapped the milk from the bowl. "I will never pet you."

She returned to the kitchen and was confronted with about a dozen banker boxes from Amity's apartment. With a couple of hours until her appointment, she might as well dig in.

Glory emptied the contents of one box labeled EPA FILINGS onto the table. There were water analyses, topography reports, a collection of environmental violations, and all sorts of records that Amity had gathered. Charts, graphs, and maps. Glory lost herself in the papers. She noted anything that she didn't understand, facts and figures she found shocking, questions, and things she wanted to research. How she would go about all of this she wasn't exactly sure, but she was starting to understand why Amity was so engaged. The more she read, the more questions she had.

And then, as if snapped out of a hypnotic state, Glory heard the slamming of a car door. She cursed when she looked at the clock and realized it was time for her court-appointed agony. She jumped up from the table, shut the radio off, and headed toward the front door. Her mouth nearly hit her knees when she opened it.

Constance Wheeler—frenemy, church gossip, and all-around pill of a woman—was standing at the front door. She was wearing a red dress that was too snug for her ample frame, and her hair was bleached in that way that a lot of black women down here do, with that hint of yellow-orange, the same color as a baboon's ass.

"What are you doing here?" demanded Glory. "I'm all settled up on my annual dues."

"Hello, Glory. I am your court-appointed community advocate. I'm here for my first home inspection as a result of your"—she reviewed paperwork attached to a clipboard—"housing violations." Her face was fixed in a triumphant expression.

"Like hell you are," said Glory.

"First things first," Constance said, emboldened. She stretched out a hand with her palm up. "Give me my earrings."

Without thinking, Glory said, "You get your earrings when your husband stops making foolish wagers."

"It seems to me you have a choice to make. Return my earrings or flunk your evaluation, which would leave you with a"—she rifled through more papers on the clipboard—"ten-thousand-dollar fine and possible condemnation of your home. I believe I have you in the catbird seat."

What a stupid expression, thought Glory. Catbird seat. What does that even mean? If it meant that Glory didn't have a leg to stand on, Constance was probably right, and she knew it.

"Here," Glory twisted the diamond earrings free and dropped them in Constance's hand. "How the hell are you my advocate? Running the DMV doesn't make you qualified to do anything but renew driver's licenses."

"I'll have you know that I have an associate's degree in psychology from Southern Louisiana Community College, which comes in handy when evaluating the underlying causes of complex hoarding situations such as yours." Constance slid the clipboard under her armpit and pressed her arms against her body as she stabbed the diamond solitaires into her earlobes. "I also have eighty hours of training provided by Lafayette Parish. You see, some people talk a big game about charity. Others actually put in the work."

"I am not a hoarder," Glory insisted. "This whole thing is a farce. And I have a pretty good idea of who called in anonymous false charges, I might add. I just need the evidence."

"You're free to chase whatever delusional fantasies you want in your free time, but according to the Superior Court of the City of Lafayette, this house is a problem," said Constance. "Luckily for you, I am a professional as well as a kind-hearted person, so this will remain confidential, as is required by law."

"Thank you, I guess," said Glory as courteously as she could muster. It was in that moment that she realized that all her business would soon be broadcast across the Acadiana Red Hat Society, not to mention the diocese. With the mouth on Constance, the pope would probably be filled in by the end of the week.

"Shall we start in the vegetable garden?" asked Constance.

"Vegetable garden? Ain't nothing in those garden beds except weeds. The produce at Sam's Club is good enough for me."

"I find that very interesting, given that you practically blackmailed me to get those fingerprints, under the guise of someone breaking into your garden . . . Wasn't that your excuse?"

Glory's face froze. She had forgotten about the elaborate backstory she had invented to coerce Constance to run those fingerprints. Immediately she realized two things: Constance was not here to play. Furthermore, Constance was sharper than Glory had given her credit for. She would need to be more vigilant in her investigations moving forward.

"I do suppose that was a little bit of a white lie," said Glory, scrambling for words. "You see, things keep disappearing from my home, and truth be told, I have reason to believe it's a family member. I don't want the authorities involved, naturally."

"I knew you were up to no good," said Constance, shaking her head in disgust.

Glory was ready to launch a barrage of insults against the woman's family and her dog. But now was not the time. She knew she'd have to keep her opinions to herself, no matter how difficult.

"I don't have all day for this nonsense, Glory. Let's get started."

Constance inspected the foyer, clipboard at the ready. The entryway had been cleared of the mountain of cookbooks and unhung art leaning against the walls. Stacks of unopened mail had been opened, considered, and shredded. A small entryway table now featured a tray for the day's mail. A vintage plate from Glory's collection had been repurposed as a home for keys. Delphine had hung the art on the walls in a pleasing gallery style. Constance was wordless and scribbled away. Glory stretched her neck, trying to read what she wrote. Constance huffed, concealing the paperwork with a manicured hand.

"Next room, please."

Glory gnashed her teeth but kept quiet, escorting her to the living room. A large leather chesterfield was flanked by matching armchairs upholstered in burgundy velvet—all procured from estate sales. Glory's own chair, a tattered wing back, had been draped with a vintage suzani. On the mantel were various decorative objects—a brass clock, books, and ceramic candlesticks from her mother. A pleasingly faded Turkish rug gave the room a cozy but collected feeling.

"This is a lot more tasteful than I would have expected from you," said Constance, writing more notes.

Glory huffed and looked out her sunroom to avoid becoming even more enraged. Every bone in Glory's body wanted to break that clipboard over Constance's head, but she managed to keep herself together.

Constance walked into the kitchen, where the laminate counter-tops were cleared except for the stained Mr. Coffee machine and a chrome toaster. Constance pointed at the lidded banker boxes near the kitchen table. "What are all these boxes?"

Glory walked from the living room to the kitchen, shielding the boxes from view with her body. "These are personal documents, Constance. They are none of your business."

She might as well have extended a calligraphed invitation to Constance with that vague but intriguing warning. Constance crouched lower to read the handwritten labels—Amity's descriptions—on the outside of the boxes. *Mosstown EPA Filings. Benoit Family Holdings. State Testimony Prep. Possible Lawsuits and Actions. Father Romero Research / Speeches.*

Constance banged her clipboard against the kitchen table. "Glory Broussard, I demand to know what you're up to."

"Fine," she said. Sometimes it was easier to tell the truth than to spin a convincing lie on the spot. "Father Romero is testifying in Baton Rouge in a hearing about environmental justice, and I am helping him prepare." This was true, as Father Romero had asked for her help after their run-in at the Lafayette General emergency room.

Constance was agog. "Father Romero has a PhD from the Chicago Theological Seminary. And he just won the Lewiston Grant. Why would he ask you?"

And not you? That was what Glory assumed she meant, but she kept her composure. In fact, it pleased her to see Constance come ever-so-slightly undone. Was it anger, or something more personal, like jealousy?

"You think you know everything about me, don't you? I've seen you and the other Red Hat members laughing at me, gossiping behind my back. You may think I'm a joke, but Father Romero does not. I have been working with him and Sister Amity, bless her soul, for many months," said Glory. Well, she was on the team now, she reasoned. "While you have been planning Easter Egg hunts, I have been a valued member of his investigative team."

Constance looked as if storm clouds had singled her out for a downpour.

"Do you know what a fence-line community is, Constance?"

"Well, I . . ."

"A fence-line community is an area situated near facilities that produce hazardous waste. Did you know that Mosstown, which is 80 percent black, is a fence-line community? And did you know that these communities are disproportionately black? Do you think it's an accident that oil refineries end up near poor black people?"

"I suppose not."

The old rope-a-dope. Like a boxer, Glory knew that when you have someone on the ropes, you keep them there. "Did you know that, according to the CDC, about 3,700 Americans get gallbladder cancer each year? It's a rare cancer. And yet there were fifty diagnosed cases in Mosstown alone last year."

"That is a shame," said Constance.

"Damn right it's a shame," said Glory. "And you know what's even worse? Black people are more likely to breathe polluted air, no matter their income. It don't matter if you're rich or poor. These polluting companies will find black people no matter where they live. And the organizations that fight for so-called environmental justice? Hardly no black people sit on those boards. So you'll have to forgive me if my picture frames are a little dusty, or if I'm a little behind on my mail, because honestly, I have been working on more important things." She paused before delivering what she hoped would be the final blow. "And I'd like to get back to this crucial work."

Constance looked every which way except at Glory, just like she had at the Red Hat member meeting. She grabbed the clipboard off the table and rustled the pages faster than she could read them.

"Well, this house is awfully cluttered for my liking, but I guess one person's clutter is another person's cozy. I will file my report with the court."

"A favorable report?" asked Glory, looking upward at Constance with a pleading smile in her eyes.

"I see no reason to file anything other than a satisfactory report."

"Hot damn, I'm done with this nonsense."

"Not quite," said Constance. "There will be at least two more inspections to confirm that you've been compliant."

Glory shuddered.

"I suppose my work here is done."

"Look, I know I'm not your favorite person, but I'd appreciate you keeping all of this confidential."

"I already told you, I am bound to confidentiality."

"I mean not just this visit, but . . . everything else?"

Constance pulled a manila envelope out of her bag. "So I got curious when you accosted me at the book club meeting. I wondered what could be so important that you would be willing to blackmail me, a decent and honorable woman. So I ran the fingerprints."

Glory lunged for the envelope. Constance snapped it back over her shoulder.

"You're not the only person with investigative talents in this town," she said. "What do you want with this Angus Valentine anyway? Does he owe you money? Or is he your hitman?"

"*Hitman?*" said Glory, incredulous. "There's only one client that owes me money, and that's your husband. And he's alive, isn't he?"

Glory racked her brain. "Angus Valentine? I have never even heard of that name before."

"I'd suggest you stay away from him," Constance said as she tossed the envelope on the table toward Glory. "He's done some prison time and was released into a work release program."

Glory computed the facts in her head, then clapped her hands when she solved the equation. "Gus!" she yelled. Noah Singleton's Gus. Flirting with the white woman Gus. Can't make a decent cappuccino to save his life Gus.

Constance dropped the clipboard into her handbag, signaling that the visit was over. With one hand on her hip and the other wagging directly at Glory's face, she said, "One of these days I'm going to find out what you're *really* up to, Glory Broussard. And when I do, it ain't gonna be pretty."

"You can see yourself out," said Glory, waving her off dismissively.

Constance marched out of the house. The door creaked open, and she yelled out, "You have a package," before shutting the door behind her.

Must be something Delphine ordered online, Glory thought. Delphine had already received several packages in her brief time in Lafayette, including the moisturizer she'd left back in New York, even though Glory told her she could use her Merle Norman products. And new sheets, because she thought the guest room needed an "upgrade."

Glory shuffled to the front door and was taken aback by the box sitting in front of the door. It had no labels or tape. The flaps were casually tucked into each other, in the way someone would store Christmas ornaments in the basement. She looked around and found the block was empty, except for Constance, who was walking toward her car and doing her best to ignore her.

Glory tugged at the box flaps, then let out a blood-curdling scream. A mist of bees swarmed her body. Constance spun around and gasped when she saw what was happening. Glory kicked the box away and jerked her arms and legs, trying to flick away what looked like hundreds of bees, but it was too late. Glory's plump hand had already started to swell. Red welts raced up her arm. Her vision grew faint. She barely croaked out "Call 911" before collapsing to the ground.

12

By the time Glory's eyes fluttered open, she was stretched across her front lawn, her body sunken into the damp grass. Hovering over her were two male paramedics and Constance Wheeler's overprocessed hair.

"Ma'am, can you hear me?" asked the paramedic as he waved a light directly into her pupils.

"Wha . . ." Glory struggled. "What happened?"

It was Constance who had called 911 in horror as Glory staggered to the lawn and blacked out. By the time the ambulance arrived, her hand was as swollen as a baseball mitt. The EMTs had pricked her outer thigh with a shot of epinephrine, which slowed the crawl of welts up her arm.

"You're in anaphylactic shock," said the paramedic. "Are you allergic to bee stings?"

"I ain't ever been bit before," she croaked. "What do you think?"

"We only found one stinger, there in your right paw."

Glory, not in the mood for jokes, shot the man a hardened glance. Had she been her regular self, she would have definitely rebuked him in the name of the Lord, but as it was, the earth felt like it was on a tilt. She propped herself up on the lawn and locked her elbows behind her. A car driving too fast for the neighborhood speed limit appeared. Delphine and Lieutenant Landry, who had been reviewing the terms of his new hunting property, flung open the doors of his patrol car and came running out.

"Mom," screamed Delphine, diving to the lawn and putting her arm around her mother's shoulder. "What happened? Landry heard a 911 call from your address, and we raced over."

"Someone put a box of bees on my doormat."

"Bees?" said Delphine in disbelief. "Why would anyone do that?"

The police radio crackled. "I'm at the scene. A large vessel containing bees was placed at the doorstep of 3763 Viator Drive. No backup requested at this time, but we do need animal control on the premises asap." Landry, as always, seemed to know what to do.

"Miss Glory, we need to get you over to the hospital," said Landry.

"No, I'm not going to the hospital," she insisted. "It's one bite. The paramedic already done shot me up with drugs. I'll be fine. Just help me up."

"I don't think you need me anymore," chimed Constance, relieved. "Feel better, Glory." She walked as fast as a high-heeled woman in her late fifties could manage and did not look back.

Landry and Delphine clutched Glory's forearms and pulled until she was upright. "I'll take it from here," said Landry, dismissing the paramedics. Delphine wrapped an arm around Glory, and they wobbled back into the kitchen through the garage, evading the bees still swarming the front door.

Glory eased into a chair at her dining room table. She may have still felt groggy from the injection, but she was clear-headed enough to want Landry out of her house. She didn't want him asking about the boxes she'd procured from Amity's apartment, not to mention the manila envelope still resting on the kitchen table. The sooner he left, the sooner she could take her investigation to the next level.

"Miss Glory, you want to tell me why someone would leave a box of bees at your door?"

"I have no idea," she said, stone-faced. "I am the victim here."

"I usually turn a blind eye to your freelance gambling activities, but do you have any angry clients? Anyone who owes you money?"

Glory scratched at the red welts still blooming around her clavicle with both hands, leaving a maze of crimson lines and slashes on her chest. "I don't run that kind of operation. You know that. Anyone who owes me money settles up eventually, and no one owes me enough money for a stunt like that." Glory visualized the ledger in her head, just to be sure. The only person who owed her any real money was Constance's husband, and that man was weaker than a gallon of sun tea brewed on a cloudy day.

"I think it's time you told the truth," said Delphine.

How do you say *Girl, shut up!* with your eyes? That's what Glory was trying to communicate with her face, but Delphine ran her mouth anyway.

"We don't think Sister Amity committed suicide. We think she was murdered, and we've been looking into it and asking around. Maybe the bees are connected to that, to someone who wants to hurt you? Or hurt *us*?"

Landry gripped the top of a dining chair and let his head hang. He looked like a man about to lose his cool, like a man who needed a few seconds to regroup before he said something he might regret. "There was no foul play associated with Sister Amity's death. Absolutely none," he said sternly. "Come by the station, and I'll hand you the autopsy report. You can read it for yourself."

Glory grinned and squeezed his hand. "Thank you, Landry. Inside information sure would go a long way in our investigation. I promise not to rat you out."

He stopped her. "Autopsy reports are public records, Glory. It's not inside information. This is the Lafayette Police Department, not the CIA." He backed up from the table, pinched his forehead, and paced the kitchen. A large van pulled up. A man dressed in head-to-toe protective overalls and a beekeeper's mask stepped out. "I'm going to do you both a favor and keep this nonsense out of my report, but you've got to drop it, Glory. You can't go nosing around Lafayette, pissing people off, and not expect trouble to show up at your front door." He walked out of the kitchen to meet animal control.

Delphine poured a glass of water for Glory. "Landry is right. This needs to stop."

The water was on top of the manila envelope, the one that contained the research that Constance had pulled. Glory grabbed the water and drank it. She slid the envelope onto her lap, careful not to attract Delphine's attention.

"Come see," said Glory, patting the table and gesturing for Delphine to sit down with her. "You never knew my friend Beverly. Everyone knew me and Amity were thick as thieves, but not a lot of folks remember Beverly, because she died when she was nine years old.

"Beverly's mama cleaned for a rich white family in Breaux Bridge. You should have seen that house. It was grand, with tall white pillars out front and a big old red door. Her mama used to bring her over to play, and she and that little white girl became real good friends." Glory stopped for a moment to scratch at her clavicle.

"Mama, what does this have to do with anything?"

"So the girls decide they want to have a sleepover, and that was real unusual back then—a black girl sleeping over at the house of a little white girl? Unheard of. Beverly's mama didn't approve, but what could she do? It was her employer, and she didn't want to seem ungrateful. So Beverly packed her little bag and spent the night, and we were jealous because that house was fancy and had its own pool. Come to find out, the next morning they said she died in that pool. It was ruled an accidental drowning."

Delphine sat in rapt attention. "That's awful."

"Yes, it was. But Beverly could swim, and I mean *swim*. During the summer, we'd go to the Negro pool because there was only one pool in Lafayette where we could go. Amity and I splashed around in the shallow end because that's all we could do, but Beverly would climb that tall ladder up to the diving platform and jump. She was graceful, just like Esther Williams. It was hard to imagine that she'd drown. Her mother went down to the funeral parlor to dress her for the wake, bruises all over her body. Half of her head was caved in."

Delphine covered her mouth in horror. "Why didn't anyone report it to the police?"

"Her family did report it to the police, and they looked the other way," said Glory, taking a long gulp of water. "This isn't law school, Delphine. This is Louisiana."

She stood up, taking the envelope with her. "I need to lie down. I know you and Landry and just about everyone else in this town thinks I'm some old fool. Maybe I am. But what I do know is that every time a crime is buried, justice also has to wait. And I'm tired of waiting. I was too young to help Beverly, but I will find justice for Amity if it takes the rest of my days."

Glory retreated to her bedroom to lie down, and by the time she woke up, it was the next morning. The soft morning light filtered through her gauzy drapes. A sandwich on a Wedgewood plate and an etched crystal carafe filled with water had somehow appeared on her nightstand. Glory had managed to sleep through the entire day and night in an epinephrine haze. Her skin still felt raw, and her hand was still puffy, but it didn't matter. Glory knew she had to get going, because evil doesn't take days off.

She showered and got dressed. Waiting for her at the kitchen table was Delphine.

"I think you're right about Amity," said Delphine. "We're not going to let another one of our own disappear without someone going to jail. I need to know everything you've learned and every hunch you've kept secret from me."

"Get dressed," said Glory. "We're going to Born Anew Ministries."

13

The town of Scott, Louisiana, hadn't changed much from the days when Glory and Amity would run around town in scuffed Mary Janes and starched pinafores. No one had bothered to tear down the defunct cotton gin, the gray metal building that stood on stilts with the rusted red roof. The town was stuck in time, but an awful moment in time. A time its black residents would rather not revisit and its white residents would rather pretend didn't happen at all.

Delphine crossed the train tracks and drove by the old pharmacy with the Rexall sign that could have been from the 1950s, or even earlier. Electrical wiring draped from pole to pole on each street, which were lined with tidy but old single-story homes with flat roofs.

"Pull over here," said Glory. "The halfway house is down the street."

Glory explained what she had gleaned from Gus's file. He was thirty years old. Four of those years had been spent in prison for possession of heroin. After serving half of his sentence, he had been released into the Born Anew Ministries, a halfway house, drug rehabilitation, and work training program. The Born Anew

Ministries was a project of Father Romero's, which sought to reduce punishment from Louisiana's notoriously harsh prison sentences for drug use. Its modest "campus" was in Scott.

Glory peered through her binoculars and narrowed in on her target. The Born Anew Ministries sounded grand on paper, but in reality it was a handful of shoddy homes and trailers in a low-income neighborhood.

At the center of the property was a tidy mint-green house with vinyl siding and darker green shutters. A half a dozen cars were lined up under the carport, with more parked haphazardly in the front yard. Behind the house was a collection of trailer homes in the same mint-green color, situated around a giant oak tree that stood in the center.

All of the trailer homes were old, but most of them looked habitable except for one. The corner of the roof was smashed in, probably from the branches of the tree. Half of the backside of this trailer had been ripped off and was decaying on the ground. The home had probably been a victim of a hurricane, neglectful tenants, or both.

Glory was busy noting the various states of decay of that particular trailer when the door opened and Gus appeared. He jumped from the trailer onto the ground, which one must do when there are no stairs. He got behind the wheel of a shiny pickup truck and steered around the other cars in the yard.

"Let's go," said Glory.

The truck was so new it still had dealer license plates affixed to its bumper. Gus drove down the uneven roads of Scott onto Interstate 10.

"I wonder where he's going?" asked Delphine.

"I suspect he's going to CC's Coffee House for his shift," said Glory. "From what I gather, he works Sunday through Thursday."

"That is one awfully shiny car," piped Delphine. "A little spiffy for someone on a work release program."

"My thoughts exactly."

Glory leaned her heavy head back against the headrest of the car. The sting of the epinephrine shot was still screaming in her thigh. Her head was thick and heavy with fog. The clanky rhythms of the frottoir blared from the car speakers. Normally she wiggled around her kitchen when *Bonjour Louisiane with Mandy* came on 88.7, but she was in no mood for zydeco music today.

"Turn that down," said Glory. They rode the rest of the way in silence, past a nonstop barrage of billboards for casinos and personal injury attorneys, the wallpaper of Louisiana highways.

Glory navigated Delphine to the parking lot in front of the Albertsons grocery store, adjacent to the coffee shop, giving her an extra minute to develop a plan of action before being detected. "You go to Landry and get that police report," Glory instructed. "I'll stay here for a while and watch that good-for-nothing jailbird." Her purse, like the burden of finding Amity's murderer, seemed to become heavier every day. She hauled both loads into the coffee shop.

Glory walked into CC's Coffee House and nearly aborted the entire mission when she saw that white woman with the long wet hair and disgraceful shorts again. And just like last time, Gus, a man who never seemed to smile at all, had a grin plastered on his face. And for what? thought Glory. What did he intend to do? Take her back to his trailer, the one with the dented roof and the vinyl siding? It was not a charitable way to look at it, but there was something fishy about the man at the very least. Maybe even homicidal.

Amber was her name. It blared out from her bedazzled keychain, a mess of keys and lanyards and charms. This time her hair was dry. A feather was dangling from her frazzled mane. The overall effect, thought Glory, made her look like a baby bird that had been ejected from its nest.

Gus filled Amber's plastic cup with ice. As he poured, Glory could see for the first time that his arm was etched with tattoos. They were barely perceptible against his blue-black skin, but Glory couldn't help staring. A topless woman. A king of spades. *Carpe Diem*. How original, mused Glory. Then she spotted the faintest of tattoos, a snake with a forked tongue.

Amber flashed her phone to pay for her drink. Glory couldn't help but think it was not the only thing she'd flashed recently. Amber looked back at Glory as she left and snorted. Was it because she was old? Or fat? Or black? Maybe it was the trifecta of it all that was so contemptible. Glory's face became hot. Was she feeling anger or shame, that she could feel so dressed down by this woman in her dirty Old Navy flip-flops? She had grown accustomed to suppressing this feeling many moons ago, and she was tired.

Gus's face sank when he saw Glory, his crankiest customer. "Good morning, Miss Glory," he said, his smile waning. He sounded like a child being forced to make small talk with an old hateful relative. "Cappuccino?"

"Well done," said Glory. She figured he'd never talk if she kept browbeating him like she had. It was time to take another approach. "How do you like working here? It's been, what, a few weeks now?"

Gus looked suspicious and surprised. "I like it all right, I guess. A lot to learn, but I like working with my hands," he said. "You normally don't come inside on Fridays." He was more observant than Glory had realized.

"I got some reading to do for my book club," she said, retrieving a flimsy paperback from her purse. "I'm not one of those people who show up ill-prepared for the monthly book club," she said, even though that was exactly who she was.

"I'll bring your coffee to your table, Miss Glory."

She thanked him, found a seat, and cracked open the book. She pretended to read but couldn't concentrate even if she had intended to. It was the first moment she'd had alone since those bees swarmed around her. Her still-swollen hand seared with pain.

That she felt unwell was only a minor problem compared to this: Who had intentionally placed a box filled with bees on her doorstep? It was not random, Glory knew. Could it have something to do with the home inspection and Constance's visit? Did someone want her to fail her home inspection? It seemed more likely that someone wanted to scare her. Did Amity's murderer know she was looking for him? And had the murderer been following her? Even more frightening, did he know where she lived and had he been at the house?

Gus clanged the coffee on the table, startling Glory.

"Sorry, Miss Glory, didn't mean to scare you."

Delphine was surprised to find herself feeling nervous as she drove to Landry's house. He had texted her to say that he'd returned home unexpectedly but had brought an extra copy of the police report and autopsy with him.

She couldn't stop thinking about their last encounter, when they met up over breakfast to review the contract for the hunting cabin. She'd been annoyed to find herself noticing the intensity of his blue eyes and that his aftershave smelled like sandalwood and vetiver. For a moment, she'd lost herself in the lines that rippled across his face when he smiled, like a stone skipping across a pond.

But now she was going to his actual house. Scenarios drifted across her mind. If he tried to kiss her, how would she respond? She would protest that she was a married woman. But did that really matter now that her marriage was over? Yes, she insisted, it did matter. And even if it didn't, *he* was a married man. With children. No, screw that, she thought. Life is messy, not black and white. Events would lead where they may. On the other hand, maybe she wasn't in the best of positions to enter into a passionate affair. She should focus on rebuilding her professional reputation, or trying to end her marriage with some measure of grace. There was a time she would have cared about both. Now, she could scarcely recognize her current situation, which involved a mandatory suspension from work and being on the verge of owing alimony to her husband.

She pulled up into the large home in the River Ranch section of Lafayette. It was one of the tonier parts of town, near Whole Foods and the good Target. The development was filled with tiny lots and big houses meant to mimic New Orleans in a suburban setting, complete with front porches with ceiling fans and windows with colorful storm shutters.

Landry's garage door was open for all to see. At one end of the garage was a long worktable littered with wood shavings and lumber of various sizes. Above the table was a peg wall with dozens of tools neatly arranged according to size. In the corner was a weight bench and a rack filled with heavy dumbbells. This was not just a place for his car but somewhere he spent a considerable amount of time.

She parked her car in the driveway and walked inside. Landry was lying on his side, his arm bent into a triangle to prop himself up. Surrounding him was a low table, tiny cups, and a miniature teapot. A small girl, around five years old if Delphine had to guess, was whirring around the space dressed in a princess dress and tiara. She poured imaginary tea into the cups and handed one to Landry.

"You wanna pour a cup of tea for Daddy's friend?"

The girl poured more imaginary tea for Delphine and handed her a pink plastic teacup.

Delphine sipped with great fanfare. "Why thank you! This is the best tea I've ever had."

"Sophia, why don't you go inside and see if your mom has any cookies for you."

Her eyes widened at the mention of cookies, and she vanished into the house.

"I have to admit, I was not prepared for this level of adorable," said Delphine.

Landry rounded up his legs and thrust himself upward.

"Everything okay? I got a little worried when you said you needed to take the day off."

"Sophia woke up this morning in tears from a nightmare in which we went to Disney World and I disappeared. Cried for an hour straight and damn near fainted when I tried to go to work this morning. Figured I'd take the day off and let whatever is going through that little head of hers run its course."

"She's beautiful. And you're a good dad."

"I try," he said. On the worktable sat his nylon, police-department-issued bag. He unsnapped the handles and handed her a folder. "I really wish you and your mama would let this go, but here's the file. All public information. I think you'll see there's nothing untoward happening. Just a sad, sad situation."

"Thanks," she said, clutching the file. "I've just never seen her like this before. She is so convinced something happened. And it just doesn't feel right, you know? I've run it through again and again, and I just can't make sense of it."

"These things never make sense. It's a dark pact between that person and another kingdom."

Delphine inhaled and looked around at the garage. The walls of an unfinished dollhouse were being held together by wood clamps on the worktable. "So is this your man cave?"

He looked down at the ground and smiled. Delphine could see that it wasn't a joyful smile but a vulnerable one. The kind you break out when you've been caught. "I guess you could say that. Kerry is always barking at me about what I ought to be doing. I try to keep the peace, so when the girls go to bed, I get to work in here."

Frazzled wires with black-and-red tubing were strewn across the table. "Is that dollhouse going to have electricity? That's outrageous."

She stroked the smooth wood of the dollhouse's slanted roof.

Landry inched closer. "I'm going to run the red wire up this wall here," he said, pointing and grazing her shoulder. A different kind of electricity jolted up Delphine's spine. "And that'll connect three light sources."

The hairs on the back of her neck were awakened. For a split second, she closed her eyes and inhaled the familiar smell. The sandalwood. The vetiver.

"Why can't I be a princess at the grocery store?" Sophia pouted as she bounced back into the garage.

Delphine and Landry jumped apart, like the same ends of a magnet.

"Hey, that's my dollhouse!" the child added when she saw the adults conferencing around the wooden structure.

"And it's gorgeous. You are one lucky girl," insisted Delphine.

Landry's wife, Kerry, trailed behind, staring at her phone while her daughter twirled in the garage. Delphine had been surprised to hear that Beau Landry had married into the Benoit family. She was even more surprised that anyone in the Benoit family, Lafayette's royal family, would marry a commoner. He was plain, simple, and earnest, and Kerry was none of those things. To Landry's credit, he hadn't changed after all these years. Delphine guessed this was why he spent so much time in the garage.

Kerry and Delphine had met just once, when she made an appearance at the funeral of Delphine's grandmother. She had the kind of effortless looks that men thought were natural and women knew came at a high price. They were sustained by Pilates on Saturday mornings and salads when you wanted a burger, and were fed and nurtured by a steady stream of Instagram influencers. The right oversized button-down shirt tucked casually in just the front of her three-hundred-dollar jeans. The It bag. A mess of bracelets climbing up her delicate wrists. Delphine could spot these possessions the way a naturalist can tell a peregrine from a red-tailed hawk—through years of study and observation in the field.

"Oh, hi," said Kerry, finally tearing herself away from her phone, a bewildered look set in her face.

"You remember Delphine," inserted Landry when it was clear to everyone that she did not. "She's Miss Viola's granddaughter. We went to her funeral. She was just picking up the final contract for the hunting cabin to review."

Kerry shivered. "If you think me and the girls are ever going to hang out amongst your deer heads, draining the blood of those animals and making jerky, you are sadly mistaken."

Delphine had quickly registered something across Landry's face. Was he embarrassed of Kerry? Or did Kerry make him feel ashamed of who he was? Delphine suspected Kerry did not want to sully her Loeffler Randall sandals at his dingy hunting cabin. Maybe she wished her husband was hipper. More esteemed. Maybe Landry suspected this, too. Delphine could see the situation more clearly now. Landry wasn't laying a trap for an afternoon hookup. He was just trying to be a good dad and a decent husband to a woman who would always want more.

"I'll review the contracts and let you know if there are any issues," said Delphine in her official law firm voice. "Have a good day."

Delphine was kicking herself on the drive back to CC's Coffee House. She vowed to focus on the mess of her own marriage before she went and made a mess of anyone else's union, just like her boss had told her to. Landry was an old friend. There was no point entertaining fantasies. And besides, she could never be happy with a cop. She'd end up just like Kerry, regretful and bitter, banishing to the garage that lovely man who makes dollhouses with working chandeliers. No, she would not do that.

She turned into the Albertsons parking lot, just like Glory had told her to do that morning. She walked past Gus's truck and stopped, scanning the area for other people, then looking up to see if there were visible cameras. When the driver's side was locked, she doubled back to check the passenger side. Bingo. She opened the door just a smidgen, pressing her body against the cab of the truck. The new car smell hit her nose first. The tan leather seats were immaculate and the interior spotless. On the passenger seat sat a book called *The 48 Laws of Power* and Ralph Ellison's *Invisible Man*. She quietly shut the door and met her mother.

After two cappuccinos and several glasses of water, Glory's head felt lighter and clearer, even if her bladder was expanding. She had kept her eyes fixed on Gus for most of the day, who still was not making much progress on his training manual or his ability to prepare a CC's Mochasippi. Glory figured his mind must be busy with other things, like the chests of his busty customers, but maybe also murder. Delphine walked in and sat across from her mother at the table.

"Did you get it?"

"Yes, it's in my bag," said Delphine.

"Girl, what does it say?"

"I haven't read it yet," she said, swatting away Glory's hand that was now reaching across the table. "Not here."

Gus pulled the CC's apron above his head and engaged in an intricate handshake with Noah.

"Time to tail him," said Glory.

Delphine picked up the car, and they waited at the neighboring Wingstop restaurant until Gus appeared. When he did, they followed in careful but distant pursuit.

The early September sun was dimming earlier and earlier, which Glory was noticing for the first time. Glory had no idea where they were driving. After the bee attack, maybe she should be more careful. Or maybe give the whole thing up. If they weren't chasing the killer, maybe the killer was chasing them. Glory adjusted her side-view mirror to see if anyone was following. They exited Highway 10 and made a series of left, right, left, right turns down country roads steeped in darkness.

"Any idea where we are? This feels eerily familiar," said Delphine.

"No idea."

They continued to keep a careful distance, and when Gus drove his gleaming truck down a grand driveway, they both knew exactly where they were. They were back at Milton Knowles's house.

14

"That Milton Knowles. Why did I believe anything that man said?" asked Glory.

Delphine dimmed the car headlights and spoke in a whisper, scared that the men a hundred yards away could hear them. "No, you've been right all along. You never for a second believed anything that Milton told you, and it's not like he claimed he was innocent. And you've been suspicious of Gus from the second you saw him. I thought you were being unfair, but you were right to be." She kept the car at a snail's pace to observe Gus, who parked his truck in the driveway. Judging by the familiar howling of dogs and number of expensive cars with blacked-out windows, another drunken evening of dog fighting was underway in the backyard. Milton and Gus greeted each other with a series of handshakes, grips, and embraces, though they never really embraced. Their complicated, ritualistic greeting was effortless and practiced.

"The snake," said Glory. "I forgot to tell you." Glory explained to Delphine that she had noticed some of the same tattoos on Gus's forearm that they had seen on Milton the night of their confrontation. The king of spades. The snake.

"The same snake that was on the fentanyl lollipop," said Delphine. "It's all him."

They watched as Gus placed something into Milton's palm, which Milton thrust into the deep pockets of his baggy cargo pants. Milton then gestured for Gus to join him. It seemed friendly, like an invitation. Gus waved both of his hands in front of him and shook his head, but it was clear that Milton would get his way. Milton swiveled abruptly, as if he heard something in the distance. He stood at attention for a few beats before hooking his elbow around Gus's neck like a crook. The men vanished in the backyard.

"Girl, let's go," said Glory. She had already been attacked by a dog and swarmed by bees. Locusts would be next.

Southern storms don't give much warning. A light mist quickly gave way to torrential rain in minutes. By the time they made it back to Lafayette, sheets of rain made the windshield wipers nearly useless. Glory was so exhausted after a day of surveillance she nearly cried with relief as she walked through the door. She yanked a clean blue nightgown out of the dryer, headed into her bedroom, and settled in for the night.

The evening *Quiet Storm* programming on the radio, slow jams from the eighties and nineties, was the only music to suit her mood. Chaka Khan's "Through the Fire" was playing, and Glory could relate. She had been through the fire lately and had felt singed by the flames. Chaka knew! She could hear that Delphine was taking a shower down the hall, and she sure was glad that she was here.

She still couldn't shake the fact that someone had intentionally placed a box of bees on her doorstep. That person was still out there and, presumably, still cross with her. She walked into her bathroom and smeared cold cream across her face.

But who would be mad at her? Sure, Glory's mouth could occasionally get her into hot water. She had regretted the time at her niece's baby shower when she'd asked about the paternity of the soon-to-be-born child, but everybody had been curious—not just her. Then there was the time recently when she'd laughed at her fellow Red Hat colleague Millie Broward. She had just bought a compact car, and Glory wondered out loud why the biggest women always drive the tiniest cars. But none of this rose to the level of sourcing bees and delivering them to her home.

Glory rinsed the cold cream off her face. She tried to remove emotion from the equation and focus on the facts at hand. Fentanyl lollipops with Milton's signature branding were found inside Amity's closet. *A fact*. Gus's fingerprints were on the doorknob of Amity's bedroom door. *A fact*. Gus was a convicted felon on a work release program who knew Milton well and appeared to be selling drugs on his behalf. *A fact*.

Was this enough evidence to go to the police? No, she decided. Not yet. The evidence had to be bulletproof. She knew that the fingerprints, secured with her Amazon.com fingerprint kit and illegally run through the computers at the DMV—under coercion and possibly the threat of blackmail—would not stand up, no matter how miserably the police had inspected the scene. Not to mention motive, for which she had nothing. Why would Gus be in Amity's apartment at all? Did they know each other, or had he broken in? Moreover, why would he want her dead?

She fluffed up her pillow, adjusted her reading glasses, and analyzed the police report. Color photocopies of pictures of the crime scene peeked out from the back, and her chest tightened, just like when she got the news that her own mother had passed. She turned them face down on her bed. All air had evaporated when she saw Amity that day, lifeless against the door, the rust-colored blood dripping from her mouth. She would never look at those pictures again because she had seen it with her own eyes. And she could never forget. Landry had warned her that she would be haunted by Amity's death scene. On this he was right.

Glory became nauseous as she read the report. Not only was Amity's death more gruesome than she had realized, but the police appeared to be more apathetic than she could have imagined. First, there was a 911 call from a prepaid phone of "unidentified origin." Glory had only ever seen a few episodes of *The Wire*, and that was only because she had a crush on Detective Lester Freamon, but she had seen enough to know what a burner was. A 911 call from a burner was suspicious as hell. She realized she had never asked this simple question . . . *Who called 911 that day?*

Then there was the official cause of death, which was suicide by hanging. The report noted several broken bones in Amity's neck, specifically something called the hyoid bone. It made Glory flash back to the funeral, when she had briefly touched the body and noticed the neck felt unstable. Were these injuries consistent with a suicide? she wondered. Or could they have been caused by something else?

The last time she'd seen Amity felt like just yesterday and a million years ago. It had been a month earlier, just two weeks before her death. *A fact.* She played it back in her head like a movie. The Acadiana Red Hat Society had been raising funds for an after-school computer room, and the proceeds of the bake sale would be used for that. Glory didn't bake but begged Miss Odile for a batch of her legendary hand pies with preserved figs, which she passed off as her own. They sold out instantly. She saved two in her purse. Amity and Glory had lingered, sipping coffee donated by Noah. The women unwrapped the wax paper of their sweet pies with delicate fingers and chatted like two schoolgirls.

"I was thinking . . . what you ought to do is set up a website to sell all the antiques you find around town," suggested Amity. "You have a great eye. I think you could be very successful at this."

"I don't even know how to set up a website. And how am I going to compete with all those professionals?"

"You're already a successful entrepreneur. If I know one person with the smarts and tenacity to start an online business, it's you." Amity had always seen the best in people, even if they couldn't see it in themselves. *A fact.*

All that talk about dreams and such got Glory thinking. "What would you have done if you hadn't become a nun? Is there anything you wish you had done before taking vows?"

Amity sipped her coffee to cut the sweetness of the pie. "I always wished I'd had one proper boyfriend, not those losers I dated back then. Someone who would have taken me somewhere romantic, like Paris." Amity had always been a dreamer but trained herself to channel that ambition for others. She seemed happy, but Glory had always questioned whether she had taken vows out of desperation, a path to security and sobriety. She could have done anything she wanted, but it didn't matter now.

"Can I tell you a secret?" Amity had asked her. Of course she could. The only person Glory truly confided in was Amity. There was no else she would have told. "Speaking of Paris, I booked a trip in April. I set aside a little bit of the money I get giving speeches here and there and bought myself a ticket. Figured I ought to see it at least one time before I die, and if I can't have a boyfriend, I'm going to take myself." Glory remembered how happy she was to share this secret news. Of course, she would never make it to France before she died.

The wind screamed as Glory paged through the report. There was a write-up of the crime scene, a list of officers present, and those gruesome photos that she could not bear to look at. She read the grim details as if they were a horror novel and stopped when she reached the toxicology findings.

Conservator declined Lafayette Police Department request for toxicology report.

This was the first that Glory had heard of a conservator. Who was this person, and why would they decline a toxicology report? None of this made any sense. Glory knew everything about Amity, or so she had thought. But maybe a person's soul is unknowable. Maybe Amity was more mysterious than she had ever contemplated.

A snapping sound nearly made Glory fall out of bed. A broken tree limb, she figured, as her heart raced. There was no point trying to sleep in this godawful weather. She might as well get to work.

Glory walked to the kitchen and stared at the boxes lined up against the kitchen wall. She had told Father Romero that she would review the Mosstown files with him on Tuesday, which was . . . tomorrow, she realized. She swung open the refrigerator door and grabbed a mason jar filled with cold coffee. Delphine had been making these ever since she arrived. Cold brew, she called it, whatever that was. Glory added a splash of almond milk, which

Delphine had insisted on buying at Rouses supermarket because she claimed regular milk caused inflammation in the body. She sipped the concoction. Not bad, she thought, not bad at all. She kicked up the footrest of her recliner and started reading.

She had no idea how much time had passed, but eventually Glory awakened to Delphine's confused face staring down at her. She wiped the moisture trickling down her chin with the collar of her nightgown and squinted at the hazy rising sun illuminating the backyard. Mounds of paperwork were strewn across the carpet and the coffee table.

"Did you *sleep* here?" asked Delphine, dressed in the black leggings and a baggy tee shirt she called pajamas.

"I guess I did," said Glory, slightly befuddled and a little amused. "I couldn't sleep with that rain and that commotion, so I studied the police report and some of those Mosstown files." She rubbed the sleep from her eyes.

"Anything interesting?" Delphine asked, twisting her legs into a pretzel position on the couch.

Glory had more questions than answers when it came to Mosstown, but focused on the police report instead. "Let me ask you, what's a conservator? And why would a person have one?"

"It's a legal agreement that allows a person or entity to manage another person's affairs. It could be for a bunch of different reasons. Maybe the person is incapacitated because of an accident or mental illness, or they're too senile to make decisions for themselves. Why do you ask?"

Glory limped out of her chair and showed Delphine the questionable line in the police report, the one that mentioned that her conservator had declined a toxicology screening.

"Whoa," said Delphine. "I have no idea why Amity would have a conservator. And a suicide case without a toxicology report? I'm a corporate attorney, but this feels unusual to me."

Glory then pointed out the part about the fractured bones in her neck. "Seems like a lot of broken bones to me."

"Let me make some calls. My old law school roommate is an assistant district attorney. She might have a different perspective on these police reports . . . maybe know someone in the coroner's office." Delphine looked at her mother in astonishment. "I can't believe you stayed up all night reviewing this. I'm so impressed."

Glory beamed. She loved her daughter, but it was always a tense kind of love, a roses-and-thorns kind of love. The only thing more shocking than hearing a compliment from her daughter was the realization that she couldn't remember the last time Delphine had said anything so uncomplicated and kind to her. Anyway, she was not about to dissolve into a puddle of emotions.

"All anyone had to do is read the report and use some common sense." She shrugged. The living room mirror reflected Glory's wild hair and haggard face. "My lord, let me get ready to meet up with Father Romero. A woman should at least draw on some brows before meeting with the clergy."

She disappeared to her bedroom. Delphine opened the refrigerator and wondered what happened to all the cold brew coffee she had made the day before.

15

Glory parked her SUV in downtown Lafayette, which she was loath to do. Broken bottles and cigarette butts littered the sidewalk. Two homeless men, huddled together, looked her up and down. She had no idea why a priest would choose to live in the dodgy part of town and not in the diocese-approved rectory with the other priests, which would have been more respectable.

She buzzed for Father Martin Romero. When the two homeless men became fixated on her, she slammed the button with her fist and did not relent.

"Who is it?" asked a scratchy voice from inside the intercom speaker.

"You know damn well it's me," she said. "Let me up this instant before I'm kidnapped and sold into a sex trafficking ring." The door buzzed open, and Glory scurried inside to the elevator, relieved to escape what she was sure was a certain death. On the top floor, the elevator door opened not to a hallway but a full-floor apartment that looked like it belonged in New York City, not Louisiana. She was intercepted by Father Romero.

"Glory, thank you for coming," he said, taking her coat. "You don't have to worry about those fellows on the street, I assure you. They're harmless."

"That's what you think. I could see the devil in their eyes. I would think you'd be more perceptive."

This was unlike any apartment that Glory had ever seen in real life. He may have had a servant's heart, but he did not dwell in servants' quarters. First, there was the opera. It sounded lush, nothing like the tinny sound that vibrated from her kitchen radio. Secondly, the apartment was a loft, one open space except for a partial wall concealing a bed. The furniture was mostly black and chrome, which was not Glory's personal preference, but she could appreciate his commitment to an aesthetic. The desk stuffed in the corner, the one flanked with awards and lined with his own books, looked familiar. It was the background he used when he appeared on MSNBC. Giant ring lights trained on this corner of the apartment confirmed her suspicion.

And then there was the kitchen, which looked like a set from a cable TV cooking show. His six-burner stove sparkled. Glory had always wanted one of those expensive stoves with a hood, and recognized the Calcutta marble backsplash from those she had seen in *Southern Living* magazine. Black earthenware dishes sat on exposed wooden shelves. Glory could tell they were not from Sam's Club. She felt a certain way about these dishes. Attractive, yes. But you can't trust black dishes, the same way you can't trust a black toilet. How do you ever know if they are truly clean?

She had no idea anyone in Lafayette lived like this. Or could afford to live like this. But then she remembered how everyone in town erupted when he won the Lewiston Grant, a one-million-dollar, no-strings-attached prize awarded every year to a handful of so-called geniuses. It was the first time Lafayette had made the national news for something positive, instead of hurricanes or a serial killer. And then there were the books and the speaking appearances, not to mention the cable TV gigs. He was a priest with options.

A custom-made island floated in the middle of the kitchen, and on it sat a mess. *Clean as you go*, Glory remembered from her mother, but he didn't care. A hand-cranked pasta machine was on one end. The entire kitchen was sprinkled in fine flour.

"Would you like a coffee? Espresso?"

Still jittery from the three mason jars' worth of cold brew iced coffee she'd drank overnight, she declined. "Smells good in here. What are you making?" She sat at a long dining table.

"*Tortellini en brodo.*"

"Tortellini in *what*?"

He chuckled. "*Brodo.* Broth. I use organic veal bones from a farm near Shreveport. You'll love it. Just needs another thirty minutes or so." A fuzzy blue sweater clung to his narrow frame, which looked a lot like the cashmere sweaters that Delphine loved. It was paired with slim dark jeans and sneakers that were remarkably white and unscuffed. It was a youthful look that felt odd compared to Glory's outfits, especially since they were about the same age. It felt strange to be in a priest's home and to see him so casual, so out of context. More than anything, she was annoyed that he was wearing shoes inside his home. She thought he might have had more sense than that, but no.

"So tell me how you became interested in Mosstown with Amity? I had no idea you were helping with the research."

Glory searched her brain. The problem with lying all the time, she now realized, was that you have to keep track of the lies. It was exhausting. She vowed to try to be more truthful in life moving forward.

"Like you, I am committed to fighting injustice. Amity asked for my help, and I would have done anything for her."

The broth bubbled. "I miss her," he said, gazing into the bottom of the pot as if he might find her there.

She unbuckled a leather satchel and plunked several stacks of paperwork on the table. Her reading glasses were perched on the tip of her nose, secured by a strand of faux pearls draped around her neck. "I have some questions about these air quality reports from the EPA."

"So do I. I just know that those inspectors are paid off by the Benoit family, but I can't prove it. Amity and I could never find a smoking gun."

"Come see," she said.

Father Romero leaned over her shoulder.

"These are the 2017 air quality reports. Look at the signature and the date."

"I've seen these files before. Aaron Jefferson, Senior Environmental Inspector. That's not new."

"Now look at the reports from 2018 and 2019." She fanned more papers across the table.

Father Romero leaned in closer and shook his head. "I don't get it."

"For three consecutive years, the reports were signed on September 5 by the same inspector. What are the odds that the same person would inspect the same facility and file his report on the same day year after year? And there's no variation in the signature whatsoever, but you can see the teeniest tweak on the last digit of the year. For three years straight. It seems to me that someone just lifted this signature line. In my estimation, these reports are forged."

Steam filled the kitchen as the brodo boiled over and scorched the stove. He pushed the pot from the burner and stirred, slack jawed.

"I think you might be right."

She knew she was. The more she investigated Amity's death, the more she realized that the people who were supposed to be smarter than her maybe weren't that bright after all. It emboldened her. He dabbed sweat from his forehead with a kitchen towel, which made Glory uncomfortable. This was not a sanitary kitchen.

"According to my research, every public company that exceeds a certain amount of revenue must also have a dedicated compliance officer. In this case, that person is Keller Benoit. I can assure you there is reason to be suspicious of his intentions."

"I'm not sure I follow," he said, ladling his creation into the matte-black bowls.

"He and I have had some . . . interactions."

"I'm sorry, Glory, but I'm confused."

She rolled her eyes. "Cut the crap, Father Romero. He's one of my customers."

"Ah, I see," he said, setting the bowl in front of her. He poured a glass of chardonnay and shaved some parmesan into her bowl. "But if he's complicit, aren't you?"

"Absolutely not. I am semi-retired and living on a fixed income. It's entirely different."

He shrugged. "That's fair . . . I think."

"At any rate, the Benoits are having an annual investor meeting at the Pelican Club later this week, open to all shareholders. And I just bought six shares, so guess who's an investor now?" she said, toasting with a glass of white wine.

"Do you want me to come with you?"

"No, it'll be weird with a priest in the audience." She took a sip of her wine. "No offense."

"None taken." He gave the pepper mill several twists. "Let me know what you think."

She had to admit that it smelled divine, even if she was deeply suspicious of his black dishes. Reluctantly, she gulped the tortellini and then swooned. "You may not keep a tidy kitchen, but this is one of the most delicious things I've ever tasted." She gulped another spoonful.

Father Romero fixed his mouth as if he were about to say something but stopped himself. Instead, he brought up Amity once more.

"Sister Amity and I were supposed to go to Europe in April. We were part of a Vatican commission on social and environmental injustice."

"I bet you would have loved that, given how much you love all this Italian crap."

"It wasn't in Rome," he corrected. "We were going to Paris together."

16

Glory straightened her taupe beret, the one that she paired with a double-breasted trench from Chico's as soon as the September fall weather allowed. It was one of her favorite church outfits. Now that mass was over and she'd already confessed her sins, it was time to accrue some new transgressions.

She moseyed up to the front counter at CC's Coffee House. Noah wordlessly sprang into action, but Glory stopped him. "I think I'm going to switch things up today. One medium cold brew coffee with a splash of almond milk."

Noah and Gus stopped in their tracks like they'd seen a ghost. "Well, I'll be," said Noah. "Glory done found a new drink."

"Just fix my drink," she said, flustered by the attention. "I didn't order a side of sarcasm."

Gus prepared her order while Noah rang up the purchase. When the total flashed on the monitor, Glory steadied her phone in front of the green pulsing light of a nearby scanner.

"Now I need to know what's gotten into you. First you've got a new order, and now you've downloaded the app?"

"Don't look so surprised. I'm quite technologically advanced. And don't be stingy. I know I get a free drink for downloading the app. Plus, I gotta keep track of my rewards points." She put the phone back in her purse. "If you really want people to sign up for the app, you need to do a better job of explaining the benefits . . . really sell it to people and say what's in it for them."

Noah added her points from his register and smiled, amused. "I guess an old dog can learn new tricks."

She was about to lay into him something fierce, but remembered she had other priorities this morning. Making money and making small talk—with Gus.

"Mornin', Gus."

He gave Glory a brief nod and smiled before nearly knocking over the container of coffee. Ain't that something, thought Glory, to be a criminal and so clumsy. That's probably what landed him in jail, she figured. The man had no attention to detail.

"Now, if you're going to keep working at my coffee shop, I'm going to have to get to know you a little," she said in a pushy but charming tone that only a woman over the age of sixty could pull off. In these parts of Louisiana, there are three questions that matter to most people: Who's your mama? Are you Catholic? and Can you make a roux? Glory decided to start from the beginning. "Where you from? Tell me about yourself, son."

Gus looked around as if he hoped someone would save him. Without a life preserver to be found, he gave up. "Grew up in St. Martinville, ma'am. My parents were farmers, went wherever the work took them. Sugarcane, crawfishing, that kind of thing."

"That's honorable work, yes indeed. But you went to Prairie Elementary with Delphine, here in Lafayette. How did that come to be?"

"I guess you could say family troubles," he said, pouring almond milk into the coffee. "Good talking with you. Your table's open."

How dare he cut her off like that? It took her a few seconds to regroup, but eventually she took her tumbler of coffee and, with a saccharine smile, said, "You have a good day." The nerve of this barista, no, *jailbird*. Talking to his elders all casual like. It was disrespectful and rude. She huffed all the way to her table.

There were two newspapers she liked to read on Sundays—the *Times Picayune* and the *New York Times*—for their positions on national sports and the local high school football teams, on which she would occasionally accept wagers. However, today she pulled out an iPad from her giant bag. Delphine had gotten her hooked on the nifty gadget, which she was growing fond of. It was better than getting ink on her fingers and wrestling with all that messy paper.

Glory was reading up on the new hotshot quarterback from Lafayette Christian Academy when she recognized the shellacked hair of Keller Benoit. She wondered how many tubes of gel he used to get his hair like that and why someone so young would style their hair with the hardness of a helmet. His gold watch glimmered under the lights. She didn't know anything about watch brands, but she knew Delphine would recognize it. It was fascinating, thought Glory, that rich people down in Louisiana will practically hand you their bank statements. Delphine's husband had just as much money, maybe more for all she knew, and was as understated as this Benoit fellow was flashy.

What was going on with Chad, anyway? Glory had not wanted to be nosy, on account of Delphine having a tendency to grow armor whenever she asked about her personal life, and especially her marriage. If Delphine was distraught about her divorce, she sure wasn't letting on.

Glory was so busy staring at the man and making up stories in her head that she hadn't noticed that he'd turned around and was looking at her. Embarrassed, she pretended to be absorbed in her electronic tablet as he leaned over her shoulder.

"You mean to tell me that you're sitting here on a Sunday reading Alvin Bixby's high school football newsletter?" he asked, pulling a seat from her table, flipping it around, and sitting with his chest pressed against the back of the chair.

"You can't be in my line of business without knowing what's going on in the world. I like to do my homework," she said, closing the cover on her tablet. "What'll you have today?"

"No, ma'am." He laughed. "I'm still recovering from that last time." The couple of times she had seen him here, he'd grabbed his coffee and left. Maybe she could take advantage of his suddenly chatty mood.

"I have a question for you."

"Go on. Shoot."

The specific words she used now mattered. "I see your family all over the news. Your last name is on a bunch of buildings here in Lafayette. How does your family decide which charities to support? Where to give your money?"

"That's a curious question. Why do you ask?"

Not sure whether to reveal her real motive or not, she asked, "Your family is just so *generous*, to everything from the hospital to smaller things. I remember seeing once on the news you gave money to that family whose house burned down."

"My father loves to see his name on a plaque or, even better, a building. And that family with the house fire, they were in the news so much that it was an easy PR win. Not a lot of cash for a whole lot of return. And that nun who was drumming up support for them had been so active with protesting and such against our business. So we like to spread it around. Now that I think of it, we haven't heard from her in a while, so it must have worked."

Straight face, Glory told herself. No tears. "You sure you don't want to place a bet on the St. Thomas game?"

He rifled through his wallet and plucked out sixty dollars. "All right, you wore me down. I'll bet the moneyline on Denham Springs."

"I'll take it."

Because it was Sunday, Delphine knew that her mother would be working from CC's Coffee House by now. It was the perfect time for her to slip away to church without her mother noticing. She had had a lot on her mind and felt compelled to visit the church where she had confessed her earliest sins. That said, she did not want to give her mother the satisfaction of knowing that she went to confession. First, her mother would want to know why she wanted to go to confession after all these years. And then there would be the question of what she wanted to unburden herself of.

A few parishioners were waiting for confession in the quiet of the church pews. Delphine waited her turn. She couldn't stop thinking about the mess she had made. Her entire life had always been about the right school, the right job, the right outfits. But lately it had felt like a wrecking ball had come in and smashed it all to pieces. It was even harder to accept that she herself was the wrecking ball.

It was the quiet of the church, more than anything, that made her uncomfortable. Being inside a church felt like meditating, and why would she ever do that? Who wants to torture themselves by being alone with their own thoughts? She pulled out her phone to distract herself from the silent misery of her own thinking. After absent-mindedly scrolling through a few emails and social media accounts, she turned to her phone's camera roll.

The pictures were cruel evidence of what she had, and what she had lost. There was one picture of Chad in their kitchen, holding up a misshapen birthday cake that he had baked for her. Then there was the one that she took when they were upstate, when they were happy and in love, and the autumn light made them look as if they were glowing from the inside out. The high points of the marriage still lived in her phone, evidence that she was married and content, if only for a little while.

The camera roll documented the greatest hits of her marriage. The low points happened off camera. They were not commemorated in pixels but in emotional scars. There were the times when Chad and his friends joked about her small-town upbringing in Louisiana, like she was some bumpkin born in a barn. What made it even worse was that she had laughed along with them. And then there was the time, on that night she would never forget, he got plastered and raised a fist, just to see her flinch. And countless other times after that, when it was just easier to work late than to take inventory of her fraying marriage. The door of the confession booth opened. It was Delphine's turn.

She took a seat in the dark room. An intricately designed metal grill separated her from Father Romero.

"I haven't done this in ages," she said.

"That's quite all right. What matters is that you're here today," he said in a soothing tone. "I'll take my cues from you. Just start when you're ready, if you remember how to start, that is?"

"Oh yeah," she said. She looked down at the laminated cards that lived inside the booth. "Bless me, Father, for I have sinned. It has been . . . jeez, about a million years since my last confession. I was probably eighteen years old."

He chuckled gently. "I imagine you have a lot of sins to confess, then."

"Maybe I'll just focus on a few this time."

He remained silent.

Reluctantly, Delphine continued. "I've been lying to my mother about why I'm here . . . and why I've stayed. I came to visit, and her house was an absolute mess, so I stayed to help out. I told her that one of my cases had been settled, but the truth is I am taking a leave of absence from work. I guess you could call it a forced leave of absence." She spilled everything. The affair, the harbor cruise, the probation from work.

"That's pretty bad, isn't it?" asked Delphine. It was a relief to unburden herself to a stranger.

"It's not great," said Father Romero.

"So what's my penance?"

"I think your penance is to contemplate the damage you've inflicted upon your husband, your colleague, and his family. I'd recommend you find it in your heart to sincerely apologize to your husband and your colleague, though I'd suggest you leave his wife out of this apology tour. That, and twenty Act of Contritions, ten Our Fathers, and fifteen Hail Marys."

Delphine returned to the pews and completed her prayers. After she was done, she stayed on her knees, wondering how she had become a person that was unfaithful to a husband she had loved. And how she had come to convince herself that being with a married man was . . . not so bad. Her knees creaked against the padders, and her head scraped against the pews in front of her. She knew she ought to be ashamed, and yet she was not sorry.

17

Like most people in Lafayette, Glory knew of the Pelican Club but had never had the occasion to walk through its storied doors. She felt a tiny thrill in her bones as she steered herself up the majestic road that led to the main house for the stockholder meeting. Ancient Spanish moss trees flanked both sides of the lane, their branches knitting together overhead and casting a shadow that looked like lace. Had she kept her eyes on the road instead of the trees, she would have noticed how her modest Honda stood out compared to all the other cars headed in the same direction. The Mercedes coupes, Saab convertibles, and Range Rovers.

The whole place reeked of money and racism. It may have been built in 1932, the same year as the Augusta National Golf Club, but it wasn't until 1979 that any black person other than staff walked through its doors. Designed by the famed southern architect Hud MacKenzie, it was meant to be the ultimate winter destination for northern snowbirds, socialites, and golf lovers. It didn't matter to the architect that slavery had long been abolished. He may have set out to build a golf course, but what he really created was a social plantation, something soothing and familiar to its moneyed membership.

The Big House stood proud, with large Greek Revival pillars that saluted guests as they arrived. Generously proportioned verandas framed both stories of the house, and much to Glory's annoyance, there was a sweeping staircase that invited guests inside. The house and all its trim were painted in a crisp white, though nothing could whitewash the sins of the past. Glory parked her car and labored up the stairs, knowing her knees would pay the price tomorrow.

Delphine was on her way but had decided to come separately, hoping to work the phones calling her contacts back in New York a bit longer. Glory decided to venture inside on her own. An old white gentleman in a tuxedo with tails greeted her at the top of the stairs. He opened the door and allowed a wave of well-dressed people inside but intercepted Glory before she reached the door.

"Good afternoon. Are you here for the annual Benoit Investor Meeting?"

"Yes, I am," said Glory. She had never been to a meeting like this before but thought she looked pulled together enough in a loose black cardigan with matching shell underneath and elegant flowy pants. If there was one thing that would give her away, she knew it would be her shoes, which were never chic but always sensible.

"Very good. That entrance is around the side and through the back." He gestured. "Have a good day."

Glory nodded. Women in expensive dresses and men with sharp jaws continued to flow in, people who looked like they belonged at an investor meeting. But what did Glory know, anyway. She had never been to a meeting like this. There were probably multiple meetings in a big old building like this. They didn't make their money by just having one meeting at a time, she convinced herself.

Feeling unsure and out of her element, she snaked her way around the building.

In the back of the Big House, men—mostly black—smoked cigarettes on buckets that had been turned upside down. A forklift beeped, then disappeared into a long truck backed into the loading dock. Workers in black pants and black button-down shirts grunted as they moved heavy boxes.

Glory pushed her way through the back door, which wasn't really a door but strips of plastic hanging from a doorway. Kitchen staff piped saffron-hued filling onto halves of hard-boiled eggs. Others chopped herbs into bits so small they became unrecognizable, like mounds of chewed-up grass from a lawn mower bag.

"Quit your gawking and get to work," yelled a large black man, bald and sweaty. "We could use another server in the lunchroom." He tossed a black vest in her direction.

The vest landed in her hands, hot as an ember. Embarrassment and rage billowed inside of her as she stood silently, watching women in hairnets set tiny plates on big silver rounds and then men lift the trays above their heads with a single hand before disappearing. In an instant, she was ready to burn this whole place down. Her first response was to march out of that kitchen, fire up the Honda and drive back home, leaving skid marks on that long driveway flanked by the pretty trees.

"I don't think I'm supposed to be here," said Glory. She was quickly interrupted by the overbearing man.

"You're from the employment agency, right?"

For once in her life, Glory stood silent. No, of course she wasn't from the employment agency, but should she be?

"Go on, then, we got a full house today. Every meeting room is packed with clients and events, even the apartment," said the man in charge, shoving a silver tray full of bloody marys in highball glasses at her. "You can put your purse in a locker in the break room."

She would neither serve nor abandon her purse in any sort of common lunchroom, but what did he say about an apartment? And every room being filled with clients? She already despised this hateful, bossy man, but her curiosity had won out, at least for the moment. She grabbed the tray and walked into the main house.

Once inside, the grandeur was revealed for what it was—a lie. Apart from the speckled terrazzo floors and marble staircases, everything else was unremarkable. A grand exterior concealed a bland corporate venue on the inside. It was best suited for a pharmaceutical sales retreat, a buffet wedding, or any occasion with a cash bar.

The silver-plated tray trembled as Glory walked down the hall. It wasn't because she was nervous but because she was not accustomed to holding ten drinks in crystal drinkware in front of her like some kind of robot. And then there was the matter of her giant handbag sliding down her shoulder into the crook of her arm. Her black shoes shuffled against the tapestry rugs, which Glory could tell were printed onto the fibers (probably nylon) and were not quality like the ones in her home. The overhead chandeliers radiated a flat light, which Glory knew indicated glass, not crystal. How disappointing, she lamented. People spend all kinds of money to be a part of this club, and most of them can't tell real crystal from the fake stuff. On the other hand, the fake opulence had intimidated generations of her people, keeping them at arm's length until this day.

"Can you point me to the investor meeting?" asked Glory to another black woman dressed in a catering vest. The woman looked at her askance, then pointed to a room on the right side of the hall.

The doors swung open, and not a soul moved from their vinyl seats. The investor meeting was technically for anyone who held a single share in the company, as Glory's gimlet eye had spotted in the last earnings report online. But typically, only the board and its biggest shareholders actually showed up. A man in a suit too big for his already big frame stood behind a podium at the front of the room, talking about market conditions and macro this and micro that. The fifty or so people in the room stared straight ahead, fixated on lines and graphics projected onto a screen at the front of the room. Glory set the tray filled with tiny sandwiches and prepared cocktails down on a table in the back of the room and looked over the crowd.

She spotted Delphine right away, perched in the back row and scribbling in a notepad. Glory guessed the usher up front had thought better of Delphine's chic navy dress and woven leather handbag. Maybe her daughter could decipher what all those numbers meant. Glory tried to keep up with the presentation, but she couldn't help looking around the room instead. Her heart skipped a beat when she saw Keller stand up from his chair. Of course he would be there, and she was furious at herself for not thinking this through. He walked toward the back of the room and straight toward her. She was afraid that her racing heartbeat was audible to the entire room.

Blend in, she commanded herself. She picked up the tray again and held it in front of her chest, like an old-fashioned cigarette girl. He was so engrossed in his phone that Glory hoped he wouldn't even look at her. He grabbed one of the drinks, and then it happened. He looked her square in the eye and said thank you. Just as quickly, he returned to his seat.

It was in this moment that Glory realized what she was to him, what all black people probably were to him. Louisiana was a state full of black people, but as far as he was concerned, they were there for his comfort. They were the servers, the cooks, the gardeners, the daycare, the women who did his laundry and the men who shined his shoes. They were the help. His help. Never mind that he and Glory had had an actual conversation just days before or that he placed sports wagers with her. After all the living Glory had seen, she wasn't surprised, but she now had a deeper understanding of why the preferred weapon of oppressed people is the Molotov cocktail.

But there was no point being in this room, or being here at all, if she wasn't going to pay attention to what the folks were saying. It was nearly impossible for her to keep up with all the charts and graphs, but her interest was piqued when a female executive walked to the podium to present about the proposed Mosstown chemical plant. It was a woman she'd seen on the local news many times.

"Good morning," she said. The woman was severe in the face, wearing an equally harsh black suit and pearls that came off more like a costume than real style. "Although this project has been delayed for more than a year, we believe that there are fewer obstacles. Public support is building, and we have done everything possible to mitigate the negative effects on the community. As I am about to explain, we have chosen the shortest routes and avoided heavily populated areas. We expect some residents to be vocal, but we can and will use eminent domain laws to achieve our goals."

The room erupted in applause, and the audience soon swarmed like ants, crawling around the room to chat and drink and grab tiny crab cakes from tiered faux-silver trays. Delphine rotated in her chair to stretch her torso, then glimpsed her mother serving cocktails to the other investors. It must have been the murderous glare from Delphine's eyes that alerted Glory, or maybe just a mother's intuition, but Glory made eye contact with her daughter and gently shook her head. It was so imperceptible that no one else probably noticed. Translated, it meant, *Now is not the time.*

The picture was becoming clearer. Not only was the Benoit family planning to build a chemical plant; as if that wasn't dirty enough, they were going to use federal laws to boot residents from their homes. Glory knew that Amity had been dedicated, but now she had a greater understanding of what had driven her. She also better grasped why the Benoit family was so willing to fund her charitable projects here and there. They wanted to make Amity go away, to buy her silence. They wanted her to shut up.

The room dimmed for the next presentation, and the investors sat back down. Delphine took this as her moment, walking past her mother and shooting her an urgent look before walking outside. Glory followed.

The doors to the conference room had barely rattled shut before Delphine started in on her. "What on earth are you doing serving drinks? I thought we were here for the investor meeting?"

"There's been a mix-up," said Glory, deadpan, before launching into an explanation of how she parked her car and found herself as part of the catering staff.

"We're done. I'm not having my mother serve drinks to these people at a former whites-only country club. Come on," she said, tugging at her sleeve.

"Hold on. I don't even know what those presentations are saying. Maybe I can just nose around here for a bit and join you later."

"You can't be serious."

"We are not going to get any real information about Mosstown or the Benoits by listening to these presentations. That's just what they want us to hear. Let me see if there's anything I can find out, and if not, I'll join you later."

"I suppose you're right," Delphine said reluctantly. "These presentations are probably written by their PR department and reviewed by thirty lawyers before an event like this. We're not going to hear anything but carefully scripted soundbites."

"Just keep your phone nearby. I'll text you if I need you for anything."

Now was the time Glory's knee decided to complain. She was creaky enough at this age, and being dragged onto the pavement by that crazed dog at Milton Knowles's house hadn't helped. The pain had been amplified by hiking up those steep stairs from the parking lot. She limped down the long corridor, peeking into each room as she went, observing what she could. There was the august library, lined wall-to-wall with books that she assumed no one ever read, books that were there to make its members feel superior to other people. And then there was the pool room, a large expanse of felted green. Men had one of two objects in their hands, a pool cue or a glass of brown liquor. She was back where she started, the kitchen. She erased the limp she had permitted her body to feel for just a few moments and walked back into the industrial kitchen.

First there was the matter of the purse, which against her better judgment and instincts as a Southern woman, she knew she needed to ditch. Under no circumstance, however, would she deposit her handbag in the lunchroom. She might as well let a cat squat over it and use it as a litter box. She pushed in the door of a chilly walk-in refrigerator and looked for a better hiding spot. At least it would be in a climate-controlled environment, she convinced herself, storing the purse behind a box of frozen shrimp.

Back in the main part of the kitchen, she spotted a list called "Kitchen Priorities" with today's date. *Devein shrimp for Fontenot wedding. Confirm champagne delivery with distributor. Coordinate cake delivery for the Fuller family reunion. Benoit family meeting in the apartment.*

Like a homing pigeon dispatched on a mission, she knew she could not leave until she found that apartment. She snatched a pitcher, filled it to the brim with tap water, and swallowed hard before approaching the shift manager.

"Keller Benoit just requested a pitcher of water to the apartment," said Glory with a decisive tone she hoped was unlikely to lead to further questioning. She knew from her early days as a bookie that moving with confidence, even if you don't feel it, is how to appear to have authority. "Remind me where that is again?"

He slung a damp towel over his shoulder and held up a bottle of wine for inspection. Without looking at her, he answered, "Up the stairs, last door on the right . . . then more stairs until there are none left."

This sounded like thirty stairs too many. Each one felt like a fire ignited inside of her knee. She imagined the cartilage tearing with each step. Once on the mezzanine level, she struggled to find the additional flight of stairs. A small, barely perceptible break in the pattern of the upholstered walls gave it away. It was a secret door, meant to be hidden, meant to stay hidden. Behind it was an even steeper staircase that Glory already detested. She struggled up more steps until she reached the top.

She limped down the hall and, still carrying a tray with a water pitcher and glasses, leaned her ear to the door. Muffled laughter filtered through the thick oak. Cigar smoke seeped through the walls. The laughter eventually lowered from a boil to a simmer, which Glory took as the best opportunity to enter.

The tray and everything on it was balanced on one hip. She opened the door and navigated her way with her available hand. Men sucked on the ends of their putrid cigars, their mouths tightening into rings and their cheeks wrinkling with each inhale. The apartment looked like the rest of the club—dark and vaguely impor-tant until you realized every antique was a fake. She placed the tray on the credenza near the door and, wanting to find a way to extend her time in the apartment, filled each glass slowly with water.

"These are the best earnings reports we've seen in a decade," said an old man in a striped suit. "Announcing that Mosstown plant was exactly what we needed."

"We're not completely out of the woods, but close," said the woman Glory recognized from earlier in the day, the one who gave the public relations update.

"And what about those activists? That pseudo-intellectual priest who's always on the news and his little sidekick?"

Keller Benoit interjected. "The priest can be managed. And the nun? She shouldn't be a problem anymore."

18

I just knew that slick-haired fool was involved," Glory said. She plopped a red fedora on top of her head and paired it with a red cape that she buttoned at the neck. Between the forgeries she found on the Mosstown paperwork and his country club revelation, the parts were adding up.

"But murder? That seems so extreme," said Delphine.

"You know what's extreme? Millions of dollars, which is how much that family stands to make off that chemical plant." Glory grabbed her keys from the kitchen table.

"Where are you going? Did you expand your so-called office hours to Saturday?"

"Red Hat Volunteer Appreciation Brunch," Glory said. "Even though they have zero appreciation for my efforts. But they will one day. And I hear they're having a big spread this year, so I figured at the very least I deserve a treat." She lugged the giant purse over her shoulder and pointed her keys toward Delphine. "I suggest we add Keller to our surveillance efforts, but we'll talk about that later. And do not move or throw away any of my belongings while I am out.

And stay out of my bedroom. Every woman deserves a sanctuary, and mine is my bedroom." She opened the garage door and backed the car out of the driveway.

Delphine had meant to visit her Aunt Shirley ever since Amity's funeral, when she'd learned that her aunt and mother were no longer talking. She found her in the backyard, her fingers laced around a machete. From a ladder, she swung the blade in the air at a tree branch with fierce determination, making little progress into the thick bark.

"Aunt Shirley? What are you doing?" asked Delphine.

Her elderly but surprisingly fit aunt was balanced on a ladder and stopped momentarily when she saw her niece. "Do you see this?" she said, pointing at the branch of a tree that skimmed her fence and floated into her yard.

"It's a gorgeous tree," said Delphine, confused.

"What the tree looks like is not what matters right now," Aunt Shirley said, gesturing wildly. "What matters is that this is my property, and that branch is crossing the fence line into *my land*." Aunt Shirley's gesticulations made her wobble.

Delphine ran to the ladder to steady her aunt.

"Don't you worry about me," Aunt Shirley said, descending the ladder. "You are just like your mama, making something out of nothing."

Aunt Shirley could be as combustible as a canister of gasoline in the hot sun, so Delphine bit her tongue, knowing that it could be detrimental to her mission. The goal? Uncovering what was really happening between her aunt and her mother.

"Why don't you finish this up for me?" said Aunt Shirley, thrusting the machete at Delphine's chest.

"No thank you. I'm not about to get charged with trespassing and destruction of property on account of a grievance with your neighbor."

The woman wiped her hands against her jeans and beamed. "My beautiful niece." Aunt Shirley squeezed Delphine's shoulder and gave her a warm smile, a smile that made Delphine instantly suspicious. Underneath her aunt's honeyed smile, she knew she was being inspected. Among the things she knew her aunt was surveying included: her current weight, the number of gray hairs that had sprouted since her last visit, the make and model of her handbag (as well as its approximate cost), her lack of makeup, and most crucially, her ring finger.

"I'm so glad you visited, unlike your mother, who doesn't visit at all. I suppose with your daddy leaving her and having to make ends meet, she's been busy."

"You look well, Aunt Shirley," said Delphine, refusing to take the bait.

"Sit down. I'll be right over."

Delphine took a seat at the patio table and wondered what her aunt was up to as her pink sneakers marched out of sight, into her neighbor's yard, swinging the machete at her side. She returned a few moments later with a fistful of thorny red roses pilfered from her neighbor's garden.

"How is your mother doing these days?" asked Aunt Shirley, taking a seat at the weathered iron table. She pulled out a pair of gardening shears from a nearby caddy.

Delphine could not tell her the truth, in part because her mother would be furious but also because Delphine was still trying to figure that out herself. The truth, as clearly as Delphine could make out, was that her mother had put on even more weight in the past year since the divorce became official, even though her father had moved out years ago. The truth was that Glory had lost both her best friend and her own mother over the past two years, and her house had become unwieldy. The truth was that Delphine was so alarmed by the quantity of orange pill bottles on her night-stand that she had felt compelled to write down the names of all her prescriptions and research them online. Most of them had to do with high blood pressure, high cholesterol, or low thyroid levels, but there were also prescriptions for anxiety medication and antidepressants. These bottles had been dispensed more than a year ago, according to the labels, but looked remarkably full. Her mother had always been competent and feisty, but that didn't mean she was well.

"She's fine," answered Delphine. "She's torn up over Amity, as you might imagine. She has taken that really hard. I caught a glimpse of you at her funeral."

"Such a shame what happened to her," said Shirley, stripping the thorns off the crimson roses. "A *suicide* . . . From a nun? If you want to know the truth, I always thought that woman was a little bit strange."

"How so?"

"Tell me what kind of nun protests and makes all that kind of noise, the way that woman did? And I hate to speak ill of the dead, but she was known to partake in various substances." It was shocking to Delphine to hear her aunt speak so callously about not just a nun but someone who practically grew up in her home. Someone whom she had occasionally shared a bed with, danced to Martha Reeves with, someone with whom she had shared sausages and grits on chilly mornings.

"That was a long time ago," snapped Delphine.

Her aunt stripped the thorns off another stem, this time jabbing her finger. She yelped, then sucked the wound with her mouth.

"Are you okay?"

"Yes, yes, I'm fine. Happens with roses sometimes. You must suffer the cuts if you want to live with the beauty. Anyways, how's New York? Did I hear that that husband of yours filed for divorce?"

"How did you hear that?"

"There is no such thing as a secret here in Lafayette. I'm sorry to hear this, but I am here to tell you that it's going to be fine. Without a man, I guess you're free to bill all those law firm hours. Won't be any different for you, will it?"

"I suppose not," said Delphine, biting her tongue yet again. At least someone still believed her career was intact and thriving.

"Say, there's this woman down in Youngsville that I've heard about. She can help you put a curse on that good-for-nothing husband if you want. You just tell her what he's done and what kind of punishment you want to inflict, and she'll get to work."

"Oh, I don't believe in any of that."

"Suit yourself."

Aunt Shirley arranged the roses together in a bouquet, standing back for a moment to admire her handiwork. "And how's your mama's house? You know, I've got a friend that works down at the courthouse. It's a real shame the way your mama takes care of that house."

"That was a mistake. Her house is fine," said Delphine, monitoring her aunt closely to see how she'd respond.

"Well, like I said, it's a real shame. You know, your grandmother had promised she'd leave the house to me, but Glory got to her with her theatrics and all. Now I'm the one on the fifteenth year of a thirty-year mortgage. They say being a good person wins in the end, but I'm not so sure."

Delphine couldn't tell if she was speaking off the cuff or with a sense of intention, but she suspected the latter. "It sure was nice catching up with you, but I better get going," Delphine said. She stood up and shielded her eyes from the sun, which had shifted position and was aiming its intense rays precisely on the women. This helped Delphine to see the shimmering Swarovski brooch pinned to Shirley's burgundy sweater.

On the drive back home, she couldn't stop thinking about how conversant her aunt was about curses. Her first order of business when she got home was to finally unpack the internet cameras she'd ordered online and install them.

19

A red thank-you banner hung across the buffet table, set up for the Acadiana Red Hat Society volunteer breakfast and fourth-quarter planning session. The holiday season would bring several important church happenings, including the Christmas Fair and their annual holiday bake sale and fundraiser—not to mention the best gossip of the year.

Glory arrived early, not for the buffet but because she had a mission to accomplish. But first, breakfast. Her nose twitched from the acrid smell of Sterno flames warming the catered breakfast. With a Styrofoam plate in one hand and clear plastic tongs in the other, she helped herself to a small portion of eggs, two sausage links, two pancakes, and a buttermilk biscuit, which was redundant because she already had pancakes. She grabbed a fistful of butter and syrup packages and sat herself on one of the long folding tables for the volunteers.

Sometimes she wondered why she continued to patronize a group that made her feel like she had the plague. She had made a few friends at the beginning, but after the episode with the bootleg crawfish, those friends fluttered away like birds migrating south for the winter. They should have been grateful that she was trying to save them money. How was she supposed to know that the crawfish truck's refrigeration was shoddy? Was she supposed to do an inspection? Ask for a license? No, she was not.

She pushed it out of her mind and focused on the task at hand—getting Sister Jocelyn Cormier alone. What she hadn't realized just yet was that Sister Jocelyn was already there, and she looked dramatically different. Instead of her drab blue skirt and white button-down shirt, she wore burnt-orange slacks and a white silk shirt, the kind that knots up into a bow at the neck. Glory nearly fell out of her chair when she saw Sister Jocelyn float across the room in a shoe with a bona fide heel. It may have been a kitten heel, but a proper shoe nonetheless. Wait—was that lipstick?

Sister Jocelyn and Constance Wheeler took their positions in front of the room on two stools. Glory would never forgive Constance for nosing around her house, insisting on taking all those notes on that damn clipboard. On the other hand, if Constance hadn't been there that day, she probably would have died on the front lawn of anaphylactic shock, drooling and heaving in the front yard for the entire neighborhood on account of those damn bees. Diamond earrings sparkled from Constance's earlobes, where neither Glory nor Constance's dim-witted husband could lay claim to them again.

"Thank you all for your ongoing support and volunteerism," said Constance, as if she were homecoming queen. "The holiday season is fast approaching, and we need volunteers to chair our various events. Let's start with the Christmas Fair. Any takers?"

Glory and two others raised their hands.

"Thank you, Vivianne. The Christmas Fair is a big responsibility, but I know you'll be up to the task."

Glory punctured a plastic square filled with butter and smeared it across her pancakes.

"Now, I need another volunteer for the holiday bake sale."

Again, Glory's hand shot into the air.

"Julia, thank you."

Glory punctured another package, this time syrup, which she drizzled over the dried-out pancakes, more to rehydrate them than anything else.

"Any volunteers to chair the holiday food pantry drive?"

Glory rolled her eyes and raised her hand again.

Constance looked around, and when no other hands appeared, her always-on smile began to wither. "Anyone?"

Jocelyn huffed and interrupted her. "Glory Broussard will be the chair of the food pantry drive," she said, catching Glory off guard. "We already have four volunteers, not to mention the sisters who manage the food pantry on an ongoing basis, so you'll have plenty of support."

The women finished discussing the rest of the agenda items, and while they did, Glory wrapped two pieces of French toast in a napkin and stuffed them in her purse. When the meeting was done, she approached Sister Jocelyn.

"I just wanted to say thank you for the committee assignment," said Glory without a trace of irony or sarcasm, for a change.

"It's true that half the congregation had food poisoning last year, but I think you can be trusted with canned goods."

Now was not the time to relitigate the discount crawfish debacle. Glory had to keep focused on her mission, and anyway, Jocelyn was not wrong.

"You look gorgeous in this outfit. I've never seen you out of your uniform. Are you . . . going somewhere?"

"The order does not have an official uniform. Although most of the nuns do dress alike, we are not strictly required to dress like monkeys. Sometimes a girl likes to dress up."

A woman over fifty who refers to herself as a girl is either delusional or up to something, Glory thought. This was not a dress-up occasion. It was a volunteer breakfast with a buffet from Dwyer's Cafe, not exactly the social event of the season. And who exactly was she dressing up for? A group of fusty old women who'd already seen her in her nun clothes a million times before? If Glory didn't know better, she'd say Jocelyn was putting on airs.

"Follow me. I'll show you the food pantry." The women walked to the other side of the church into a surprisingly large room lined with wire shelves teetering with tins of pork and beans, various soups, paper towels, and diapers.

"We have a pretty good system set up for the food drive," said Sister Jocelyn, pulling out a compact from a humble purse and examining her hair. "If you want to get started, you can put together some lunch kits. The ingredients are here on this list. When you're done, put the box on the bottom shelf."

"Will do," said Glory, examining Sister Jocelyn's getup. It wasn't as if she didn't look good. It was just that everything, from the quilted black purse and the compact with cabbage roses on it to the scratchy-looking fabric of her slacks, looked like an outfit from a 1978 Montgomery Ward catalog. Glory needed to move beyond her fashion critique and focus on important matters.

"I met up with Father Romero the other day," said Glory, placing one jar of peanut butter, a jar of jelly, and a loaf of Evangeline bread into a box. The mere mention of his name was enough to snap Jocelyn out of her grooming spell. "He mentioned something about Amity's conservatorship."

He had made no such mention of this, though Glory had noted it in her reading of the police report. How does one politely bring up that they are investigating a murder, anyway? You don't. You skate and glide around it.

Jocelyn snapped her compact shut so hard that Glory worried she had shattered the glass. "He of all people should know that it's common for nuns. We don't have any children, rarely any next of kin. By the time most nuns are old and dead, the only people we have left are each other."

Glory counted the orange plastic rectangles of dehydrated ramen, feeling dumb. Of course Sister Jocelyn was right. Or was she? Wouldn't it have been sufficient to have a will or . . . a different kind of document? She'd have to remember to ask Delphine.

"I'm sorry, I didn't mean to upset you," said Glory, genuinely contrite. Maybe she should leave the old woman alone. She had managed to get all gussied up, for whatever reason, and even though she was disinclined to trust the woman, there was no evidence that Sister Jocelyn was up to no good. The only reason Glory could think of to dislike the woman was because she was always swanning around the church, singing her solos, and acting like she was a member of Sister Sledge instead of the Sisters of the Holy Family. Even Glory understood these were petty reasons to dislike a person.

"It's just that Father Romero said that the conservator did not sign off on the toxicology report . . ." Not only was she lying about what Father Romero said, or rather, did not say, she was also lying to a nun. It was a daily double of sin. Why stop now?

"The only reason we declined the toxicology report was because it would have taken weeks for them to release the body, and we had to align the funeral with the cardinal's schedule. The diocese insisted we make it work. And if Father Romero has any questions about my handling of affairs, he should talk to me directly instead of spreading rumors."

Glory, thankful that she hadn't been struck down on the spot for lying to a nun, relaxed.

"You know," said Sister Jocelyn, her rigid expression softening, "you're not the only one who misses Amity, and you're not the only one who thinks there's something suspicious about it."

Glory, who had been occupied with packing lunch kits, stopped abruptly.

"She was my confidant, too, the only person I could talk to about things. Like how hard Mother Superior had been on me, getting ready for me to take over the order," she said. "Or how lonely this life is. You can't say that stuff to the other nuns because they think you're losing your faith or losing your mind. But that Amity, she was a real one. It just seemed so out of character to do what she did."

They were friends, Glory realized. It made her feel foolish for disliking the woman so much.

"At any rate, I have to get going. I have a meeting with a contractor about our new food pantry." Jocelyn straightened up a few boxes of pasta and then made her way to the shelf-stable sweets. She inspected a box of shortbread cookies with a thick slab of chocolate on top, tore open the package and stuffed a cookie in her face.

20

The server's face was flushed and dripping wet from the rising steam. She placed the pot on the table with a thud that caused the glasses of sweet tea to shudder. The server tipped the pot over and bright pink, freshly boiled shrimp slid across the newspaper that covered the table. She returned moments later and did the same ceremony with a smaller pot of tiny potatoes and cut-up ears of corn.

Comeaux's Seafood was situated on a busy intersection of University Avenue, next to a hunting store with a bunting of plastic multicolored triangles strung around its perimeter. Dozens of diners crowded onto picnic tables on the restaurant's patio.

Delphine shielded her eyes from the sun and turned to Landry. "This will and testament looks like pretty standard stuff. Just one question, though . . . Any specific reason you've made your minor children your beneficiaries and not your wife?" It had seemed that as soon as Delphine arrived in town, Beau Landry had needed several legal documents reviewed.

"If something happens to me, Kerry is taken care of with all that Benoit family money," he said, knotting a bib around his neck.

"She'll be fine no matter what. So I figured I might as well leave everything I have to my girls instead." He tore into a shrimp shell with both thumbs.

"I see. I guess that makes sense. Remind me . . . How did you two meet again?"

"That's a pretty good story, actually." He wiped his hands against the bib on his chest and took a long swig of iced tea before answering. "It was at the George Washington Ball. Petroleum Club of Lafayette, except Kerry was a debutante and I was parking cars that night."

Officially, the George Washington Ball was a yearly celebration to mark George Washington's birthday. At some point, whoever was in charge tacked on the anniversary of the Tomb of the Unknown Soldier into the festivities. Unofficially, it was a sad little debutante ball that the so-called finer citizens of Lafayette insisted on keeping alive. Debutantes squeezed into plouffy A-line gowns and tiaras, and their escorts, or "patriots," were there to . . . Well, that part was unclear. All Delphine could remember was that Kerry's mother chaired the local Daughters of the American Revolution, and it was a known fact that her grandfather was a grand wizard, something they adamantly denied publicly. She imagined at least one hood hiding somewhere in the Benoit residence.

"Kerry was the queen of the ball or some shit," said Beau. "And she hated it, every second of it. I found her leaning against my car at the end of the night, hiding from her parents and smoking a cigarette. And so began a love affair for the ages." He didn't even try to hide the sarcasm.

"I'm sure that was a lot better than our sad little prom."

They had both attended Acadiana High School, home of the Rams. Delphine remembered the purple, skintight dress that she had bought at The Limited and that her mother objected to. She could still hear the objections. "Oh no you don't," Glory said. "My daughter is not getting impregnated on prom night." But Delphine had convinced her to buy it, on account of Beau Landry being her date and because everyone who knew a teenage Beau Landry understood that he could barely look a girl in the eye let alone plan out more advanced logistics.

Delphine could hardly walk in the three-inch stilettos she'd bought for the occasion. It didn't matter, though, because two songs in she gave up and danced in her bare feet. A hand-painted banner that read ALWAYS AND FOREVER was strung up above the stage. Silver balloons skimmed the gymnasium ceiling. She could distinctly remember sipping punch from a damp paper cup when "All My Life" by K-Ci and JoJo came on, and Beau grabbed her hand and led her to the dance floor. They had stared into each other's eyes during the entire song, and Delphine had wished that it had been a real date, not a friend date.

"You were always such a nice kid," said Delphine. "I don't know that I ever thanked you for taking me to the prom. It was such a kind gesture." Delphine had thought that Shaun Donovan would ask her out after weeks of frenzied flirting. He later left a dozen roses in another girl's locker. Beau had asked her to prom the next day, and she had been thankful for his admirable brand of pity.

"What do you mean by kind gesture?" he asked. His face sharpened into a question.

"Oh, everyone knew you only asked me because you felt sorry for me. And because you were such a nice guy."

"That's not what happened," he said, confused. "I asked you to the prom because I wanted to go with you."

Had the server brought another pot of shrimp over? Because suddenly Delphine felt as if she were standing over a boiling cauldron on a summer day. All these years she had thought that Landry had taken pity on her, that she had never had a real prom with a real date. The gap between her remembrance of that night and the reality of it were a continent apart.

"Anyways, how are you holding up, divorce-wise?" he asked after a long awkward silence, and Delphine was thankful for the sudden change of topic. She figured he could sense her panic by the look on her face and took pity. But then again, why had she always assumed he was pitying her?

"Oh, holding up, I guess. I kind of messed that up." Delphine pinched more shrimp open and scraped the meat out with her forefinger.

"Forgive me for prying, but you don't seem too broken up about it."

She popped a salty boiled potato in her mouth and thought a moment before she answered. She wasn't stalling, but in the rush of leaving New York for Amity's funeral and her mother's subsequent shenanigans, she hadn't had the time or headspace to process the state of her marriage, let alone how she felt about it.

"When I was ten years old, I had been dying to go to New Orleans. I had never been, despite living only three hours away. Then somehow I convinced my mother to take me for my birthday. You know that old department store, Maison Blanche? We walked in, and I spotted this purple fuzzy sweater with puffed sleeves. And I didn't dare ask for it, because I had already asked for the trip, which felt miraculous enough, but my eyes must have been pleading. My mom told me to try it on, and she actually bought it for me.

"I probably looked like a Muppet in that sweater, but I loved it so much. But what I didn't realize was that angora is extremely scratchy, and of course it's rarely cold in Louisiana, but I loved it so much that I just kind of suffered through the discomfort. And I never stopped loving that sweater, but eventually I had to stop wearing it because I broke out in a rash. I guess you could say that my marriage was a lot like that sweater—beautiful on the outside, but it never sat well on my skin."

They sat for a long stretch, silent on the wooden picnic table. It was one of those perfect, late-September days in Louisiana, when the air was dry and cool and scented with the last of the magnolias. Her head swirled with images of prom night and the angora sweater, and she closed her eyes, hoping it would quiet her brain. She inhaled the perfumed air and let her shoulders fall for the first time in ages.

"What about you and Kerry?" asked Delphine. Her eyes fluttered open and landed on a family dressed in matching camouflage in the parking lot. "You guys doing okay?"

"I love my girls. I love being a dad." He stared onto Johnston Street, as if there was anything to see other than traffic.

She decided not to press. He deserved the same courtesy he had given her just moments earlier, when she needed a moment to pull herself together. Instead, she picked up her phone and started scrolling.

"I imagine you must get work emails at all hours," he said.

Her eyebrows wiggled as she pinched the screen of her phone to magnify the picture. "No, not work. Just checking in on my mama and wondering why she's at some auto repair shop. That woman takes her car in as soon as any lights come on."

"You're tracking your mother? You better hope she doesn't find out about that." He laughed.

"I'm not tracking her," Delphine confirmed. "Well, I guess I am. Only because she's been obsessed with this Amity Gay situation and has been acting so secretive. That night after she got stung by those bees and went to bed early, I went into her phone and added her as a contact I could track."

"I've told both of you to stop this. Please tell me this isn't still going on."

Delphine ripped the plastic bib from around her neck. "Look, I don't know if she was murdered or not. There's just something that's not right about this. It's not a thing a nun would do, you know, and especially Sister Amity. There's something about this that stinks."

She put her phone on the table. At that very moment, Landry grabbed her hand. "Please. Both of you, stop this. You two are going to get into trouble over this, and I'd hate to see it."

Delphine did not want to admit it, but she suddenly felt as if she were sixteen years old, swaying to a slow song in a gym and wishing it was real.

Somewhere between the Best Buy and Lowe's, Glory heard what sounded like an explosion, and her car veered to the right. She pulled over and, before getting out, made sure her door would not get ripped off by an oncoming car on Ambassador Caffrey Parkway, Lafayette's busiest road. This stretch of town was the lifeblood of the city, if only because the proliferation of chain stores connected its residents to the rest of the world. Bed Bath & Beyond. Ulta. Olive Garden. If you needed something—anything—you either bought it online or found it on Ambassador.

It was a terrible place for a blown tire. Glory tried to make herself small, pressing herself up against the passenger side so she wouldn't be flattened in the turn lane/emergency lane of the road. Her front passenger tire was as limp as a sixty-year-old man without his Viagra.

"Ain't this a blip," cursed Glory, inhaling exhaust.

She got back into her car, this time from the passenger seat, and searched through her cavernous handbag for her AAA membership card, not entirely sure it was current. In a panic, she started to empty her bag. The ledger, a wallet (stuffed with defunct store credit cards she applied for only to get 20 percent off a first purchase), and a handful of single-serving jams taken from Cracker Barrel were strewn across the seat. It was a mad, desperate search. She was on the verge of tears when she heard the sound of knuckles rapping against her window.

She clutched her heart and sighed when she saw Noah Singleton. He was bent at the waist, and his hand formed a visor over his eyes. "You okay, Miss Glory?"

She rolled down the window. "Jesus Christ, Noah, you scared the shit out of me," she said, sounding more ungrateful than she meant to.

"Looks like you got a pretty nasty flat."

"The light for my tire pressure came on a few weeks ago. I normally go to the dealership straightaway, but lately I've just been too busy. I'm looking for my AAA card."

"This car ain't but two years old. It should be under warranty with Robichaux Honda. Lemme give them a call right quick."

In less than thirty minutes, the car had been towed and Glory and Noah were sitting in the waiting room of the local Honda dealership. Vintage arcade games lined one wall, and a pool table with ripped felt occupied the center. Glory clutched a Styrofoam cup that read NEW ORLEANS ORIGINAL DAIQUIRIS and stabbed the straw up and down, producing a shriek that sounded like a cheap, out-of-tune violin.

"I can't believe you talked me into the drive-through daiquiri place," said Noah. It was a Louisiana tradition. A Styrofoam cup filled with booze, made into a legal, closed container by applying a smidge of clear tape where the straw goes.

"You'd need a taste, too, if your car blew a tire on Ambassador. Leave me alone. My nerves are shot, and this day ain't even halfway done." The sound of *Ms. Pac-Man* losing a life wailed from the corner.

Up until now, she hadn't gotten a good look at Noah. He was wearing navy slacks and a crisp white button-down. His brown dress shoes were glossy with polish. Had she ever seen him out of his coffee shop uniform since he'd opened his CC's Coffee House franchise? She could not remember the last time she saw him wearing civilian clothes.

"What are you doing so gussied up, anyways?"

He tugged at the knees of his slacks. "Today is five years since my Sarah passed away. I don't go to church per se, but sometimes I like to sit in the pews for a long while. I just like the quiet." He turned his head toward the service bay. A man with a welder's mask on his face took a giant rotary cutter to a hunk of steel. Sparks enveloped the worker like a rainstorm.

Glory tried to come up with the right words, but there were none. Instead she held up the Styrofoam cup as a peace offering.

He took a sip from her straw and flinched. "What is this?"

"Something called 190 Octane."

He looked at her with suspicion, took an even longer sip, and handed the cup back to her. "I'm not religious like you, and I know this is probably going to sound crazy," he said, "but sitting in that church is the closest I feel to her. I don't think I'll ever get used to not being her father anymore."

"You will always be her father. Ain't no one that can take that away from you," said Glory, putting the cup on a table between the two of them, alongside ancient issues of *Sports Illustrated* and *Highlights* magazines.

"Sometimes I think about joining that church of yours, but I know it's not going to bring her back."

Glory couldn't disagree. And at this particular moment in time, she was questioning her own commitment to the institution. First, there was Father Romero and his loft apartment with the six-burner stove, which Glory found unpriestly even though she could not articulate why. Then there were those uppity Red Hat ladies who pretended to be social and welcoming even though they were as prickly as a roadside armadillo. She couldn't find the words to convince Noah that becoming a churchgoer would fix his problems or lessen his grief.

"What is it that you get from it, from church?" he asked.

"I don't know if I can answer that question, if I'm being honest with you. I guess I've just always gone and don't know any better. Let me put it another way. Does anyone truly like king cake? No, but we all buy one every Mardi Gras, don't we?" This produced a hint of a smile from Noah. "It's what we do, and I guess we all just want to feel like we're part of something bigger. That there's a point to all of this."

"What 'this' are you talking about?" he asked.

"Life, I suppose." She watched as her car was hoisted into the air over a work bay. "I find talking to Mama helps. Sometimes I go down to St. Martin de Porres, that little cemetery where she and Amity are buried, and I talk to them. I know it's silly, but I tell them what I'm fixin' for supper, all the gossip and goings-on with the Acadiana Red Hat Society. Just regular stuff."

"And that helps?" asked Noah.

"I can't explain it, but yes, I think it does."

Glory took the cup again and finished the rest. Icy crystals tickled her throat. A man with a gray beard and matching overalls walked into the waiting room.

"Glory Broussard?"

"Yes, that's me," said Glory, standing up and tossing the cup in the trash. "Is my car ready?"

"You sure are lucky we had that tire in stock. You got the last one."

"You couldn't just change the tube?" asked Noah.

"No, sir, you can't just change the tube when you're dealing with a slashed tire."

Glory's mouth fell open, and Noah darted up from his chair.

"By the looks of that tire, I'd say someone with a knife and a score to settle wanted to send you a message."

21

Noah had insisted on following Glory back to her house after the news of the tire. The automatic garage door creaked open, and she parked alongside Delphine's rental. Glory turned around at the sound of Noah's horn honking.

"You sure you okay?" Noah asked from a lowered car window.

"Yes, yes, I'm fine," she lied. "And thanks for everything this afternoon."

He raised his window and drove away.

Inside the house, Delphine sat in the kitchen working on her laptop.

"Where have you been all afternoon?" Delphine asked, seemingly absorbed in her computer.

Glory sat down at the table next to her. She slumped in the chair as if she had just been through an obstacle course. Her eyes blinked heavily. "Oh, just got a flat tire on Ambassador," she said, not mentioning that the car was intentionally sabotaged by a knife-wielding vandal. She wasn't in the mood to deal with Delphine's inevitable dramatics about the situation. And besides, she thought, what was

Delphine going to do, call the police? The same police that spearheaded a shoddy investigation of her dearest friend? No, Delphine
didn't need to know the specifics at this particular moment. "How
was lunch with Landry?"

Delphine continued to type without looking up. "Oh, you know.
Just reviewed his will and testament."

"There ain't no lawyers in Louisiana that can do that for him?"
asked Glory.

"Always good to have a second pair of eyes on all your important
documents," Delphine said. "Speaking of which, I spoke earlier this
morning with the assistant medical examiner in New York. He had
some interesting thoughts about the autopsy report."

Delphine explained that even though there was no toxicology
report, the autopsy itself had raised several questions with the
pathologist her paralegal had introduced her to. The hyoid bone in
her neck had been fractured, which was consistent with a hanging.
But there were nearly a dozen other fractures in her neck, which
could be consistent with hanging but also strangulation by force.

"He told me that given the circumstances, he understands why
it was categorized as a suicide," said Delphine. "But in the context
of a different crime scene, it could also be consistent with someone
choking her to death."

There is a strange dissonance sometimes between what you believe
to be true and that moment when it becomes true. It was the confirmation Glory had been waiting for, but instead of triumph, all she
felt was shattered. She told Delphine that she needed to lie down
and closed her bedroom door. She slept for twelve straight hours.

Glory awoke the next morning, unsure for a moment where she
was or how she got there. Crumpled-up tissues were a new addition to her bed, along with the books and paintings and abandoned

sewing projects that took up most of the space on her quilt. When she turned over in her bed, she could see that Delphine had been in her room, and recently. A paper cup from CC's was steaming with coffee. On a saucer was a scone, the kind Glory liked, with the sugary crust on top. Beside the scone were two blue pills. Delphine, being Delphine, had apparently gone through her bedroom and its contents with surgical detail, and Glory knew her secret was out.

What did it matter anyway? she thought. Was there any actual pride left to preserve? Any dignity left to save? Just about everyone in town knew by now that her ex-husband had abandoned her for that woman with the taut skin. That part was for the best. Glory had long grown tired of the constant cigarette smoke and the velvet, drawstring Crown Royal bags she found around the house. She was relieved to have peace in her home. Let Little Miss Short Skirt deal with his cheating ass.

But she had been able to hide the darkness, the one that seized her bones and wouldn't let go. At least, she had been able to hide it until now. On the outside, she wore her berets and sparkles like a shield. It really didn't matter if Delphine knew or not. The girl wasn't dumb, she reminded herself. One look at her house, which had always been full but at least tidy, should have been a clue that something was amiss. It must have been obvious to Delphine the second she stepped inside.

She blew on the hot coffee and looked at the pills with suspicion. Two pills, twice a day. This was the correct dosage, if Glory cared about that. Seeing the medicine lying there reminded her of everything she wanted to forget. She opted for the scone instead.

She hobbled to the kitchen and saw the cat through the window. He—or she, come to think of it—was in the usual spot atop the patio table. It was skinnier than she had ever seen it, each rib silhouetted and sharply defined against its short black fur. One eye was nearly swollen shut, and a gash spread across its face. Glory could empathize.

She filled a dainty bowl with milk and sprinkled some dry cat food, which she'd thought twice about buying, onto a plate. If you feed a cat, it belongs to you, and Glory definitely did not want a cat. But she got the distinct sense that no one else was caring for this animal, and everyone ought to have someone looking out for them in this world.

Glory felt unmoored. And whenever Glory felt especially adrift, or when she needed a special prayer to be answered, there was one place that made her feel a little better—the monastery of the Discalced Carmelite Nuns. At first, she'd misread it as the Displaced Carmelite Nuns, and that's what initially drew her in. She could relate to a group of displaced people because that's how she felt most of the time. As it turned out, *discalced* just meant barefoot, and disappointingly, these nuns wore shoes. Without waking up Delphine, she got in her car and drove east on West Congress toward the Carmelite campus.

The area was a lot like the rest of Louisiana, a zoning disaster. There was a junkyard with a rusted car on a platform, which was next to a tract of new homes, which was next to some kind of maze that people paid good money to get lost in for reasons Glory would never understand. But once she turned into the oversized oval driveway of the Carmelites, everything was orderly. Each blade of grass was crisp, and the flowers were always in bloom.

The chapel itself was plain with redbrick walls on the inside and outside. Painted white beams over the altar pointed to heaven. Because she needed her prayers to really be heard today, she lowered herself down onto the padded kneelers, even though every bone in her body protested. The cartilage in her knee made an unpleasant crackling sound.

Praying was a lot like that one time she saw a therapist. You spend most of the time talking about pleasantries and then get into the deeper stuff at the end of the session, if you're feeling brave enough. First, she prayed she would be able to get back up from these kneelers. Then she prayed that Delphine would divorce that useless husband of hers and find herself a nice, normal man. She prayed that Delphine would have more sense than to get involved with Landry. Glory had always thought he was a good egg, but the situation was messier now. Then Glory worked up enough bravery to pray for the big stuff.

She prayed that the darkness that had gripped her would lighten. She prayed that Amity and Beverly would one day find justice. And she prayed that when it was her time to go, let it be because the Good Lord had summoned her and not dispatched an axe murderer to do the job. She prayed that she'd leave this Earth under natural and sudden circumstances, like a heart attack or a brain aneurysm that takes you straight up to heaven, not brutalized and drowned in a pool like Beverly had been. Or found hanged from a doorknob, which Glory didn't even know was possible until it happened to Amity, not that she believed it anyway.

But was there any difference between being called up by the Lord in an orderly fashion and being hacked to death by an axe murderer? Were some events ordained by the Lord and other deaths unsanctioned? Or worse, were some events ordained by evil? If that was true, she would also have to believe that the Lord was not all powerful, and she wasn't sure if she was ready to go down that road. Even more frustrating, why was it that a woman her age hadn't sorted through all these issues? She was a woman of faith, yes, but why does faith have to be so foggy? She wanted her faith to be like the beams of a lighthouse, clear and strong and definite. Instead, they were more like the headlights of her Honda CR-V, able to take her a short distance and then another short distance. She just had to hope that that was good enough to deliver a person home.

After her prayers, she drove to St. Martin de Porres, her childhood church and Amity's home base. The grass at St. Martin de Porres was always damp and muddy, even when it hadn't rained. Glory had worn her black, beat-up sneakers because of it. She had been here enough to know that fancy footwear was a bad choice. The graves here were not lined up neatly, probably a result of the makeshift rules and regulations of colored cemeteries from back in the day, assuming there were any rules at all. Glory made her way through a maze of aboveground graves and traditional tombstones until she found her mother.

As always, her mother's grave was neat and attended to. Glory made sure that was the case. The artificial yellow flowers were replaced the moment they looked dingy, and fresh flowers were brought for all the big occasions: Mother's Day, Easter, and Christmas. Glory had paid extra for one of the modern tombstones with her mother's photo on it, which none of her siblings had wanted to chip in for. And at least once a month, Glory came around to intimidate the groundskeeper and make sure the grave site was cared for. The weeds were always pulled, the grass trimmed, the tombstone polished. It may have been the tidiest ten square feet in the entire cemetery.

Because it was at the edge of the cemetery, Glory had had a bench installed, and no one had told her she couldn't. There was just a single plot remaining in the entire cemetery, which Glory had purchased years ago for herself. Delphine would have to make her own arrangements for the afterlife. Glory sat on the bench and caught her mother up on everything.

She told her mother about everything that had happened. And how Delphine was in town and how things were always going to feel strained between the two of them, on account of Delphine being a New York City lawyer and Glory being someone who had struggled to make ends meet most of her life. Even if Glory did have a steady gig now, Delphine would never look at her as reputable. She wondered out loud if the two of them might be closer if Delphine had never left, if she'd gotten some normal job down at Costco, and admitted she was ashamed to have those thoughts. She fluffed up the fake yellow plant and got ready to leave.

Then she had an idea. She took the yellow flowers from her mother's grave and sought to find Noah's daughter, Sarah. She had a rough idea of where she might be because she had attended the funeral. It didn't take her long to find the simple marker. She bent down and left the flowers with Sarah. She figured Noah, being a man and all, probably didn't think to leave offerings, and vowed to add Sarah to her list of visitations.

Glory then headed to the opposite end of the cemetery where Beverly Malveaux was buried. Her headstone was grand when it was first installed. Everyone in the black community was so enraged that even folks without two nickels to rub together found a way to contribute. But now the once-grand headstone looked small. The weeds were overgrown, and folks had stopped leaving flowers a long time ago. Glory made a mental note to talk to the groundskeepers about stepping things up in that part of the cemetery. She would also need to remember to bring flowers next time.

The ground seemed extra wet as she made her way to Amity's grave, each step made a slurping sound as she trudged her way over, like she might be swallowed up. There was little traffic this early on a weekday morning, so it was even stranger to see the shiny pickup truck parked along the perimeter of the cemetery. She was startled to see what appeared to be a young black man praying at the edge of Amity's grave. She was even more startled when that young man looked up and it was Gus.

22

"T he maintenance of these trailer homes is a disgrace," said
Glory. The silence of Father Romero, Delphine, and Noah,
who walked behind her, was all the confirmation that she needed.

"They were damaged in Hurricane Emily. We're replacing them
as soon as we raise the funds."

She wanted to point out that Hurricane Emily was five years
ago. She also wanted to point out that he had been awarded a one-
million-dollar prize to use at his discretion. *Don't ever let anyone tell
you that Glory Broussard can't censor herself when needed*, she wanted
to say. She was pleased with herself for holding back but reserved
the right to speak out if anyone started working a nerve.

"I hope you didn't tell him we were coming," Delphine added.
"Suspects need an element of surprise to break them down."

After Glory had seen Gus at the graveyard, she went straight to
Father Romero and told him almost everything she knew—the drugs,
the cavorting with Milton Knowles, and Gus and the matching tattoos. Father Romero relayed everything to Noah, his work release
sponsor, and the men agreed that Gus needed to be confronted.

Where there's smoke there's fire, and there was a big old forest fire blazing around Gus.

"No one is a suspect," said Noah in a way that sought to bring down the temperature of this entire expedition. "The man's been a good employee. We need to give him the benefit of the doubt and not treat him like he's on an episode of *Cops*."

They agreed that Father Romero would be the one to knock on the door and start the interrogation. It was his ministry that had advocated for Gus's early release, that owned the land and the house and the trailers on it. Maybe a priest in his vestments would break him.

The trailer was unchanged from the time Glory and Delphine surveilled him. It was dented on the backside, its roof damaged from countless storms. What was once sparkly and mint green was now just dusty and gray. The six trailers made a half circle. In the middle was a tree with a tire swing that one would be wise not to test out given the general condition of the property. Chickens strutted in the yard, clucking and pecking at nothing but air.

When Gus opened the trailer door, Glory noticed that his eyes were red and his face was puffy. If she were a person quick to judge, she might have assumed drugs were the culprit, but could he have been crying? She knew from her line of work that most folks were capable of leading more than one life, and she wasn't about to be distracted by his dramatics.

"We'd like a word with you, son," said Father Romero.

Gus let everyone in, as if he had been expecting this. The interior of the trailer wasn't fancy, but much to Glory's surprise, it was clean. An old-fashioned speckled bowl was filled with fruit, and his bed was made with crisp hospital corners. Glory figured it was from all those years in prison and not because of any self-discipline. She would not give the man an ounce of credit or goodwill, not after what she'd seen. Not given what she knew.

Gus sat in a chair, and everyone else remained standing. He couldn't bear to look at anyone, which Glory took as a sure sign of his guilt. He fidgeted with his hands and then his shoes, and then he came out with it. "I guess you're here to talk about Sister Amity."

Glory snorted in disgust.

Noah held up a hand, as if he were trying to hold her back, and said, "Son, you need to tell us what you know."

He closed his eyes for several seconds before he started. "I'm a different man today, but back then I really didn't have no choices. We were so poor that most of the time we didn't even have electricity, no running water half the time. So I started selling just to make ends meet, help my family out. And I was good at it, real organized, you see. I was professional.

"At first, it was to help out my family, and I guess it got to my head. Started thinking I was a mogul or some mess. Some kind of Cajun Scarface," he said, with a quick smile on his face like he was reminiscing about the good old days. "I had a team covering everything from Duson to Breaux Bridge. And that's when everything went down.

"But when you become a baller, you start to feel that heat. Cars following you everywhere. Lights on your street at night where they ain't never been before. You start to get real paranoid. It started chipping away at me, making me all anxious like. That's when I decided to get out."

Even Glory was absorbed by this story. No one was expecting Gus to talk, let alone spin a tale that sounded like . . . it might be true? Glory didn't even notice that her back was starting to complain or that more chickens had ambled into the yard and that the sound of the clucking was getting louder. She was as captivated as everyone else standing in the broken-down trailer.

"What I didn't know was that the cops weren't following me as much as they was following Milton Knowles. They got me and tried to get me to flip on him, but I wouldn't. He gave me a job when no one else would. So I stood strong, did the time."

Father Romero walked over and put his hand on his shoulder, "I see, son. This is what they do to our black children. Charge them as adults without any grace whatsoever, without any regards to the inequality that forced them into illegal activity in the first place. I'm so sorry, my child."

"Sorry my ass," said Glory, leaning into Gus's face. "You may be able to fool this liberal bleeding heart with his Prada shoes and manicured fingernails, but you can't fool me. I know for a fact that your fingerprints were on the doorknob of Amity's bedroom. And I seen you out there at the graveyard, praying for salvation and kindness when I'm pretty sure God is sending neither your way. How do you explain that?"

Father Romero removed his hand from Gus's shoulder, as if Gus were the devil suddenly spritzed with holy water. Glory had shared with the crew about seeing Gus at the cemetery, but apart from Delphine, she had not shared the results of her questionably obtained fingerprint analysis.

Gus stuttered, his eyes tearing up. "I wanted nothing more than to stay out of trouble when I got out. I had big plans. Become a real legit entrepreneur. But if you know Milton Knowles, you know how he can pull you back in. The first thing he done was give me a new truck, a sort of thank-you present for time served, I guess. I suppose I could have said no, but this is Lafayette, not some big city. You need transportation. How was I supposed to get around? And then he asked me to do some runs, but only to Amity. Once I found out she was a nun, I refused to give it to her, told her I wasn't turning no nun into a junkie, but the way she explained it made it feel like I was doing her a favor. That Mother Superior was in her final days and needed that fentanyl for the pain."

Father Romero buried his face in his hands, and Noah clenched his fists, unsure where to direct his rage.

"You lie!" screamed Glory. Delphine grabbed her shoulders as if her mother might jump him, the way you see victims do sometimes in court.

"My fingerprints were probably on the door because the last time I saw her, she had all these boxes around the place, on her kitchen table, in the hallway. She asked me to help her put them on the top shelf of her closet. So I opened her bedroom door and lifted them up there for her. Then one day I came to her apartment for our scheduled drop-off, and she wasn't there but the door was unlocked. I walked in and saw her just . . ." His face twisted, and the grown man dissolved into tears. "I didn't do it, I swear. I just walked in and she was like that."

Father Romero pressed the side of Gus's face into his chest, and he sobbed like a child. Glory turned her back on him and began to pace, unsure if any of this was true but reconciling the very accurate details in his story with Amity's apartment. Noah jumped in.

"I gave you a job at my business under the condition that you keep your nose clean and be honest. I can't tell you how disappointed I am in what you're confessing right now."

"I'm sorry, Mr. Noah. I just . . . didn't know what to do. I couldn't tell no one. You know how Milton is."

Glory's rage subsided for a moment to fire off a few more questions. "And you called 911?"

"Yes, ma'am."

"And why didn't you come forward and tell anyone?"

Delphine handed Gus a tissue. He blew his nose and dried his eyes with a shirt sleeve. "I'm on five years' probation. The Lafayette PD will toss you in jail for jaywalking. You not supposed to have any interaction with the police whatsoever. If I came forward, they'd send me back, and I just can't go back. I can't." The tears started anew.

Glory and Delphine sat at a weathered table underneath the giant oak, allowing grown men to deal with a grown man's emotions. A chicken pecked at Glory's ankle.

"I'm going to snap the neck of one of these chickens, bring it home, and fry it if they don't leave me alone," said Glory, waving her purse at a rooster that was getting a little too close for comfort.

"I believe him, Mama," said Delphine, who was perched on the bench as lightly as she could, so as not to stain her expensive jeans or get a splinter in her rear. "Not that it was right to stay quiet. He should have spoken up, but he's not wrong. They definitely would have sent him back to prison for this."

Glory took a wild swing at a chicken with her purse, striking her target and sending a handful of feathers into the air. "What's the point of keeping roosters anyway? No eggs, just trouble."

"Mama, leave that poor animal alone."

Glory put her purse on her lap. What she wanted to do was call the police and report Milton's ass for bringing all that vice and damnation into Amity's life. And yet there was a ring of truth to Gus's story that she couldn't deny. She knew Amity would have done anything to ease Mother Superior's pain, even if it meant calling up that no-good Milton Knowles. Somehow, Glory would see that Milton got his in the end.

23

"Thanks for coming to the closing with me," said Landry, his callused knuckles fastened around the steering wheel of his truck. The interior smelled of leather and was simple and squared away, just like him. It was empty of any contents at all except for the maps tucked inside the passenger-side door, an energy drink in the cupholder, and a sheriff's pin on the visor. The rain poured in sheets over the window, so much so that Delphine didn't know how he could even see.

"I've noticed the banks requiring additional information at closing these days, throwing a wrench into everything. Always best to have a lawyer onsite if you can," she said, despite not even practicing this kind of law or knowing if any of this was true. She hated to admit it, but she really was her mother's daughter. She dangled a set of keys. "You are now the proud owner of a hunting cabin."

They chatted about his plans for the cabin until the rain became so intense that both needed to focus on the road. Delphine didn't want to distract his driving in this heavy rain, and she was afraid of what might come out of her mouth. They hydroplaned over a slick spot on the road. Thunder cracked in the distance.

"Look here," he said, finally breaking the silence. "The cabin is about twenty minutes away. Lafayette is two hours away. Why don't we go and wait out the rain there, rather than risk our lives out here in this storm? We ought to be good here for a little while."

She agreed.

He drove carefully the rest of the way. Slowly, the highway disappeared in a vast landscape of partially drowned trees and marshes so watery and overflowing that Delphine had no idea if the storm had done that or if the land had come that way. The truck navigated a steep incline, and after a final bend, a wooden A-frame house appeared.

"Here she is. Casa Landry," he said. Landry went first. He grappled with the keys in the rain, and when the door was open, Delphine sprinted from the cab of the truck into the home.

Delphine shook off the rain like a wet dog and looked around. On the first floor were all pine boards and a futon, with a small kitchenette in a corner, along with a few piles of boxes. The wood-paneled walls slanted inward. A small, lofted space was visible from the ground floor.

"I know it doesn't look like much," he said, "but I'm going to refinish these floors, update the kitchen a bit . . ."

"I love it," Delphine said. "Awfully small for the whole family, though."

"I don't really see Kerry and the kids coming up too often. She hates the idea of me hunting in the first place."

"I have to admit I agree with her on that point."

"Anyways, probably won't be more than me and a couple of buddies. You see that marsh over there," he said, guiding her toward a giant window, his hand in the small of her back. "Duck hunting for days."

"I thought that was just flooding from the storm."

He laughed. "I guess it does look a little flooded out there." And then he did something he never really did with Delphine. Looked straight into her eyes.

The modest thing would be to look away, but she didn't want to. She couldn't name what she wanted from him, other than to stop all this pretending. Maybe it was time to stop censoring her life. Maybe that would start right now.

"Let me find something for us to eat." He backed away and rummaged through the boxes. "But don't get your hopes up for a gourmet meal," he added. She slipped off her wet shoes and curled up on the futon, where she closed her eyes and listened to the rain on the roof. It wasn't long until she drifted off.

Some indeterminable time later, she woke beneath a striped camp blanket. The sky had grown angrier and darker. Landry was busy in the efficiency kitchenette, a single piece of furniture that combined a sink, one burner, and a compact fridge in one. It occurred to her she had not seen him in casual clothing in years. He was always in his cop uniform. Today he was just himself, in dark jeans and a loose black tee shirt that showed off his strong arms.

And how long had she been in disguise, too? She didn't wear a uniform, but hadn't she costumed herself to be accepted at work, by Chad, by their friends and family? She policed her clothing and manners and words, and what had become of her life? It had already been washed away along with the dirt roads that led to this cabin.

"How long was I asleep?" she asked, inhaling the aroma of something satisfying in the air.

"Couple of hours."

"Two hours!" She jolted upright from the futon and made a weak attempt to gather herself, but she stopped herself when she saw Landry's wide grin, which put her at ease.

"I texted my wife to let her know that I'd be staying here tonight. That storm's bad, and there's a severe weather warning until tomorrow morning. Lived in New York City so long you almost forgot about hurricane season, didn't you?"

"Where did you get food from?"

"I brought some basics down a couple weeks ago. Some tools, cleaning supplies, some kitchen stuff, and some MREs. That's 'meals ready to eat,' like the military uses out in the field. The chili's pretty good. Powdered eggs, not so much, but I know how to doctor it up. Here." He handed her a glass with a decent pour of whiskey. She did not object.

The rain battered the windows as they ate their chili and drank whiskey out of juice glasses, and Delphine loved every second of it. The much-needed nap in the rain. The slightly scratchy blanket now wrapped around her shoulders. The not-bad-at-all chili. She felt more like herself than she had in a long time.

"You better text your mama. I don't need her yelling about how I abducted you or putting an all-points bulletin on my ass."

"You're such a Boy Scout." She grabbed her phone and then shrugged. "It's dead."

"Gotta charger out in the car," he said, the winds rattling the windows. "I'll text her in the meantime and grab it once things calm down. Of course, she's going to think we're up to no good up here alone."

"On the other hand, it will provide her with hours of delicious speculation and worry," she countered. "Do it."

He texted and put the phone down.

She let the full weight of her body rest against the edge of the futon, which was folded up into a sofa. A large sip of whiskey eased its way down her throat, warming her body and reducing her inhibition.

"You and me . . . would it be the worst thing?" she asked, lacing her hand in his. His hands tensed inside of hers for a second, then relaxed. She tried to read his face as he stared out the window deep in contemplation, as if he were trying to solve a puzzle.

He shook his head slowly, deliberately, as if he had made up his mind. He turned away from the window to look at her and said, with clear-eyed intensity, "It would not be the worst thing. It would be all I've wanted since the second I learned you were back in town."

He leaned in so close that she couldn't tell whose whiskey she was tasting anymore. He kissed her in a way that was more intoxicating than the scotch, as smooth as any high-end whiskey. He lingered at the spot on her neck, just above her clavicle, that made her feral with desire. With Chad, she was always choreographing their sex. *First this and then that, and then he'll do that thing and it will be over.* With Landry, she was present. She savored the sensation of his tongue lapping her shoulder, so much so that she didn't even notice him unbuttoning her shirt.

His arms reached behind her back to unhook her bra, and she wanted to pause time. She wanted to remember what this felt like. Remember what it was like to be wrapped up with a man who she wanted and who felt the same way about her. His eyes were full of desire. She shivered as he kissed her breasts, lightly at first and then slightly rougher, like a man who couldn't control himself. Then he slid further down the futon, peeling off her black lace underwear and delighting her even more with his tongue until she could no longer suppress an explosion so loud she was glad that they were deep in the Louisiana woods.

With the clarity of mind that comes from a stupendous orgasm, she thought that some degree of reciprocity was warranted. It did not feel like a chore like it had so many times before. When she finally got a good look at the entirety of his body, taking him into her mouth did not feel like an obligation. She craved him. She savored the saltiness of his skin and the smell of his body as he let out a moan. He clenched the blanket beneath him with his fists and insisted that she stop immediately so he could be inside her. Nothing had ever felt as satisfying as being with him. After all these years, she began to think maybe Beau Landry was what she'd needed all along.

By the time she woke up the next morning, the rain had stopped and the sun shone straight into her eyes. Landry was already awake, making coffee and stirring oatmeal in a pot. They rode back to Lafayette in near silence. Delphine finally charged her phone and saw the texts pour in from her mother. There would be plenty of time to deal with that. For now, she slid over in the cab of Landry's truck to be close to him, her head on his shoulder and his hand on her knee. They drove back to Lafayette, held together by the silence.

24

E ast Simcoe Street had seen better days. It was once the hub of Lafayette nightlife, a place where women donning pinafores could steal a dance with a gentleman with sweet-smelling pomade in his hair. Nowadays it was mostly a street of desperation. It was also a place where Glory could confront Milton Knowles without a pair of canine incisors sinking into her flesh.

You knew you were on East Simcoe when you saw the Evangeline Maid sign, the famous one that declared their product "Stays Fresh Longer," with the massive spinning loaf of bread. On the other end was Blackie's Four Corners Barber Shop. There was little of note in between. A boarded-up beauty supply shop. An auto parts store. A car wash with neither cars nor water. And then there was Miami Moon.

Glory had texted Delphine to ask her what to wear, but her phone was dead for some reason. She knew that Delphine had gone out with Landry to close on his hunting cabin and that a big old storm was headed that way. Maybe the reception up there was spotty. At any rate, she would have to do her own homework. According to the Facebook page for Miami Moon, of which there were

682 members, it was Denim and Boots night, and DJ Big Shaun would be presiding over the turntables. At least it gave her a direction for what to wear.

The pointy toes of her red cowboy boots scraped the gravel. They were adorned with fringe along the calf, which flapped in the breeze. Loose jeans bunched around the top of the boots and stretched high above her waistline. She'd decided on the sequin top because she wanted to look festive and not dowdy, but she'd left her cowboy hat at home. That would have been too much.

She parked her car in the gravel parking lot and had second thoughts. Low-slung sedans with blacked-out windows screeched in and out of the parking lot around her. Rap music—and not the cheerful kind of rap that Glory could abide—made her windows shake even though the music was not coming from her car. She held tight to her steering wheel, hoping it would fortify her enough to go inside. What the hell, she thought. Ain't no one going to be looking at me anyhow. Cloaking herself with the shield of invisibility that comes from being a woman of a certain age, she summoned herself to go inside.

Glory handed the bouncer twenty dollars for the cover and noticed the tattoo on his hand. This is why you can't get a real job, mused Glory. You can't show up at any reputable job with a king of spades tattoo that looks like it was drawn with a ballpoint pen inside Angola State Penitentiary. Then it dawned on her that she'd seen that tattoo before, first on Milton and then on Gus. It reminded her why she was here in the first place.

The floor of the club was coated with varnish as thick as nail polish topcoat. The low ceilings were painted black, as were the walls. It was probably easier to paint the whole place black than to clean it. A mirror stretched the length of a small dance floor, which was surrounded by round tables with foil-like tablecloths that reached just a couple of inches below the tabletops. It appeared to be mostly unchanged since the 1960s, but not in a charming way—in a raze-the-whole-thing-down kind of way.

Inside, plus-sized women were squeezed into flimsy clothing with a breathtaking amount of stretch. Men in loose tee shirts and even looser pants huddled together, staring into the glowing screens of their cell phones. What was the point of a theme night if no one was going to participate? thought Glory. Furthermore, she could remember coming here a couple of times before she was married. She could really cut the rug back then and was tempted to show these kids a few things, but knew they'd just see her as some old fool.

Glory ordered a 7-Up and grabbed a seat at one of the round tables. Whatever faint hopes she had for DJ Big Shaun faded when he started to play some of that filthy heathen music that seemed popular. One thing remained consistent, which was that Miami Moon was a spot where people could indulge in the current dance trends.

Unfortunately for Glory's blood pressure, these customers were not dancing the locomotion. The women pushed their derrieres into the men's groins and made their rear ends vibrate. Then they bent their upper bodies toward the ground, still thrusting their buttocks toward the man's genitals. Glory had seen this before on the BET Awards and wondered why a network that catered to families would encourage black women to degrade themselves like this. It was one thing to see Megan Thee Stallion acting like this on TV. It was another thing entirely to see it in person.

She felt nothing but profound sadness for these women. She hoped they would find the Lord and redemption, but she mostly hoped that these women would not be cursed with a yeast infection from the too-tight unitards. She hoped their feet would not be misshapen with bunions from wearing heels that did not fit their plump feet. But more than anything, she hoped that one day they would get some sense and love themselves.

Glory was busy tearing off bits of her cocktail napkin to stuff them in her ears when a woman nearly her age motioned at her, asking to share a seat at her table. Curious, Glory obliged.

"You must be here for the mixer," said the woman in the demure pink blouse and pleated beige slacks. "This place is . . . not what it used to be."

"No, no mixers for me," she said. "I'm just here to see my son deejay. Tried to get him a job at FedEx, but no, he wants to be a *musician*." She waved at the man behind the table, his laptop connected into speakers the size of a teenager. He waved back with a bewildered look on his face.

"This is some original dancing, don't you think?" added the stranger, twisting a faux-pearl bracelet around her wrist.

"They might as well be fornicating in the devil's bedroom," she said, letting her guard down.

"Remember what this place was like back in its heyday?" asked the woman, who must have asked only because she was sure Glory could commiserate. "I used to practice the latest dances with my sister on the weekdays and used nearly all my babysitting money to come here and dance. Now people hardly interact with each other. You've got the men on one side and the women on another, like it's a middle school dance. And when they do decide to dance, they're damn near procreating."

"You know that's right." This begged the question: What was a woman of Glory's age and understanding of the world doing here, long past the time when the Miami Moon had any grandeur or respect? "What kind of networking event did you say you're here for tonight?"

"My daughter forced me to join this dating app. Love Never Expires. For people our age, I guess. Some speed-dating event. I regret the whole thing."

"Do you *want* to be here?" Glory asked.

"I would prefer to be in bed with my dog."

Glory tapped her hand in recognition. "You know, I think at our age it's about unlearning things. Society been telling us all the things we're *supposed* to want since forever. It got us believing that if you did all the right things—work hard, save money—you'll be guaranteed peace and security. But we're old enough to know that isn't the case. We both know ain't no one coming to save us or fix a damn thing. So I say do you want you want, even if that means getting in bed with your dog."

"You don't want to be married?"

"I've been married, and there is one thing I know for sure. I don't want anyone living in my house ever again."

The woman, who until now seemed very tightly held together, relaxed and stood up. "I think I'm gonna go home and see about my dog. You have a good night, you hear?"

Glory took a long sip of her 7-Up and looked at her phone. Landry had texted to say that Delphine's phone was dead. They were apparently caught in a storm three hours away and were going to wait it out at his new cabin. Glory knew where this was headed. There was no way those two were going to stay shacked up in a cabin toasting marshmallows and sipping hot chocolate, but it was Delphine's life. She'd have to deal with the consequences.

While she was fretting over Landry's text, a man with a gray tooth and a belly too large to be contained in a tucked-in shirt walked over. She glanced around to make sure this moth-eaten man was not coming for her. Her heart sank when she realized he was.

"Now tell me, what's a pretty young lady like you doing here by yourself?"

Glory grabbed her purse as if she were protecting it from a pickpocket. "I'll tell you right now that you're wasting your time. I am not here to dance, and I am not here to make friends, so you just skedaddle."

"You must be here for some kind of company, because you can drink alone at home for free," he said. "My name is Lawrence." To Glory's great annoyance, he seated himself at her table. "Say, you want to dance?"

"I done told you, I ain't here to dance or stroke the ego of grown men who should know better than to continue to harass a woman when she says she doesn't want to be bothered. Now go on."

"Okay, okay, I'll leave you alone," he said, amused by her gruffness. "But I am curious. What are you doing here, then, if it ain't for fun?"

"If you must know, I am looking for an acquaintance."

"I know just about everyone here. Wanna tell me who you're looking for?"

Glory hesitated, but he did have the look of one of those men. One of those men who came every week and chatted up the bartender even when she was busy with customers. One of those men who yukked it up with the doorman. One of those guys who, if he were lucky enough to get a phone number, would start planning candlelight dinners because he had been alone for too long.

"I'm looking for Milton Knowles," she said.

He looked as if he might get struck by lightning. "Look, you seem like a nice enough woman. You'd be smart to stay away from that man. Nothing but trouble."

Glory laughed with sarcasm. "I've known that man for thirty years and don't need any lectures. Is he here or not?"

He nodded at the bar. "In the room behind the bar." Glory began to stand up, but not before he pleaded one last time. "One dance?"

She was wearing her best boots, the pair she bought on that home shopping show but only wore twice because her sister Shirley had mocked her and made her feel embarrassed by them. It would be a shame to waste this stellar outfit on just tracking down Milton Knowles. Her mind was made up when she heard the opening notes of the "Cupid Shuffle."

It had been ages since she had kept up with the dances, but this one she knew. The song was recorded by a musician named Cupid, which was how the kids knew him, but Bryson Bernard was Loretta Bernard's son, and everyone was surprised when it became a TikTok dance trend. Loretta couldn't stop talking about it, and Glory was tempted to tell her that enough was enough. But it's not often that anyone from Lafayette makes a name for themselves, so Glory let her have her little moment.

Glory knew the dance because everyone in Lafayette seemed to know the dance. Some of the young people at church taught her. She lined up on the floor with the gray-toothed man and what seemed like the entire club. Glory stepped to the right when the song demanded it, then to the left. When it got to the part of the chore-ography where you tap the heel of your shoe into the floor, the fringe of Glory's red boots swayed. She regretted ever putting those boots in the closet. For a brief three minutes, she lost herself in the dance, forgetting about the death of her friend, the bees that someone left on her doorstep to intimidate her, the curse that plagued her, and someone knifing her tire. With her practical purse slung over her sequined blouse, she shimmied and scooted and danced.

And when it was over, she came to her senses, like a hypnotist snapping their fingers in a client's face. She'd come to see Milton, not shake her ass on the dance floor. Her dance partner was sweaty and smiling. He leaned into her and whispered, "You know what they say about a man with rhythm . . ."

Why couldn't he leave a perfectly pleasant moment alone? This was why she was single, because there were no gentlemen left in the world. Maybe there were never any in the first place. She shook her head in disgust and decided it was time to confront Milton so she could go home. She walked past the bar and into a short narrow hallway guarded by a muscle-bound man in a Beyoncé concert tee.

"I'm here to see Milton Knowles."

"No, ma'am."

She looked up at him to better see his face. "Henry? Henry Sonnier? Yes, I remember when you used to run down my street with your pants off, your daddy running behind you trying to catch up."

"Miss Glory? What you doing here?"

"I have business to resolve with Milton Knowles."

"I'm afraid I can't let you in, Miss Glory. That's not how he operates."

The door opened. Black-and-white checkered tile lined the small footprint of the room. The men gathered on improvised seating, a couple milk crates, a few fold-up chairs, while Milton sat on a leather-upholstered chair behind a rolltop desk. He saw Glory and sneered.

"Clear out," he barked. "I need to have a private conversation."

The men scattered. She could feel their eyes on her and stood up straighter, determined not to buckle under their gaze. She walked in the room and tried not to look scared when Henry closed the door behind her.

"I see you came back for more," he sniped.

"I need to know if she was using." She tended to believe Gus's version of events, but maybe she could rattle Milton and get closer to the truth of what happened that night.

"That ain't none of my business," he said. "And it ain't none of yours." He swiveled around in his chair, occupying himself with a sleek laptop instead.

"There are two kinds of people in this world. Those who give a damn, and then there's people like you. Your kind takes and takes, it doesn't matter who gets hurt. It doesn't matter who dies, as long as you get yours."

He rested his elbows on his spread knees and looked straight at her. "I see you're still on that do-gooder kick, all high and mighty and shit." He leaned back in this chair, lacing his fingers behind his head. "People out here in pain, the kind of pain you know nothing about. Pain because they were born poor and black and always gonna be poor and black. Pain because they saw their buddy get blown up in the war and ain't no therapy gonna make them clean again. And what I give them is a little bit of relief. Lecture all you want, but none of the sanctimonious crap you be touting ever made anyone feel better."

"Did you visit her apartment?"

"Nah, I ain't visited her apartment."

"Did you visit her apartment and hit her, like you used to hit her? You were using the drugs to try to force yourself on her and she said no and then you hit her and got carried away . . ."

"Glory . . ."

"And then got carried away and you choked her. You choked her until she was dead, and then you made it look like she did it!"

He stood up and yelled. "You done lost your everlasting mind, Glory Broussard. Now I'm going to say this just once, and then you're going to walk your fat ass out of my office, leave my club, and never come back again. I only seen Amity once in the past twenty years. She came to me to ask me for some fentanyl for that Mother Superior of hers. She had cancer, and the drugs they was giving her didn't even take the edge off. So I helped, and that's all."

Glory could feel blood rushing through her ears. A second later, she could actually *hear* the blood rushing in.

"Now, hold up your end of the bargain and take your ass home."

She would have a good cry on the way home but couldn't fall apart in front of Milton. She turned around and walked out of the room toward the dance floor. She could barely hear the pulsating music on the way out. Her heart was thumping louder than DJ Big Shaun's speakers, and her vision was blurred from the tears. Her cloudy vision made her doubt what she saw next, but there was no questioning what was happening.

Sister Jocelyn Cormier, dressed in a low-cut dress with cleavage spilling out in an unholy way, was making out in a corner with the sweaty, gray-toothed man. He pressed her into the corner while his hands explored every nook and cranny of her body. Her eyes were closed and she smiled, taking it all in.

25

She was doing *what?*" asked Delphine, shocked. She had slipped into the house the morning after her rendezvous with Landry and headed straight to her bedroom. Glory and Delphine had been tiptoeing around each other ever since.

Glory was behind the wheel as they drove to Baton Rouge, at the point where the interstate gave way to the Atchafalaya Basin Bridge. Here, the highway levitated on steel stilts. Below them, a swamp teeming with alligators, snakes, and other catastrophes swam in a soup. They had been busy, so Glory was glad that they could connect in the car ride on their way to see Father Romero testify before the state legislature. After the storm, she decided not to make a fuss about Delphine and Landry at the cabin. Even if what she suspected was true, she knew Delphine would never tell her the truth anyway.

"Isn't that illegal or unethical or something? She's a nun!" said Delphine.

"I would imagine that she has taken vows of celibacy, but where does celibacy start and end?" Glory mused. "Does getting felt up in the corner of a dingy bar count? Or do you have to do the full Monte Cristo to get disqualified by God?"

"This is the time you choose to concern yourself with nuance?" said Delphine. "Are you telling anyone about it?"

"How many times do I have to tell you? Glory Broussard ain't no snitch. And besides, I'd rather have the leverage." She popped a butterscotch candy into her mouth.

"Leverage? First the gambling, now you're Don Corleone, extorting the nuns and shaking down corner stores for protection money."

"It'll come in handy one day. I just have to choose the right moment to strike." Glory chomped the candy into shards between her molars and tried not to look down. She was always afraid that if she glanced over, she might take the car with her and *splat*, instant death. Creatures of death lurked under that thick brown water. She remembered that man she saw on the news a few years back who made a running leap into the water during a traffic jam. He should have been alligator supper. Yet he walked the streets of Lafayette as a free man, when he should have been locked up in a mental institution. It defied all logic.

"So let me see if I understand this," Delphine said. "I'm gone for *one night*, and you . . . go to a nightclub, confront an angry drug dealer, and witness a veteran nun sucking face with a strange man?"

"Oh, I did the Cupid Shuffle, too. You know, if you listen closely enough, the lyrics tell you how to do the dance."

"I guess someone leaving a box of bees wasn't enough to scare you. Or a drug dealer kicking you off his property, but not before one of his vicious dogs sunk its teeth into your leg and sent you to the emergency room. No more unsupervised visits, no confrontations with anyone else while I'm here, you understand?"

Good thing Delphine didn't know about the tire. Glory scrunched up her face and mocked her, the way school kids do to their teachers once they turn their back.

Delphine reached into her bag and pulled out a manila envelope, which she seemed to have an unlimited supply of for every occasion. Glory wondered if she had a file folder on Chad that she could dig into. She must have a divorce file. She made a mental note to look for that when Delphine left the house again.

"Everyone who is testifying today had to submit their opening statements in advance. Here is Keller Benoit's statement."

Delphine summarized his statement. The plant was crucial to Louisiana's oil industry, and assuming ownership of the homes was legal under the federal laws of eminent domain because of the critical and much-needed infrastructure the project supplied. They understood the hardship those affected would face in relocating their homes, but they would be fairly compensated.

"So the usual bullshit," said Glory, keeping her eyes squarely on the road and trying hard not to think of the water.

"Pretty much. High-priced attorney talk, fluffed up by publicists."

"Well, looks like they have a surprise coming their way today."

Father Romero was unmissable on the steps of the state capitol in Baton Rouge, tall and noble in his vestments. It was easy to see the godliness in him in that clothing, but Glory had now seen him in his home, barefoot and sweaty and not cleaning as he cooked in the kitchen. Had it made her feel differently about the man? Maybe. Faith is an easier sell when the candles are flickering, when the sun shines through the jewel-toned stained glass, casting luminous shadows on the walls. It was a tougher sell in the harsh light of day.

Glory and Delphine met him on the steps.

"Delphine, it's nice to meet you. Your mother told me you were able to take a little break from work to stay with her a while. It's so great they give you that kind of flexibility."

Delphine gave an awkward smile, and Glory wondered what that was all about. It wasn't like her to be so reserved around people she hadn't met.

"I hear the two of you have been cooking up something explosive for today's testimony," Delphine finally said.

"Has anyone ever told you how incredibly smart your mother is? If you ever need a paralegal at that New York law firm, don't overlook your mother."

"Erin Brockovich got nothing on me," said Glory. "You ready to roast some Benoits today?"

"I have never been more ready."

Inside the rotunda, Glory and Delphine took their seats. On the other side of the aisle sat men in suits that might have looked more expensive if they had bothered to get them tailored correctly. The women wore pearl necklaces and tweedy jackets. The Benoit family. Beyond the barrier that separated them, Father Romero sat on one side of the table, alone except for a boxy briefcase on wheels. Keller was flanked by two wrinkled lawyers that looked three times his age. The men whispered and scribbled on yellow legal pads.

The long lenses of about twenty cameras were pointed directly at Keller and Father Romero, from journalists crouched on the floor in the front of them. Thanks to Twitter and Father Romero's appearances on MSNBC, the Mosstown plant had transcended Louisiana politics. National news crews had flown in to cover the day's testimony, causing a stir even among the lawmakers. Murmurs filled the room until the sound of a gavel reverberated, and the proceedings began.

Father Romero read an eloquent statement about the value of human lives and community over corporate greed, the ecological destruction the refinery would wreak, and the toxins that would inevitably leach into the soil and water. He cited indisputable data about the poor health of those who lived close to similar plants and how rare cancers somehow became commonplace in the presence of chemical plants like these.

Once he was finished, a ragtag group of protesters erupted into applause. Then, in what was clearly a pre-planned display of outrage, a dozen or more people who had been seated stood up and hoisted signs above their heads. In unison they chanted, "Cancel Big Oil. Cancel Big Oil," causing a stir until they could all be rounded up by the capitol police and escorted out.

By the time the frenzy in the room simmered down, Keller's brow was glistening under the hot TV lights. His lawyers poured him a glass of water, and he gulped before he delivered his predictable remarks.

"He's rattled," whispered Delphine.

"Oh boy, he's gonna be shook by the time this is all over." Glory beamed.

The lawmakers lobbed question after question at Keller Benoit and Father Romero. Both men were ready for this moment. Father Romero delivered fiery responses that bordered on church sermons, and not the demure Catholic kind but the bombastic Baptist kind. Keller Benoit was just as prepared, but his tenor was calm and deliberate. He came off studied and glib, like he was prepped by three-hundred-dollars-an-hour lawyers, which he was.

Then came the question that Father Romero had been waiting for, from a partisan state representative he knew was in the pocket of the Benoit family. These hearings weren't about getting at the truth. They weren't about hearing both sides and making an informed choice. For the lawmakers it was about getting on television, especially since Mosstown was now a national cause. It was rare for a state senator to get on local Louisiana TV, let alone national cable news. As a cable news personality himself, Father Romero knew they'd all be acting up, trying to get the spotlight to stay on them.

State Senator Chassier spoke. "Father Romero, you sit here today and tell us that this is a moral issue, not a political one. But aren't you the one who is making it political, with your appearances on MSNBC—a socialist, left-wing network? The oil industry employs nearly 10 percent of people in Louisiana. Isn't your presence here, attacking Benoit Industries, just a cynical ploy?"

Glory and Delphine could barely contain their excitement, trusting that Father Romero would find the right opportunity for the incendiary evidence, hoping that time was now.

"I am here not only because I believe it is the right thing to do morally but because I have evidence that Benoit Industries has lied to the public about its compliance with Louisiana state laws."

Keller Benoit writhed in his seat and whispered in the ears of his lawyers.

"I present five years' worth of inspection certificates from the Mosstown chemical plant. Each one signed on the same day, by the same person, with the same exact signature. Furthermore, I have a signed affidavit from the signatory that he only visited the facility once, before he was mysteriously reassigned to another part of the state. The Mosstown chemical plant has been operating on falsified EPA reports."

The room let out a collective gasp. Keller spun around in his seat and searched for his father. A few minutes ago, he'd delivered poised and confident answers in front of a gaggle of press. Now he looked for his daddy to swoop in and fix everything for him. Glory unwrapped another butterscotch and leaned back into her chair. She enjoyed it the same way an arsonist enjoys returning to the scene of the fire—to see their handiwork up close.

The lawmaker banged his gavel for order, but there would be none. Instead he was forced to call the room to recess. Keller, his attorneys, and his family formed a huddle to strategize their next move. Glory reveled in the chaos.

After the break, Keller was subjected to more grilling. His composure was long gone. His face was at times crimson. Other times he stumbled over his words, as if he were trying to formulate an answer that would not get him into any more trouble. His standard response to the tough questioning was, "I don't recall," which cable news replayed on a loop later that night.

When it was over, Glory and Delphine rode the elevator down to the parking garage. Keller Benoit was waiting for them in the vestibule. He lunged at Glory until his face was uncomfortably close to her.

"It's funny. You come into my life, and everything turns to shit. There's your illegal gambling business, although I guess I did seek you out at the coffee shop. But then next thing I know, you're poking around at the Pelican Club, and now this."

Glory couldn't hide the surprise on her face. She was certain that he had not recognized her at the investor meeting.

He snickered. "What? You think a big old black woman is just going to blend in at the country club?"

Delphine muscled her way between the two of them defiantly. "Don't you dare talk to my mother that way. I don't care what your family name is. We will not be intimidated."

"I will destroy both of you."

26

Delphine was alone in the house. In just the last week, the tree in the backyard had dumped all its leaves onto the ground. The sky was gray and desolate. It was getting past the point in the year when folks opened their windows, but Delphine had always loved the sensation of cold, bracing air. It invigorated her, made her feel like a fresh start was around the corner.

Ever since the chaos in Baton Rouge, brought to a head by her mother's eagle-eyed snooping, Glory had spent most of her time volunteering at the church pantry. Delphine decided to use the time to deep clean as much of the house as she could without interference. This included Glory's en suite bathroom, where she was strictly forbidden. Once she entered, she understood why. Delphine would have raised hell at the dingy bathtub and the vanity, which was buried under so many Mary Kay products that Glory's rep surely owned a pink Cadillac by now.

She had just finished scouring the bathtub and mopping the floor when she was startled by a knock on the front door. And without as much as a call or a text, there was her husband, Chad, his hands shoved in his pockets and a duffel bag strap digging into his shoulder.

"You could have told me you were coming," she said.

"Can I come in?"

They walked into the living room, and Chad took a seat on the leather sofa. Delphine sat across from him on a coordinating wing-back chair. The beige living room carpet had recently been cleaned, each twisted strand of wool springier than before. Glory's figurines were nestled inside the curio cabinet that was wedged into the corner of the room. Neat stacks of books and magazines covered nearly every inch of the coffee table.

Even though they were at least six feet apart, Delphine could smell Chad's shaving cream. She always teased him about it, that little stiff brush that he used to emulsify the balm that he'd first bought during their Italian honeymoon and continued to seek out. Oakmoss and cinnamon. It made her want to press her cheek against his and inhale him, hit the rewind button back to those early days when it felt like love would be enough.

"I'm sorry to come here unannounced. I really am," he said, "but I didn't know what else to do, Delphine. We've worked out the terms. I've dropped the request for support. Everything is more than fair. It's time we both move on."

"So what exactly is happening here? Are you going to shove a pen in my hand and make me sign these papers?"

"No. I would just rather this be over sooner than later, and as I said, I don't want any alimony. I want to apologize for that. I guess I was just angry about everything that had happened," he said in a tone that was rehearsed. "I was hoping we could just make things official. What would you advise a client of yours to do?"

A chilly, clarifying breeze raced around inside the house. Delphine knew exactly how she would advise a client in this situation: make a deal, sign the papers, move on. None of the property would go to her because it belonged to his parents. She would forever miss those fifteen-foot ceilings, the original moldings, the herringbone floors. But as it turned out, she was just as comfortable sleeping on the futon at Landry's hunting cabin. Or here with her mom.

The wind rattled the windows, and there was more knocking at the door, snapping Delphine out of her brief fugue and back to reality.

"Was that the door or the wind?" asked Chad.

"I think it was the door," she said, standing up and walking through the foyer to the front of the house.

It was Landry, with his graying stubble and baseball cap, and eyes that seemed to lay his soul bare. They hadn't seen each other since that night at the cabin. No calls, no texts. She had wondered whether she had been ghosted by someone whom she had known since childhood, or if that night in his cabin was something that she'd hallucinated in a fever dream.

"I ran into your mama at the coffee shop this morning. She was on her way to work at the food pantry," he said. "Thought this might be a good time to head over and talk things through."

A cough echoed from the living room. A few minutes ago, the two men in Delphine's life were nowhere to be found. Now, they were both improbably in her mother's house: the man whom she had always wished would give a damn until she had given up hope and stopped caring, and the man with whom she had shared one of the most passionate nights of her life but was married.

Landry tugged his baseball cap closer to his eyebrows and lowered his voice. "Is that your husband?" Said husband must have heard, because no sooner had the words escaped his mouth than Chad was making his way over to the both of them.

"Chad Murphy," he said, as if they were exchanging business cards in a Manhattan conference room.

Landry's rough, callused hand engulfed Chad's smooth hands and buffed fingernails. "Lieutenant Landry."

"Is . . . something the matter?" asked Chad.

Delphine smoothed the front of her yoga leggings and began to nervously twist a lock of hair around her fingers.

"No, sir, not at all."

Delphine winced at the word *sir*. It was probably just an old Southern instinct, but there was no need to address Chad like that, especially after everything that had gone down between her and Landry.

"I was just stopping by to . . . uh . . . update your mama on some news from the Amity Gay investigation."

Delphine was relieved for the cover. Landry had been steadfast in his refusal to participate in what he called "this nonsense" many times, so Delphine knew he must have been picking up on the tension, the way that most people in Louisiana can detect a tropical storm by smell.

"Tell her I came by, won't you?"

"Yes, of course," Delphine said, relieved that she sounded normal. She watched him get into his truck and drive away.

"Is your mother involved in an investigation?" Chad asked.

"No, well, it's complicated. A friend of hers recently passed away."

Chad walked back into the living room and dug into his backpack, as if his patience for chitchat had run dry. A stack of papers thudded on the table.

"Here, I've printed it all out for you. I know you're the lawyerly type, so you're going to want to make sure I didn't pull any fast ones on you. I included a prepaid overnight label, so you can just drop it in the mail once you're done."

Delphine didn't understand why she had hesitated. This marriage was not a fixer-upper. It could not be mended by a few therapy sessions, which they had already tried. It was more like a piece of cheap furniture you buy at IKEA. It looks pretty on display, but the flimsiness of it is just below the surface. Underneath are a bunch of ill-fitting dowels that don't quite match their holes. There is no rubber hammer good enough to make it all work. It holds, until one day when you move it slightly and everything tumbles to the floor.

As if he could read her mind for the first time in their marriage, Chad said, "Remember, you were the one who cheated on me."

She wondered if those so-called "working sessions," with the Sichuan delivery and beers in Styrofoam cups, smuggled in from a favorite bartender at the dive bar downstairs, were worth it. She wished she felt worse about it, that she was in tears, or that Chad was in tears. It was surprising how cordial and professional the unwinding of their marriage was in the end, making her wonder if it had been a sham from the start.

"I'll read it and send it by the end of the week."

He unzipped his backpack and held out a glistening pair of keys. "I moved your stuff into storage. Don't worry, it was packed up by the best movers in Manhattan. Everything is climate controlled, wrapped or hung up the way it should be. I paid for six months' storage."

"I guess this is it, then," said Delphine.

"I guess so." He nodded and gave a little wave, as if she were a stranger, before walking out the door. It was the second time that day she'd watched a man drive away from her.

27

Glory smacked Delphine's hands away. "Get your grubby little fingers out of my eyes. I've had enough."

"Hold on, old woman, I'm almost done." Delphine glanced back and forth between her laptop on the kitchen table and her mother, dabbing her mother's face until she was satisfied. She plopped a pointy hat on Glory's head, wiped her hands on a tattered kitchen apron, and then held a mirror up for inspection.

Glory's face had been smeared with green face paint. Her eyelids and cheeks were contoured with a bit of dark brown, giving her a patina like an old watering can left outside in the rain. And thanks to an online makeup tutorial, black moles jutted from her chin and her forehead, as if evil was sprouting from the inside out.

"Good gobbledygook," said Glory. "I only agreed to pass out candy for the children. Now you got me looking like some kind of demon spawn."

"Oh, lighten up, it's almost Halloween. Have some fun." Delphine untied the apron to reveal her costume. A black leotard was paired with a crinkly black skirt. A headband with felt mouse ears squeezed her temples. She had painted a nose and delicate whiskers onto her own face. The getup had been hastily secured from a roadside tent along Ambassador Caffrey. These roadside tents dotted the major arteries of Lafayette, and beneath them one could find an array of seasonal needs, like pumpkins or Christmas trees, and, for some reason, fireworks 365 days of the year. This time of year, they had Halloween costumes.

"Let's add some cobwebs to your dress," said Delphine, who was having more fun than she ought to, given the divorce papers sitting on her bedroom nightstand.

"Girl, this is my good funeral dress. I'm not letting you put any doodads on it. We're late as it is."

The cat meowed loudly as they were getting into the car. He was still thin but stronger, on account of Glory's regular feedings of kibble and milk on fine china. He meowed again, and Glory bent down slightly in his direction and pointed at Delphine.

"You hungry? Get her. Pounce!" Glory cackled and got into the car.

The distribution of the Halloween candy had fallen under Glory's official Red Hat duties because she was now in charge of the food pantry, and the food pantry was somehow in charge of Halloween candy. Moreover, candy duty was universally loathed by the Red Hat members because it was four hours long and there was always some greedy child who inhaled all his candy before he left the building and vomited inside the church. As a result, the trick-or-treating had been permanently moved into the parking lot.

Glory and Delphine lugged vats of candy onto a fold-up table among the many fold-up tables for the Halloween festival—one for face painting, which Glory had had quite enough of, balloon tying, pumpkin carving, and to Glory's surprise, palm reading. She shook her head when she saw a child with an extended hand, palm up, sitting on a tiny chair. She wondered how the occult had passed muster for a children's Halloween festival and decided to bring it up with Father Romero, who needed to be reviewing these activities with a closer eye. And then there was the corn maze, which Glory also did not approve of. First of all, it was Louisiana, not Iowa. There wasn't enough corn in the world to make folks forget that they were in a parking lot off West Congress. And who wants to get lost, anyway? Seemed like people were desperate for stuff to do, Glory figured.

Constance Wheeler and her granddaughter, who was dressed as a frog, were the first to make their way up to the candy station.

"Ribbit," said the girl, clutching a pillowcase.

"You are a very cute frog," said Delphine, dropping a few pieces of candy into the sack.

"Grandma, can I go to the bouncy house?"

"Go on ahead. I'll catch up with you." When the girl was out of earshot, Constance turned to Glory. "I was so sorry to hear that progress on the house had been sidelined."

"Sidelined?" said Glory. "Like hell it is. My house is outstanding."

"The City of Lafayette has received another complaint. I'm afraid we'll have to increase the regularity of my visits until we have ninety days without complaints and three satisfactory visits."

Delphine walked over. "That's outrageous. I'm going down to the courthouse. This is straight-up harassment."

"You're welcome to do that, but until that house meets the city's standards, I'll have to keep conducting inspections as part of my role as community advocate. Have a good day." Constance huffed off in search of her granddaughter.

"I tell you, once I have proof that your Aunt Shirley is behind this, I am going to sue her for harassment and defamation of character." Glory ripped into a candy bar and sank her teeth into layers of crunchy cookies, caramel, and chocolate. "I'm gonna have a walk around, see if any children have lost a finger carving those pumpkins."

"They make safety blades for kids," said Delphine.

"A girl can dream." Glory's witch hat cut a strange figure across the parking lot, and her long black dress seemed like it was weighing her down. She unwrapped another pilfered candy bar, balling up the wrapper and letting it fall to the ground.

A woman sat at a small card table, the kind you might unfold for a weekly poker game. She wore a satin tuxedo with the bow tie alluringly untied around her neck. Her skin was tight and glossy, despite the deep-set wrinkles across her face. Her red lips jumped out under the brim of a top hat. Glory stared hard at the woman's face, like she was an actress in a film whose name she forgot. When she saw the turquoise ring on her finger, the memories flooded back.

It was Felice. The psychic. *CreoleIntuit52, if you're paying by Venmo.* Glory marched over to the corner of the parking lot. The autumn wind raced up her dress. She wrapped herself in Delphine's black pashmina, which she made a mental note to keep. The next gust of wind nearly carried away her witch's hat. The sirens of police cars bellowed from the highway.

"I'm Glory Broussard. We've met before. My daughter brought me over to your trailer. You probably don't remember me on account of this green makeup I put on for the kids." Glory didn't want to come on too strong or reveal too many cards, since what she wanted most from the woman was answers.

"Prefabricated home."

"Huh?" asked Glory, confused.

"That's what they call it these days. A prefabricated home. And of course I remember who you are. You're the woman who didn't want to put her purse on the floor because you thought my house was dirty."

"No, it wasn't that," Glory stammered. "You know that old Creole tradition—can't leave your purse on the floor or your money will up and run away."

Felice was not amused. She picked up a deck of tarot cards and pretended to shuffle them.

Glory, eager to take advantage of whatever insight she might have, sat down at the table. "I want to ask about the curse you said was placed on me," said Glory.

"That'll be seventy-five dollars."

"Are you insane? Robbing children at a Halloween festival!"

"I'm not charging the children. I tell them something delightful and positive and send them on their way. You on the other hand . . ." She raised an eyebrow. "Make it a hundred."

"Fine," said Glory, momentarily defeated. "I don't have cash on me but go ahead and bill my daughter with that bank app you use."

Felice tapped her phone, and when she heard a cash register *cha-ching* noise, she put it facedown on the table. "How may I help you?"

"First off, I need to know who keeps placing calls to the City of Lafayette complaining about my house."

"I believe you already know who placed the call about your house. As I am sure you understand, there are some people who will never be happy in this life, and so they make it their personal mission to destroy others."

"So it *is* my sister, Shirley, isn't it?"

"It is not for me to say or not to say, and as I believe I told you before, the matter at hand is the curse. Because unless you weaken the curse, you will have nothing but misfortune in your life. Now it is the house, but eventually it will be something else. Do not focus on petty revenge. That is meaningless. Focus instead on breaking the curse."

"But how? How do I break the curse?" said Glory, almost whining.

"I already told you," Felice said, with impatience around the edges. "You cannot remove it, but protection against the curse is all around you. It has already arrived. You must have faith. I want you to do something for me. Close your eyes."

Glory looked around to see if anyone was watching her. It was one thing to be participating in this act of godlessness. It was another to get caught.

"Oh, quit worrying about what people think," said Felice. "I am an invited guest. Turns out those stuffy Red Hat ladies can have some fun, at least on Halloween."

She had a point. Glory shut her eyes.

"I want you to manifest a protective symbol."

Glory opened one eye. "I thought you said it was already here."

"It is, but I need you to *believe* it. Now close your eyes."

Glory obeyed.

"Imagine what it feels like to be safe. To be covered in a veil of safety. To let go of what no longer serves you and create space in your life for the shelter and armament true faith can provide. I really mean this, Glory. Sit here and imagine what that would look like."

Glory brushed the sirens aside and tried to imagine this. She wasn't into any kind of hocus-pocus nonsense, but even she had to admit there was no harm in trying. Faith. It was such a steadfast thing, so solid sounding. Glory had been raised to have faith, but if she was honest, what had faith ever done for her? It hadn't kept her third-grade friend Beverly alive, nor had it kept Amity on this

Earth—and she had more faith than anyone. Father Romero had faith, but he also had money, which is the best protection of all. Maybe folks are always going on about faith because it's something you can have when you can't afford anything else.

"I just got an alert on my phone," interrupted Delphine, who had apparently had enough of passing out candy and had found her mother.

Glory opened her eyes and could see the children descending on the candy stations like vultures on a carcass, picking off tiny boxes of Junior Mints and Milk Duds.

"Don't worry. I'll pay you back," said Glory, motioning to Felice. "Remember our friend?"

"Nice to see you again."

Felice tipped her hat.

Delphine turned to Glory. "I don't care about the Venmo request. You hear these sirens? I think I know what they're for. I got an alert on my phone that Keller Benoit was just arrested for fraud."

28

Glory and Delphine were in the parking lot of Olde Tyme Grocery, just off Johnston Street and around the corner from the University of Lafayette. A pile of green tissues were crumpled up on the dashboard, a few on the floor.

"I should have had more sense than to let you put this crap on my face," said Glory, erasing the last of her witch-face makeup after what seemed like twenty minutes and twice as many tissues.

"It would have melted off with soap and water, if we'd just gone home first."

"We can't go home first, because I've been working all day at this ridiculous Halloween festival and I'm hungry. And now I'm shook over this Keller Benoit news and need a muffuletta to calm my nerves."

They walked past the red bistro tables and the giant rainbow-colored Snowball cutout to order sandwiches. The place had opened in 1982 but looked as if it could have opened in 1972, or even 1952. The deli floor had red-and-white checkerboard tile on one side and wood floors on the other. Its varnish had been worn thin by foot traffic and spilled beer.

"The usual?" asked the tired-looking man behind the counter. Glory nodded, and Delphine placed an order for a shrimp po' boy.

"You want that dressed?" he asked.

Glory stepped in. "I'll have mine dressed. She won't."

The man squirted mayonnaise and shredded lettuce into Glory's sandwich and wrapped both in white butcher paper. Glory and Delphine filled their red plastic tumblers with unsweetened iced tea and sat down in the cramped dining room.

"Tell me what the *Advertiser* says," said Glory as she splashed Tabasco sauce on her dinner.

Delphine summarized the online story for her. After Keller Benoit's testimony in Baton Rouge, an EPA investigation confirmed what had become clear during the hearing: the agency's certification of the chemical plants were forged. As a member of the plant's board, and moreover, its top compliance officer, the responsibility had fallen squarely on Keller's shoulders. He had also leaned on the shift worker that day to take the fall, and that shift worker fell all the way to the FBI and sang to the nearest agent he could find. Between the lies, the money paid to support the lies, and the intimidation and various other crimes, he was facing a number of federal charges. The sirens they heard during the festival were for him.

"And get this," said Delphine, reading from her small cell phone screen. "It mentions Father Romero and Amity as the originators of the protest against the plant."

"What else does it say about her?"

Delphine scrolled. "Nothing."

"Motive," Glory said. She put her sandwich back on the tray and gulped her iced tea. "That was his motivation. Amity was all up in his business, trying to expose his dirty deeds, and he didn't want the heat. Now, they'll stand to lose millions of dollars if this plant gets closed."

"That's a pretty solid motive, I'll give you that," said Delphine. "But where's the proof? And what, you think that man killed Amity with his manicured hands? I don't know, he just doesn't strike me as the murdering type."

"They're never the type until you mess with their money. And when you do, they snap."

Delphine got a glimpse of herself in the security mirror wedged in the corner and was reminded she still had whiskers drawn on her face. "Are you done with this sandwich? Let's go home and wash our faces."

Green water circled the drain as the hot shower steamed the last bit of Glory's makeup off. Delphine had retired to her bedroom to do whatever it was she did late at night. Maybe she was texting Landry. Or maybe she was fighting with her ex. All Glory knew was that the light stayed on for a long time.

It didn't matter anyway, because Glory liked to watch the evening news in peace without Delphine sniping at her. Nothing but car accidents and drunks and stupid high school sports, Delphine complained. Not much happened in Lafayette on a daily basis, and usually nothing had changed between the evening news and the late-night news. Except this night was different.

Keller Benoit being led away in handcuffs was the top story. She had just assumed that because of his name and his money that it would never be so public, that he'd turn himself in downtown with a big ole group of attorneys that charged more by the hour than most folks in Louisiana make in a week. But no, they snatched him out of his office on a Saturday, wearing jeans and a polo and flip-flops.

Glory shook her head. What kind of man wears belted jeans and flip-flops? If you're going to go through the trouble of putting on a belt, you can at least put on some shoes with laces. They must have got him by surprise, because his hair swooped over his eyes, which meant he didn't even have time to apply any gel.

The lawyers may not have been there when the cops snatched him up, but they were waiting at the courthouse steps not too long after. They were all in suits and sweaty, despite the fall weather that was growing cooler every day. Kerry Benoit-Landry was off to the side with the family. Glory couldn't tell if the steely look plastered across her face was concern or annoyance.

Next up was the weather and a looming report about so-called Tropical Storm Victor. Ever since Hurricane Katrina, the weathermen put on a hysterical display anytime there were raindrops on the horizon. Like most of Louisiana, Glory had learned to tune it out, for the most part. Always been raining in Louisiana, and it was never gonna stop. And what kind of name was Victor for a storm, anyhow? Victor was the name of the guy who drives up and repairs the chipped glass on your car windshield. A storm should be named Damien or Lucifer. Something formidable.

After the update on the Keller Benoit arrest, the weather report, and the high school sports, it was time for "Lafayette Crime Stoppers." Each Saturday night, KADN Channel 46 showed videos of people committing crimes and asked the public to call in and identify the perpetrators. The criminals featured in this segment were never masterminds but more like mental midgets. Glory peeled the plastic wrap off a popcorn ball she'd bought the other day at Don's Boudin, the kind of popcorn ball held together with that Steen's cane syrup— the good kind. She tore the popcorn ball apart and fed herself small pieces while she watched.

First, there was the man who broke into the Whataburger on Pinhook Road after-hours and dropped his phone in the vat of grease while cooking up some French fries—and then stuck his hand in the blazing oil to fish it out. Then there was the drunk woman who dozed off at the garden center in New Iberia, fell off a bench, and tumbled into a koi pond. Unlike Keller Benoit, most Lafayette criminals were simpletons.

Watching all these dumb criminal videos reminded Glory that Delphine had installed those video cameras, but she had never checked them. They had been installed around the perimeter of the house and near the garage door that led inside the house. She opened the cover of her iPad and reviewed the Post-it Note with instructions that Delphine had scribbled down. Delphine was always leaving instructions on how to do this or that, not to mention passwords for various apps and websites. Glory always recoiled, like a cat that had just cleaned its fur and didn't want anyone sullying it, but she was secretly glad her daughter had done so.

She turned the TV off and the radio on. Then she opened the app for her web-connected cameras. A pop-up warned, "You have eight notifications," and she got excited. She clicked on the notification and watched the grainy video. She brought the tablet closer to her face, trying to discern the figure moving in the dark. What she hoped would be the culprit was that skin-and-bones cat, licking its bottom.

She clicked on the rest of the notifications just to be sure, but it was just more of the same. The cat yawning. The cat stretching on the patio. The damn animal leaping onto her patio set and making itself at home. Glory knew better than to feed a damn cat, and now she couldn't blame anyone but herself for that flea-bitten vertebrate with a tail taking up residence in her yard. She vowed never to feed that filthy animal again.

She wasn't expecting to ever have any proof, but there it was, on the very last alert. Last week, exhausted from all the drama that had recently entered her life, she took a quick nap and surprised herself by waking up after four hours. Later in the day, she found that her large gray trash cans, normally on the side of her house, were strewn in the street. And no, it was not windy, and there was nothing to explain it away. She figured that someone must have taken them and flung them there. But who? Was it the same person who put the box of bees at her doorstep? What did one have to do with the other? At any rate, the answer to the trash can terrorist was right at her fingertips.

Glory was surprised at the clarity of the video streaming from her tablet. She had expected it to look grainy and black and white, like some corner store footage that police watch down at the station on *Law & Order*. Instead, the colors were saturated and vivid.

First, the woman drove a lap around the block, presumably to see whether anyone was at home or not. Satisfied that it was safe to proceed, she parked the car in front of the house and then peered inside. She went to the back of the house and jammed her keys unsuccessfully into the doorknob. Delphine had insisted on changing the locks when she'd installed the cameras. She thought that if Glory was worried enough to install cameras, she ought to be worried enough to change her locks. This seemed to set the woman off, because she wheeled two oversized trash cans, one with each hand, behind her until she reached the curb. She twisted her face and screamed before tossing the garbage cans into the street.

Apparently, throwing the trash cans into the street wasn't even, though. She reached into her back pocket, and Glory had to zoom into the video to see that she'd pulled out a set of keys. The woman messed around with her keys for a moment, unfolded a Swiss Army knife, and stabbed Glory's tire.

"Well, goddamn . . ." said Glory in a measured tone. And that was when the cat came back into view. That skinny cat arched its back and then clung to the woman's leg. She tried to shake it off, but it held tight for at least thirty seconds. By the time it loosened its grip, the woman was clutching her thigh and limped off screen. Now that's loyalty, Glory thought.

It was her sister, Shirley, and now she had receipts. She closed the cover of the tablet and let her head fall back into her recliner. Two lines of thought battled in her brain: sadness and revenge. She was saddened that her sister had been stealing from her, and heartbroken she had slashed her tires. Yet at the same time, Glory felt white hot with rage. She wanted revenge. If she knew her sister was stealing from her and did nothing, what did it say about her? She didn't want to hurt her sister, but she thought there must be a middle ground between enlisting someone to break her legs and forgiveness. The right level of revenge was somewhere in between.

It really do be your own people, mused Glory, coming to terms with the fact that a street cat had been more loyal than her own blood. A certain kind of clarity happens late in the night. The quiet clears the mind the way a rainstorm purifies the air after a storm. Her psychic intuitive Felice had been right all along—Glory really did know who had placed the curse all along. It could only be Shirley.

She hadn't noticed until then that her favorite Quiet Storm radio program was playing. Glory went to the kitchen to straighten up, knowing full well that that good-for-nothing busybody Constance Wheeler was going to be stopping by again soon for another of her so-called inspections.

Amity's boxes had somehow crept from the side of the kitchen to the middle. The path from the oven to the refrigerator, once clear, was starting to narrow again. Glory pushed the boxes to the side, knowing that that big-mouthed Constance would have something to say about it. She shoved a pile of boxes nearly as tall as herself back toward the wall with both hands, until the entire tower spilled its contents across the floor.

She kicked the pile of papers out of frustration. It is too late for this shit, thought Glory. She shoved the papers back in the boxes, one beige envelope after another. Water reports. EPA filings. Louisiana Water Board statements. All of Amity's work in a heap on the floor. Among the inky xeroxed copies, a bundle of hand-lettered gray envelopes stood out, tied together by red-and-white kitchen twine.

Glory had not yet made her way to this bundle of letters. She slid a pair of reading glasses onto her nose and read one.

Dearest Amity,

I hope you do not misinterpret my persistence as obstinance. You said that I should stop writing to you, but I cannot. In just a few months, we will both be free to live our lives precisely as we desire, in the arms of one another. Until that day, this is just a brief reminder that I cannot sleep, and I will dream of you nightly.

With a limitless love,

Martin Romero

29

What a fool she had been, she now realized. The shelves stuffed with Danielle Steele and Jackie Collins novels should have been the first clue. They were a key to the inner workings of her friend, a mirror to her real desires. Apart from the tumultuous relationship with Milton Knowles, when it came to love, Amity was always on the outside looking in. She was a cheerleader to everyone else's happy moments—weddings, babies, family vacations—never having tasted any of life's sweetness for herself.

And Father Romero. She shook her head ruefully, ashamed at herself for getting swindled by such a smooth talker. She always had the feeling that Father Romero wasn't right but chalked it up to him being one of those intellectual kinds of clergy. But her first impression of him had been correct. He showed up at his first Acadiana Red Hat Society meeting in slacks and a button-down, which would have been bad enough, but he was also wearing shiny black leather shoes with a strap. She later dismissed it because she knew that the former pope had a pair of fancy Prada shoes, so she figured if it was good enough for the pope, it was good enough for him. But now she saw the entirety of him in a different way. The makeshift TV studio in his apartment, the opera music, the wine collection. He was a man of God but also a man of capitalism. She could hardly sleep that night, working out what she intended to say to him about the letters.

The next day, Glory barged into Father Romero's office just before Sunday mass. She would have preferred to leave this sordid mess outside the walls of St. Agnes, but it was the only place that she could think of where she could confront him privately but not get herself killed in the event he lashed out.

The looming storm had darkened the skies. Father Romero was in quiet contemplation in his office when Glory found him, reviewing what was probably the sermon he was preparing to give. In the brief seconds before she spoke up, she imagined a lifetime of stories between him and Amity. How close had they actually been? Had they kissed? Had they made love?

"Glory," he said, looking up from his papers. Behind him was a shelf with expensive-looking books, and he sat in a chair that Glory just knew was expensive too. "How are you?"

In her trembling hands was the bundle of letters. She peeled one away from the stack and, surprising even herself, slammed it against his desk. "You did it, didn't you?"

"Did what? I'm sorry I. . . ." Terror set in his face at the sight of the letters.

"Do you mean to tell me that a man of God was carrying on, breaking his vows of celibacy, and besmirching a nun's good name? Have I assessed this situation correctly?" Glory had become so animated that her black felt hat with peacock feathers had fallen to the dingy, carpeted floor.

He put his face in his hands and disintegrated. His shoulders slumped, and his proud chest caved in, making him look small. After what seemed like an eternity, he looked up at Glory with reddened eyes. "It's true, everything in those letters is true. We were in love."

"What kind of priest are you?"

"A human one. I am a human being like everyone else, weak and flawed."

By now, the outer rings of the storm were making their way into Lafayette. The sound of rain bounced off the air conditioner, which jutted out of Father Romero's office window. Thunder cracked the air, the lightning still a ways off. Glory paused and gathered herself. She knew that once she crossed this chasm, there would be no going back. "Why did you kill her? She changed her mind, didn't she? Didn't want to leave the Church, and then she had leverage over you, your career, and that million-dollar crusader image."

He stood up quickly. The chair beneath him crashed to the floor. "Now you've got the wrong idea here, Glory. Yes, Amity and I were in a romantic relationship, but I had nothing to do with her death. Nothing whatsoever."

Glory wasn't ready to believe him just yet. She had watched enough of the Investigation Discovery channel to know that it's always the lover, the boyfriend, the husband. She felt possessed of something she hadn't felt in a long time. She felt bold and righteous and would not back down until she got the confession out of the man. "So tell me, then . . . what was the plan? You were going to leave the priesthood to do what? Get married? You know those cable news shows wouldn't like that . . . The former priest who won a million dollars and then shacked up with a nun? How did you think that was going to play out?"

The usual bravado had drained from his face, and maybe his entire soul. He picked the chair up off the floor and sat in it. Despite his vestments he didn't look like a priest anymore. He just looked pathetic. "We didn't have a plan exactly. And yes, I knew that leaving the Church would cause a brouhaha, not only here in Lafayette but on all those hateful conservative news channels that despise me. It would give fuel to the fire. You know, own the libs. But I told her I didn't care, that I'd find a way so that we could be together. But she said no."

"Of course she said no. She was a woman of faith."

He sighed. "Yes, she was a woman of faith, but she loved me, too. We were together, Glory, in all the ways. She didn't want me to leave because she didn't want her name caught up in the news, in all the gossip we knew would come with the ferocity of a fire hose, so we decided not to formalize anything or make any announcements. There was no need. It became a partnership, a romantic one, a professional one, a spiritual one. I loved her with my entire heart."

Glory's skin went cold. The revelations left her woozy.

"But it's my cross to bear now. I have to live every day with the pain of knowing that she took her own life, and it was the anguish she felt over our closeted relationship that led her to do it. So you go ahead and do whatever it is that you intend to do. Report me to the diocese, call the newspaper, or whatever it is that you're cooking up. Because I deserve it. It's not any worse than the suffering I already live with."

The clumsy sound of an untuned guitar interrupted them. It was Sister Jocelyn with her instrument around her neck, waving sheet music. "You're late for mass, Father Romero," she said.

Glory shook her head in disgust and walked out, leaving her good hat with feathers on the floor.

30

Glory was too rattled to go to mass after the confrontation with Father Romero. She couldn't bear to see him standing behind the altar, reading some sermon about community and valor and sacrifice. And she definitely did not want to see Sister Jocelyn strumming that stupid guitar.

She headed to CC's Coffee House instead, meeting up with her regular clients, tallying the lines and overs and unders, and taking money most of these men would never see again. Faith is a strange thing. The same regulars shuffled in week after week, filled with belief in themselves and this ritual that left them empty-handed most of the time. It was those rare times when they came out on top that validated the losing streaks.

Maybe church was a lot of the same thing, Glory pondered. She had prayed every night for years and kneeled at church on Sundays her entire life, but none of that shielded her from the hard times, from the long hours or the cheating husband or the solitude that had become her life. It was the handful of good things that kept her believing. Her daughter turning out mostly right kept her believing, even though she didn't want to believe what she suspected about Delphine and Beau Landry. It was getting harder to ignore, like a gnat chewing on your leg.

She was snapped out of all this cursed thinking when Noah refilled her coffee.

"You seem rather subdued this morning. Did someone put a curse on you?"

She tilted her head back, stared at him, and without an ounce of sarcasm answered, "Why yes, I do have a curse on me. My spiritual intuitive says I have to put my faith in something to break the stronghold of the curse, but I'm not sure there's a whole lot to believe in anymore."

Noah stared at her in confused silence.

"Anyways, what's your Wi-Fi password?"

"Wi-Fi? First you download my app, and now you're asking for the Wi-Fi password?"

"Just give me the goddamn password."

"Right there on the table tent by the sugar. You just open your camera and scan the code to connect."

"I know how to use it," declared Glory, despite not actually knowing how the codes with squiggly lines and bars had actually worked until now.

Noah raised his hands in defeat and walked back behind the counter.

Glory's hands were shaking so much that she had to put her phone down on the table. She could barely hold it straight. Between the confrontation with Father Romero and running into Sister Jocelyn, her nerves were rattled. And the nerve of Sister Jocelyn, running around the church with that guitar and her sheet music, like she hadn't been allowing that gray-toothed man to slip his hands into every little nook and cranny. How were these two people in charge of shepherding the spiritual livelihood of Lafayette?

Once her hands were still enough, she picked up her phone again and downloaded the Love Never Expires app. She remembered it from her conversation with that nice woman at Miami Moon and wondered if Jocelyn was a member, since she was at the mixer. Everything she had heard about dating apps was from TV documentaries, and from what she could tell, these women on them usually ended up being swindled by some criminal or picking up a stalker. She needed to see for herself.

She filled out just enough information to sneak a look. There was a man posing with a tiger, and another one with jet-black hair the color of shoe polish that Glory recognized immediately as hair dye, because there was no man over the age of sixty with hair the color of piano keys. Each profile reeked of lies and desperation. Glory might have been lonely from time to time, but not lonely enough to date one of these guys.

She looked out the window, where there was enough rain to form a giant puddle between the curb and Glory's car. The storm was picking up, and she knew she ought to be getting home, but being shell-shocked is not just something you can shrug off with a few cups of coffee. Noah approached, offering another refill like a peace offering. That was when Glory got the idea.

Right as Noah tipped the coffeepot, Glory snapped her phone at him. The flash ricocheted off the front windows.

"What . . . Did you just take a picture of me?" he asked.

"Just a little something to remember you by."

"Woman, you sure are acting strange today." He finished refilling her coffee and walked behind the counter, a slight scowl over his face.

She filled out the fake profile with Noah's picture. Interests: fishing and hunting. Political leanings: fiercely independent, which was something vague enough to appeal to everyone in Louisiana. Desired partner age range: 45–60. Glory snickered. She knew full well that no man really wants a woman in that age group, not even men in that age group. But the lure of a man wanting to date an age-appropriate woman would be enticing bait.

Noah Singleton was soon matched with more than eighty possibilities, which was not surprising. Glory knew there weren't but five eligible bachelors that age in Lafayette Parish.

This dating app was more entertaining than "Louisiana Crime Stoppers." There were at least three married women Glory knew, not to mention that old woman who boiled and served the crawfish down at Comeaux's. Within minutes, several women in their thirties were also vying for Noah's attention, which really did show how desperate the women of Lafayette were for some decent male company.

The screen of her phone was smudged by all the swiping left and right. She nearly turned her phone off until she stumbled upon the profile she had been hoping to see. *JustJocelyn*. It was unmistakably Sister Jocelyn. Hobbies: singing, nature, and hiking. Glory nearly cackled. As far as she could tell, the only hiking Jocelyn had ever done was hiking up her skirt that night at Miami Moon. Her lips were painted in mauve gloss, and she wore a low-cut blouse that showed off her ample bosom. She scrolled through the pictures. JustJocelyn with a cigarette in one hand and a martini in the other. JustJocelyn leading the church choir in a red wrap dress. JustJocelyn with a dog that did not belong to her, licking her face.

In the last photo, there was JustJocelyn in what Glory could clearly recognize as the Sisters of the Holy Family's community garden, tending to a hive of bees.

31

Glory drove back to St. Agnes, her car struggling against the whipping winds. In the warmth and dryness of her car, she tried to think through her strategy. She did not want to bring anything to the police just yet, although she wasn't exactly sure why not. She propped her elbows on top of the steering wheel and rested her head, struggling to think it through. A knocking on her window, loud as thunder, snapped her back to the here and now.

She rolled down the window a couple of inches. The rain slid in sideways. "Glory, my dear, what are you still doing here? Mass finished three hours ago." It was Jocelyn in her non-uniform uniform, struggling to hold an umbrella in the midst of a storm that maybe the Weather Channel had been right about. "I assume that you know the Red Hat meeting has been canceled today, on account of Victor that's going to blow through later tonight. It was just upgraded to a hurricane."

Glory stalled. "I was just thinking that I'd come and take inventory of the food pantry in case we need to set up a relief center once the storm goes through. Might be good to have a plan in place to get folks some water and some pantry items."

Sister Jocelyn cocked her head in surprise, as if she had never considered that Glory might be capable of such foresight. "I hadn't thought of that, but it's an excellent idea." Jocelyn's umbrella staggered from side to side. Rain pelted Glory's forehead, even inside the car. "I told you about the cotton gin renovation, right?"

The only cotton gin still standing in these parts was the one in Scott, if that rickety old thing qualified as standing. It looked as if a strong wind might blow the whole thing down, and yet it had endured countless tropical storms and hurricanes. It was a miracle it was still there after so many decades.

"Father Romero raised money to restore the old cotton gin as headquarters of our food pantry service. Even chipped in some of that millionaire money of his own, on account of it being a historic site and all that. It's gotta be restored in a certain way to preserve historic detail and all. Not that there are any historic renovation experts down here."

The wind turned Jocelyn's umbrella inside out, like a worn tee shirt. Sure was a funny time to suddenly turn chatty, Glory thought.

"You know how he is. Plays by the rules," said Glory, nearly choking on the irony of what she had just said.

"I was just headed out there, as a matter of fact. We have a trailer all set up for interim community outreach as a gesture of goodwill during the construction." She had to raise her voice to be heard above the winds and rain. "You know how it goes . . . trying to prevent folks from calling the city while all that noise and disruption is happening at the construction site. I was loading up my car if you want to follow me."

She didn't have an end plan yet, but Glory conceded. She and Sister Jocelyn dodged the deluge of rain to make multiple trips from the food pantry to their cars, loading their respective trunks full of diapers, gallons of Kentwood water, saltine crackers, and canned tuna. When their trunks were so full that they could barely close, they drove down Highway 10 toward the town of Scott.

Glory ran her windshield wipers at maximum speed and turned off the radio to better concentrate on her driving. She thought about texting Delphine to share her whereabouts but needed both hands on the steering wheel with all this rain. She focused on the road, and eventually her mind drifted back to the cotton mill and those hot summers when she was a kid and her fingers were raw from labor. People think that folks picking cotton is a relic of the Antebellum South, but Glory could still remember the smell of sweat on her skin and the heat of the sun beating down on her neck.

Under a darkening sky and winds that seemed more powerful by the minute, Glory followed Sister Jocelyn onto the bit of asphalt to the side of the mill. Weeds had sprouted through the blacktop, a patch-work quilt of neglect and disrepair. The mill stood tall, erected of corrugated steel that looked brittle with rot. Broken glass was sprinkled on the ground level like confetti.

Jocelyn got out of her car first and walked to Glory's driver side. "Right over there is where we're storing the food temporarily, until the mill restoration is done." Jocelyn pointed at something that looked like it belonged more on a dock than in the hinterlands of Lafayette Parish. "Want a tour?"

Glory jumped at the crackling of lightning. It was too loud and too close for comfort. "Maybe we should just put this food in the container and get going, before we're stuck out here in this storm . . ." said Glory.

"Please, you know how they are with the weather down here. Always a five-alarm fire for some two-bit nonsense. Come on."

Against her better judgment, Glory shielded her face with her hand and followed the nun through monsoon-like rain. Rain slid down Glory's back and into her shoes until they were able to take shelter below the mill. Water poured from the holes above them, from what was supposed to be the mill's floor.

Sister Jocelyn had to yell to be heard over the weather's roar. She shielded her face with her hand from the rain. "We're going to use this area as a loading dock, you see. For food deliveries and pickups. You won't even have to get out of your car for pickups. Volunteers can just load directly into people's vehicles."

"I see Father Romero has thought of everything," Glory said, wondering what she was doing out here with a woman that had to be Amity's murderer.

Jocelyn crossed her arms. "Father Romero isn't the only one with a brain. The rest of us make important contributions."

"I didn't mean . . ."

"Did you know that I was admitted to Rice University? It was my parents that decided I'd be better off in the sisterhood. No one ever asked what I wanted," she said, offering a fragile, tenuous smile, as if she had said too much. "Anyways, let's go upstairs so I can show you how the pantry is going to be set up."

Steadying herself against the wind, Jocelyn unlocked the door, leading to a spiral staircase. Nails stuck out from the floorboards. Dead cockroaches lay upside down, bellies up. Glory wanted to be anywhere to be here but could not let Jocelyn smell her fear.

"Come on, you old woman." Jocelyn laughed. "I know you and I haven't always seen eye to eye, but I gotta say, you're the only one who really gives a damn about the Red Hat Society. For everybody else it's a social activity, a place to gossip and eat those terrible petit fours from Sam's Club. I can't stand those bitchy old women, always trying to act like they're better than anyone else. But you, I think you're the only one who is in it for the right reasons, to help the community."

Involuntarily, Glory puffed her chest. "I am so glad you noticed that. People dismiss me because of my . . . *profession* . . . even though half their husbands are spending Sunday mornings with me instead of at church."

"Ain't that the truth. And don't even get me started on Constance's husband. That man has more girlfriends than a rooster in a hen-house," conspired Jocelyn. "Come on, let me show you the new pantry. You're going to love it."

Glory followed behind Jocelyn, gingerly navigating a spiral stair-case so narrow that the heel of her foot could not fit on a single step. At the top of the stairway, Jocelyn held the door for Glory.

The loft of the cotton mill was riddled with trash—needles, discarded food containers, and empty bottles of store-brand liquor. A rat scurried across the floor, disappearing into a hole in the floor that led to lord knows where.

Jocelyn started laughing. It was a sour, repugnant laugh that reverberated off the tin walls and sounded even more sinister set against the cat-and-dog weather. "You dumb, dumb woman. They say you're good with numbers, but you're pretty stupid when it comes to showing some common sense. In the future, you really shouldn't follow people into an abandoned building, where no one can hear you scream. Oh well, I suppose there's not going to be much more of a future for you, Glory Broussard."

Glory's knees buckled, as if they would give way and she would fall through the floor. Her throat seized when she saw the deranged face staring back at her. She convinced herself to fight through the fear and willed her body to function. "I know about the bees," said Glory. "What I want to know is why you put them at *my* door?"

Jocelyn laughed that vile little laugh again. "There are no secrets in Lafayette. You of all people should know that." She kicked an empty beer bottle against the wall. The glass shattered, exploding in the air, barely missing Glory's face. "Fine. I guess you deserve to know. You've turned out to be a worthy opponent at the end of the day. Gus dropped off a couple more shipments of that pain candy for Mother Superior after Amity was gone. He didn't want to do it anymore after he overheard you talking about Amity's murder to Noah. That's how I knew you were up to no good. Now I have a question for you. How did you learn about my bees?"

Glory tried to scan the room without moving her head or even her eyes too much. She looked at the door, and the only object that stood in her way—Jocelyn. "I saw you at Miami Moon doing despicable things with that man in the corner of the bar. I put up a fake profile on Love Never Expires, and that's when I found you, drinking martinis with your chest hanging out. Next time you're going to attack someone with bees, don't put a picture of your bee-hive on the internet."

"Ah yes, I'll have to be more diligent moving forward. Thank you. You know what we tell the children in Sunday school, don't you? Feedback is a gift."

"There's not going to be a next time. This is over." Glory walked slowly, feeling the loft floor give a little—no, a lot—with each step. The sky rumbled with thunder and lightning, and probably the devil, by the sound of it.

Jocelyn reached into her cardigan and pulled out a pack of ciga-rettes. She flicked the lighter with her thumb, lit one, and inhaled. A plume of smoke curled in the air. "When you become a nun, you become a caricature. You dress the same and look the same, but I was never like the rest of them. I had smarts. I had passion. I wanted to do things, big things." She pointed the cigarette at Glory, its menacing tip illuminating her face. "But I did what I was told because that's the way. You know who didn't do what she was told? Amity. I was the good one. I was the *responsible* one, the one who would take over for Mother Superior. And somehow Amity got all the acclaim, all the attention, and you know what, I was fine with that. But when she got Father Romero, I could no longer abide.

"I know you think that I'm the scandalous one, Glory, but you should have seen your girl Amity that night," said Jocelyn, shaking her head and laughing ruefully. "All laid out on Father Romero's desk, their arms wrapped around each other."

"You knew?"

"Not only did I know, I suppose I promised to keep their secret."

Glory's heart slumped in her chest. Father Romero had fessed up to their affair but had conveniently left out the fact that there was an eyewitness.

"But they kept going, kept taunting me, kept throwing it in my face, what with the hearings and charity and research. And that's when I began to think . . . why should I be the only one who toes the line? Why am I the fool that sacrifices and suffers while those two go to Baton Rouge and testify? They were going to go to *Paris*. I should have been going to Paris! I should have been the one he wanted."

Glory jumped. The lightning seemed so close that she worried the mill might combust into flames. The rain battered the tin roof. It sounded like the building was being pelted by nails.

"So you were jealous? Jealous of their love, angry that they were out in the world in a way that you weren't?"

Jocelyn took a long inhale of her cigarette and flicked it in Glory's face. Glory could feel where the smoldering tip grazed her cheek.

"You are misunderstanding me!" Jocelyn screamed. Her hands were balled into fists like a child.

Glory walked slowly, almost imperceptibly toward Jocelyn. Her gaze was fixed to the door.

"I didn't set out to kill her that day. I merely intended to let her know that I was no longer going to participate in her little charade. But when I got to her apartment, I saw all those romance novels on her bookcases. I saw a passport lying on the kitchen table. And it wasn't fair, you know? And I guess that's when I lost it and went for her throat."

As if it was timed with the disclosure, Glory leapt to the door, leaving a gaping, treacherous hole in the thinning floor where she had just stood. She rattled the doorknob with both hands, but it was no use. Locked.

"Tsk, tsk, tsk," said Jocelyn. "Haven't I proved myself more than capable by now? Haven't I shown you that I'm two steps ahead of everyone?"

Glory panted and looked around frantically for any kind of escape.

Jocelyn took a deep breath, paused, then took another. A hardened, decisive look settled into the lines of her face, and she began to sing "Peace in the Valley."

Oh well, I'm tired and so weary
But I must go alone
'Til the Lord comes and calls
Calls me away

Glory threw the full weight of her body against the door, but it would not budge. The door was the only solid construction in the building. Glory's desperation seemed to ignite something in Jocelyn. She walked across the loft floor toward Glory, gingerly avoiding the many small holes, as well as the big one left by Glory's running sprint.

"You don't want to do this. This is not who you are," Glory said, trying to appeal to whatever meager godliness remained in the woman.

Jocelyn's voice grew even stronger.

> *There will be peace in the valley for me, some day*
> *There will be peace in the valley for me, oh Lord I pray*
> *There'll be no sadness, no sorrow*
> *No trouble, trouble I see*
> *There will be peace in the valley for me*

Jocelyn's eyes reminded Glory of that gruesome day when she found Amity lifeless, her eyes open and streaked with broken capillaries. At the end of the song, Jocelyn brushed her cardigan off and straightened herself up. "Good night, Glory."

Hands around her throat. Gasping for air. Rain echoing like gunfire. These were the last moments before Glory lost consciousness.

32

Machines near Glory's bed whirred and buzzed. Glory's eyes fluttered open. Two blurry figures came into focus—Delphine and Lieutenant Landry. She removed the oxygen mask from her face and struggled to talk. "Is this hell? Did I die and go to hell?"

Laughter forced the tears out of Delphine's eyes. "No, Mom, you're in the hospital."

"So I am in hell." She looked down and saw herself in an ill-fitting hospital gown which had not been tied properly in the back. The unfolded part of the gown flopped near her neck and over her chest, leaving a hint of bosom exposed. "My lord, they can't even see to it that you're decent in the hospital of all places."

Delphine knotted the strings tightly, then caressed the side of her mother's face.

"I'm going to have to take a statement, eventually," Landry chimed in. "I have a lot of questions for you, and I'm still pretty mad you two were gumshoeing around Lafayette like some kind of amateur Cagney and Lacey, but thank god you're okay."

"What happened?" Glory coughed, and then her whole body was taken over by coughing.

"What do you remember?" asked Landry.

"I remember that deranged woman luring me to the cotton gin, locking the door, and choking me. Memory gets a little fuzzy beyond that point, if you know what I mean."

Delphine offered her a paper cup with water, which she gulped.

"When the storm got bad and you weren't home, I got worried," said Delphine. "I looked up your location on my phone and got more worried when I saw that you were at that old cotton gin. I had a hunch something was wrong and called Beau. We got there just in time."

Glory looked as if she had seen a giraffe in the room. "Looked up my location? You mean to tell me you put a tracking device on me?"

"It's not a tracking device. It's just a feature on your phone," said Delphine. "I set it up that day you got taken out by those bees and went to bed early. Figured I could use it for emergencies, and looks like I was right."

"I do suppose this was an emergency." Glory straightened herself up and looked at the various machinery. "So what's the verdict? Internal bleeding? Traumatic brain injury? Am I dying or what?"

"You lost consciousness when she choked you, but your vitals are fine. They're going to keep you overnight for observation."

"No they won't. I'll be damned if I'm going to sleep in this scratchy nightgown on sheets that someone has probably died on. Take me home."

A nurse walked in and settled Glory back in the hospital bed with the skill of someone who had witnessed this kind of petulance before. "You need to stay in bed until you're discharged, which will be tomorrow morning at the earliest. Might as well make yourself comfortable." She flipped through a chart and then looked at Glory's face again, this time more closely. "Weren't you in here recently? A dog bite if I recall?"

Glory imagined that this would be quite the topic of gossip in the nurse's break room and was reluctant to give her that satisfaction. But as it turned out, she was too tired to be witty. Being plucky was for the rested. "Yeah, that was me. Y'all can go ahead and yuk it up behind my back."

The nurse checked the machines and scribbled a few notes. "From what we've heard, you were quite brave." She turned to Landry and Delphine. "Now, why don't you two leave me alone with Ms. Broussard so I can run some tests in private."

"We need to talk," said Delphine to Landry. They had left Glory's hospital room and sat down on a hallway bench. Fluorescent lights hummed overhead.

"We do," he confirmed.

They were both waiting for the other to start.

"We can't be together. Not that you're suggesting that should happen," she stammered. "There are a lot of things happening in my life. Many of them bad. I am in the middle of a divorce, and I'm not entirely sure if I'll have a job when I get back to Manhattan."

"Delphine . . ."

"Let me finish," she demanded, looking down at the hospital floor. "I have a friend with a house in Upstate New York, out in the country. When she bought the house, the backyard was infected with something called Japanese knotweed. It's pretty enough, but it's invasive. Ruins everything in sight. And you have to get rid of every little bit because it will take over. Even the tiniest bit of root will sprout and contaminate all the other plants."

"Delphine . . ."

She continued. "That's me. I'm that plant. I take everything good and ruin it, until there's nothing left but the bad."

Landry cut her off. "I love you," he said, rubbing her knee. "I've always loved you. I'm not embarrassed by that or by our night together. Now, it doesn't mean I'm leaving my wife, and there's absolutely nothing that could tear me away from my girls. But I thought you should know. It feels good to finally say that out loud."

33

Even though Glory had witnessed the fall of Jocelyn Cormier in real time, she wasn't conscious during the most crucial moments. There was no trial on account of Jocelyn's guilty plea, but there were court dates for pleas and hearings, and Glory attended each one.

Jocelyn's end happened exceedingly fast. The Lafayette Police Department was finally forced into action. Between Glory's first-hand account of the confession and Beau Landry's firsthand account of Jocelyn's hands tightened around Glory's neck, Jocelyn lost her will to fight. Perhaps even her will to live. Glory would later see video of her in the interrogation room, and she was listless, barely following along with the conversation. Her defense attorney apparently even told her to snap out of it, to gear up for the fight of her life. But there was nothing to gear up for. The fight had already left her. She pleaded guilty, and was condemned to spend her retirement at the Louisiana Correctional Institute for Women in St. Gabriel for the murder of Amity Gay—as well as the attempted murder of Glory Broussard.

The news set Lafayette aflame like a wildfire during a drought. In the days that followed, Glory couldn't take the trash out or go to the mall because all the local news crews were staked out on her lawn. She even had to stay away from CC's Coffee House and her business for a few weeks because of all the attention.

"A woman can't even take the trash out in her own home," she grumbled to Delphine on video chat.

"Mom, you need to hold the phone up higher so I can see your face. All I can see is your chin."

"I'm holding it like you told me to," said Glory, who only pretended to be exasperated by Delphine's orders. "When do I get a tour of the apartment?"

"When are you coming to New York again?"

"Never," said Glory, entirely serious. "But I demand a video tour."

Delphine flipped the phone's camera and showed her around on FaceTime. "I'm still unpacking, and it's a lot smaller than my old place, but it's mine. Here's the living room." A gray sectional was lined with overstuffed pillows that didn't match but also matched perfectly. A large ottoman, covered in a rug that Delphine explained she'd bought years ago in Morocco, anchored the room. The kitchen had white lacquered cabinets and one of those big expensive refrigerators that you see on the Food Network. Spices lined up on a rack above the stovetop made Glory relax. Anywhere there are spices means that real cooking is happening. And anywhere with real cooking is a real home.

"What neighborhood did you say you live in again?"

Delphine turned the camera toward her again and rolled her eyes. "I've told you a thousand times. I live in Brooklyn now."

"I'm just asking. Don't get all mad at me. I don't know these neighborhoods like you do," said Glory. "Be nice to your mother. I was almost murdered."

"And how long do you intend to play the attempted-murder card?"

"Well, Jocelyn is serving a fifteen-year sentence for my attempted murder alone, so at least that long. Or until I die. Whichever comes first."

Delphine plopped herself down on the couch and hugged a paisley pillow to her chest. "I was thinking . . . maybe you should get a license and become a private detective. You do have a knack for sticking your nose in other people's business, and now that you're a semi-celebrity in Lafayette, maybe it's time to make it official."

"Girl, I am not paying good money to get permission to do what I already know how to do."

For a few weeks, Glory stayed at home, nestled in the safety of her recliner. Even though she had solved the death of her friend, which she knew from the beginning was not a suicide, she struggled with the aftermath. She tried to focus on the parts of Amity that still felt alive. The time she chased that boy down the street for peeking in her bedroom window. The time they ate an entire coconut cake during recess that was meant for their third-grade class at Westside Elementary—and not for just the two of them.

But eventually the spotlight dimmed, as spotlights tend to do, and Glory returned to regular life—with a few extra benefits. Because of the attention, renovations on the decaying cotton gin got accelerated. As the volunteer head of food pantry services, Glory was actively involved. She could be found most weekdays at the site with a hardhat atop her head. When she wasn't at the site, she was coordinating with local restaurants and grocery stores for excess food donations.

And eventually she found her way back to CC's on Sundays and her regular routine. She sighed when she saw the old pine table in the corner. It was like the old bosom friend that you haven't seen in ages, but no matter how much time goes by, the affection is unbreakable. Noah was wiping down his espresso machine behind the counter.

Glory coughed. "What do you have to do to get good service around here? Solve a murder?"

He smiled. "What are you drinking these days? Cappuccino or cold brew with almond milk?"

"Cappuccino. Old habits die hard."

His usual serious face softened as he sat down to join her. "I must say, I thought you were crazy when you were talking about Amity being murdered. And who would have guessed Jocelyn Cormier? Jealous over a love affair between Amity and Father Romero! I need to know what they're pouring over in that church, because I gotta get me some of that."

Glory cut him off. "People are complicated, Noah. Even good people. You ought to find it in your heart to cultivate a little more tolerance and empathy," she said. She wrapped herself in Delphine's black pashmina, grateful that she forgot to return it.

He stood up. "Can't ever win with you, Glory Broussard." He took the damp towel permanently slung across his shoulder and wiped down her table. "And by the way, thank you for the flowers. For Sarah."

She shrugged and wrapped the fuzzy pashmina around her shoulders more tightly. "I have no idea what you're talking about." The bell of the coffee shop's front door jangled, and a group of middle-aged women in full hair and makeup waved at Noah. "Looks like you have some admirers," said Glory.

"The strangest thing been happening lately," he said. "All of a sudden, women have been coming in here, all dressed up, asking for me and talking about *love never expires* or some nonsense. What do you think that's about? Is that a song or something?"

"Who knows?" said Glory, making a note to remove the fake dating profile from the app. Or maybe she'd leave it. He was grumpy, but a decent man. One of the good ones. He'd make someone happy.

Glory sipped her coffee. "Hot damn, that is some good coffee. Is this new? You could trot a mouse over that."

"You've been complaining about my coffee for so long I thought I'd try something new. Been getting compliments on it all day. I guess you were right," he said, trying not to acknowledge the beaming smile across her face as he headed back into the kitchen.

The bell jangled again. This time it was Gus, lugging a handcart piled full of boxes. He opened the boxes and started stacking jars in the merchandise section.

"You got a new job? First time I seen you not behind the counter," asked Glory.

He reached into the front pocket of his coveralls and handed Glory a business card. "Miss Glory, you are now looking at the CEO and founder of Gus's House of Bees. This is my first shipment right here."

"CEO? Look at you!"

"You know I was never any good at making coffee. And then I heard that the sisters were looking for someone to take over the bees, on account of Jocelyn Cormier being . . . well, you know. But I'm a farm boy, and I knew what to do with them. They gave me the entire colony."

"As long as those bees never find their way to my doorstep again, I'm happy for you," said Glory.

"I got big plans for Gus's House of Bees. I'm starting with honey. I got lavender honey, jalapeño honey, and blueberry honey. And next summer I'm offering pollinating services to local farms. Gonna be real big, Miss Glory, you wait and see."

"You just stay away from that Milton Knowles. I hope you learned your lesson."

"You didn't hear?" asked Gus. "One of his fighting dogs escaped the backyard and attacked a neighbor. Brought the whole operation down. He's back in prison until the trial."

That night, there was a special Red Hat gathering at St. Agnes. The women whispered when Glory walked into the meeting room, but that was nothing new. Those hens had always treated her like an outsider. Glory fixed a plate at the buffet in the back, relieved that no matter what budget cuts they endured, there always seemed to be money for a spread from Poche's Market. With a plate piled high with pork backbone and dirty rice, she tucked herself into her usual table in the back of the room.

Constance Wheeler and her frosted hair cleared her throat and stood at the front of the room. "We know that the past few weeks have been . . . a lot," she said, with a morose look on her face. "The first order of business is a new priest for St. Agnes. Now, this is ordinarily the business of the archdiocese, but we are brainstorming ways to insert a member of our organization onto the search committee. It is obvious that their discretion was sorely lacking with the selection of Father Romero.

"Secondly, leadership has met privately, and we have decided that, despite prior grievances that were well founded at the time but now seem petty given all that has transpired, that we would like to award Ms. Glory Broussard with a plaque of distinction for her heroic efforts in solving the murder of Sister Amity Gay, as well as for her long-standing service to the Acadiana Red Hat Society and new role as executive director of the food pantry."

Glory froze, just as she was dousing her plate with hot sauce. When she looked up, she saw the women's faces smiling at her, their applause ricocheting off the walls. She was so unused to this kind of attention, or at least this kind of positive attention, that her food was soaked in hot sauce before she snapped out of it.

It was the first time in her life that Glory had ever received an award. She intended to hang it in her home office, next to the profile story about her that had run on the front page of the *Advertiser*. Delphine had already sent a copy off to some fancy online framing shop, and she was just waiting for it in the mail. She thanked the women for the award and was about to head back to her seat when Constance cleared her throat.

"Now, one more thing. Because of your long tenure in the organization and your exemplary work thus far in the food bank, leadership has also decided to do away with our vote for the head of the Mardi Gras committee. You will lead it this year, though the board retains final say over the food vendors selected, as well as the decorations and all activities." It was good enough for Glory.

>

Bone-tired by the time she got home, Glory collapsed in her chair and turned on her favorite TV show. She clapped her hands when she realized what was happening.

"Tonight's Mystery of the Week comes from Lafayette, where a terrible person has been knocking over the trash cans of a resident, who also reports that a number of pots, jewelry, and brooches have disappeared from her house. Could the events be connected? Let's roll the tape."

The program cut to images of her sister, Shirley, looking around as if she were trying to avoid getting caught, then hurling the trash cans out into the street with the determination of a discus thrower.

"If you've seen this Awful Annie, call our crime stoppers hotline. Lafayette deserves better than this." Almost as soon as she turned her TV off, frenzied texts and calls started flooding in from Shirley. Satisfied, she declined the calls and turned off her phone. As luck would have it, there were never any more calls to the City of Lafayette about the condition of her house.

In the kitchen, she surveyed the boxes of research from Amity. She thought about putting them into storage, just in case. These may have been the boxes that brought Amity and Father Romero together, but it was also their legacy, as much as Glory hated to admit it. Without their partnership, and without this research, there was no doubt that another chemical plant would now be operational in Louisiana. Because of their work and Father Romero's testimony, Keller Benoit's deceit was uncovered and countless lives would be saved. No matter how upsetting Glory found their relationship, at least she could take peace in that.

A familiar sound from the backyard came through the window. The cat seemed a lot less raggedy, mostly on account of a giant bag of Meow Mix that Glory had hauled from Sam's Club, as well as bowls of milk that Delphine lectured her about being bad for its digestive system. But all of it seemed to be agreeable to the cat. Its bones were less sharp, its stomach no longer concave. She looked at the cat and felt sure. This had been her symbol of protection all along, the one Felice had told her to open her heart to.

Hadn't the cat appeared shortly after Amity had died? It most certainly gave her sister a good wallop when she slashed her tires. She had placed faith in Father Romero and the Church for so long, and while she intended to remain in good standing at St. Agnes and with the Acadiana Red Hat Society, she thought it might be advantageous to spread her faith across a few different buckets. Maybe faith can take an unexpected shape.

Patti LaBelle was on the radio, singing about having a new attitude, when Glory opened the door. The cat sauntered in and tucked itself into her leather recliner. "Not on my chair you don't," she ordered. It relocated to the sofa and yawned, as if it understood.

"I think I'll call you Patti."

ACKNOWLEDGMENTS

Glory Broussard came about in a circuitous way, over many years. I marvel at the twists of fate that nudged her into the universe.

Many thanks to Jeff Ourvan and the various members of the Write Workshops who read the earliest iterations, especially Vicky Vidalaki.

I have been supported by a wonderfully kind and attentive team spearheaded by Alice Speilburg, who championed Glory's messy, petty ways from the very beginning. Throughout the publishing process, I have felt so wonderfully heard by the Pegasus Crime team, including editor Jessica Case and public relations and marketing lead Meghan Jusczak. I am grateful to everyone who has supported my book behind the scenes—from design, proofreading, copy editing, and more.

My mother, Barbara Arceneaux, is determined to introduce Glory Broussard to everyone in Lafayette. My brother, Shaun, will be foisting copies into the hands of strangers. Be on the lookout for eager members of the Arceneaux family.

Lastly, I am immensely lucky to have a ride-or-die friend in Kerry Bennett, who, in addition to being an endless source of enthusiasm and support, is a talented editor who read multiple raggedy drafts and shined this book up considerably. I really can't thank you enough.

Coming Soon—Fall 2024
A New Glory Broussard Mystery

T he day had started harmlessly enough. Glory strode through the heavy doors at CC's Coffee House, the one on Ambassador Caffrey Parkway and West Congress, in the same shopping center as the Albertsons grocery store and Soulhaus, a restaurant that had just opened. She hadn't tried this new restaurant yet, but her daughter Delphine had texted her some videos of a local sportscaster consuming piles of food on TikTok. Why her daughter had wanted her to watch a video of some man eating piles of food was beyond her, but Glory had to admit it looked pretty tasty. So far Glory had been able to resist because she had received a stern lecture from her doctor about her numbers, and by "numbers" he meant every number that can possibly be measured by science, but when she inhaled the aroma of fried catfish, she could sense her resolve weakening.

By the time she sat down, Noah Singleton, owner of this particular CC's franchise, was walking her way balancing a tray of small paper cups on an upturned palm near his shoulder. "You have a good Christmas, Miss Glory?"

"Sure did, and you?" Small talk was the glue that held the South together. No matter one's political affiliation or personal beliefs, the connective tissue of Lafayette Parish had remained intact with benign questions like *How's your mama doing? You having people over for Mardi Gras? What you fixin' for Easter?* Not that most people minded. It was preferable to questions that might upset the peace. "You just *look* mischievous today. I can already tell you're up to no good," she added.

Noah swung the small tray in front of her. "Try this."

She gave him a skeptical look, took a small sip, and coughed dramatically, like she had ingested poison. "Noah Singleton, I don't know what is in that drink, but I suspect I might have a case of sudden onset diabetes. What in the name of the Good Lord is this?"

"I'm still working on the right level of sweetness," he said, looking disappointed that he hadn't yet found the right balance. "I'm trying to create a signature drink to go viral on social media. I call it Praline Perfection. Chicory coffee and six pumps of praline syrup topped with whipped cream and a praline candy crumble."

Glory had no idea why anyone would ever want to go viral. She had had a moment in the spotlight last year and she wasn't eager to experience that again, thank you very much. "Here's an idea," she added, "for an extra two hundred dollars, you can serve it with a vial of insulin." Noah was always trying to make his store stand out, but sometimes he was doing a little too much, thought Glory.

"Did you know that there is no actual pumpkin in a pumpkin spice latte? Not one drop." And before Glory could even answer he chimed, "And do you know how much money Starbucks has made off that drink? Over a billion dollars! Yes, ma'am, I just need to calibrate my recipe a tiny bit."

Noah gestured for the barista at the counter to bring Glory another cappuccino, on the house. Before walking back to the kitchen he pointed at her and said, "I'm going to perfect this recipe. You watch." He disappeared behind a pair of swinging doors.

Glory had just returned from church and the monthly meeting of the Acadiana Red Hat Society. As was tradition, all members wore red to these meetings—a sign of solidarity and sisterhood. Today she wore wide-legged red pants with a coordinating blazer and a red hat. This particular red hat was purchased by Delphine, who lived in New York City. It featured a wide brim with an exaggerated rosette to one side. Glory nearly squealed when she had opened the bundle, packaged in a stunning black-and-white box and wrapped with the most perfect ribbon she'd ever seen. It was the kind of finery that Glory had always craved, but that only Delphine would spend actual money on.

Her clients had been streaming in at a steady pace, waiting for their turns at the table, because Glory only allowed one client at a time. They bought coffee, chatted with the barista, and when there was an opening, sat themselves at Glory's table, placing their money in an unsealed, unmarked envelope. Glory recorded their wagers in pencil in her book. Business was always strong during football playoffs. Glory worked year-round but made a good chunk of her earnings in January and February, when amateur betting and foolishness collided. She had also been busier than usual since everything went down a little over a year ago. Glory had become somewhat notorious in Lafayette after the murder of Amity Gay and her role in solving it. She had relished the attention at first, but now it made her itchy with discomfort. Word of mouth had brought a whole new slew of customers, and when you're working in the world of unsanctioned and illegal betting, publicity is generally not welcomed. But Glory had always been good at vetting her customers and those instincts had not faded.

That is why when a Black woman with caramel highlights and carefully layered hair walked toward Glory, she did a double take. She did not know this woman. Of this, she was certain, because she knew everybody who walked through those doors, but there was something about her that felt familiar. She wasn't Glory's age, but wasn't her daughter's age, either. Judging by the slight laxity of her jawline, Glory judged her to be somewhere in the middle. This woman could no longer rely on her youth to be naturally firm without trying, and though she had a few lines that feathered around her eyes and just a couple along her forehead, Glory knew that her still-pretty looks would be deteriorating at a rapid clip from here on out. Glory had been there herself, many years ago.

"Are you Glory Broussard?" asked the woman. Glory sized her up even further, now that she was close up. She wore a patterned blouse that was too busy for Glory's taste, jeans that were tight but looked good on her slender frame, and stiletto heels, which Glory noted was not a reasonable thing to wear on a Sunday before noon.

"I'm afraid not, miss. You must have me mistaken for someone else." There was something about the woman that Glory did not trust. She had more customers than she knew what to do with anyway, so she wasn't about to take any risks. Glory peered over her reading glasses and did some calculations on paper to signal she was not interested in any further conversation, not even the polite, Southern kind.

"Actually, I'm pretty sure you are. I saw your picture in the *Advertiser*," she fired back.

Glory pressed the lead of her pencil harder and scratched away in her notebook, as if the woman did not exist. This was another reason Glory had hated all the attention: it had shaken all the crazies loose from the trees. Old men showed up who wanted her to investigate the chattering voices that echoed in their balding heads. Throngs of women pleaded for her to investigate husbands who might be stepping out on them. There was a part of Glory that enjoyed listening to the sordid affairs of others, because the best kind of gossip is from the mouths of strangers. It satisfied her desire for drama, but because she didn't know the parties involved, it allowed her to claim she was minding her own business. But one thing Glory knew from personal experience is that if you think your husband is stepping out, he most definitely is. You don't need to spend hard-earned money to figure that out. She gave these women the same advice: *Don't go throwing good money at bad men*. And besides, Glory Beverly Broussard was not for hire.

"I'm real sorry to bother you, ma'am," insisted the woman with the pretty face. "But my husband has gone missing and I thought you'd like to know."

That was it. Glory snapped. "Let me tell you something. I've done had it with you people showing up here with all this nonsense. What I do know is that I can't help you, and I definitely don't know who your husband is, so please leave me to my business. And support a Black-owned business on your way out. Ask for the Praline Perfection. It's a special, off-the-menu item." She shifted her focus back on her ledger as if it could save her. She had never formally studied math beyond basic algebra, but somehow had developed a pretty spot-on way of developing scenarios for a slate of games and estimating her earnings by the end of each weekend. Glory called it her special arithmetic while her daughter called an algorithm, which must have been one of those ten-cent words Delphine learned working at that law firm.

"I'm Valerie LeBlanc. My husband is Sterling Broussard."

Glory pressed down so hard on her pencil that the lead broke. The shattered lead lay on the paper. Graphite dust smudged her algorithm.

Valerie took a seat across from Glory. "Look, I know I'm the very last person you ever want to talk to, but I don't know what else to do." Her voice ached with weariness, and there was not enough concealer and tinted face powder in the world to camouflage her exhaustion. "Sterling went out to see some friends four days ago and I haven't seen or heard from him since. It's so unlike him."

Glory huffed. "I was married to the man for twenty years. Sounds exactly like the Sterling Broussard I know . . ."

"It's not the Sterling I know," the woman said, leaning her body halfway over the table as if it were a confrontation.

Noah's barista delivered the on-the-house cappuccino at this moment, allowing Glory a few moments to regroup. She took a sip, then delicately placed the small cup on its saucer. "Listen, I unsubscribed from all that Sterling drama years ago. I'm sorry you've gotten yourself tangled up, but you of all people knew what you were signing up for." She shoved her notebook into her cavernous purse and stood up.

Panic raced across the woman's face. "I thought maybe you'd want to look into it . . . for your daughter's sake."

Glory glared down at her. With fire pulsing through her veins, she said, "Don't you mention my daughter again. She is no one to you."

"Sterling wrote her a letter. I have no idea what it means, but I have a feeling she might. Here." She rummaged through the purse on her lap and pulled out a small square envelope. It looked like an invitation. Scrawled across it, and in handwriting she could recognize in an instant, was the name *Delphine Broussard*. The woman thrust it in her direction, like bait. Glory could not resist taking it. She unfolded the paper. With each word she read, her composure and her posture seemed to dissolve. By the time she was done, Glory was hunched over the table.

As much as she wanted to tell Valerie LeBlanc to disappear into the hole she had crawled out of, there was no denying the handwriting was his. She had recognized it immediately on account of her receiving his clientele as part of their unofficial, unmediated divorce settlement, in which she had received his gambling book and all the clients that came with it. The way they had worked it out, she had had two options: he'd pay her in installments, or she could have his book. Glory knew he was better at making money than keeping it, and that book was how he brought in cash. She figured if he could do it, then she could learn. She bet on herself, literally and figuratively, and it had paid off. Maybe not enough to buy designer hats from Madison Avenue, but enough.

"Where did you get this?" said Glory, shaking the pink, lined paper toward her face.

"When he went missing, I went through all his papers and found it on his desk. It was in an envelope with a stamp on it. I guess it was something he was gonna send, but he never got around to it . . ."

Glory stared out the coffeehouse window. Valerie watched expectantly, as if she sensed Glory was on the precipice of deciding and didn't want to say the wrong thing. Finally, Glory stood up. "Listen, I've known Sterling a lot longer than you. I'm sure he's out cavorting or getting into some mess. One day you'll grow tired of it, and for your sake, I hope that day is sooner rather than later. But there ain't nothing I can do to help you."

She walked out the door, cupping the note in her palm.

The last thing she wanted to be doing on a Sunday was driving. It was after noon now, with a bunch of football games about to start. By now half of Louisiana would have their meat on the grill and two to three beers in them. Some of them would be hitting the road to pick up something for their potato salad or wings, or another case of beer to replace the one that had already been consumed. Glory should have been at home.

But because of That Woman, and the disturbance she insisted on dragging through Glory's door, she was now on I-10, heading west to Jennings—and she would give Sterling a piece of her mind when she got there. Extracting herself from that man had been hard enough. He didn't deserve to trample on her hard-earned peace with his shenanigans.

And Glory was certain that whatever he was up to, it was definitely she-nanigans. She had seen it happen enough during their marriage. He'd have a "gig," even though he hadn't managed to make his trombone sound serviceable in years, and disappear for a few frantic days at a time. Then one day he'd stagger home, reeking of cheap scotch. Or one of the many times he owed his clients money and had "gone fishing" with his buddy Maurice, only to have angry folks expecting a payday to show up pounding on their door. In fact, it was the sloppy way he ran his business that inspired Glory's no-nonsense professionalism. It had all gotten to be too much. She had gathered him up and dried him out too many times to remember.

Valerie must not have known that he had something of a crash pad in Jennings, which didn't surprise Glory, because Sterling was full of secrets. But Glory knew about the place through the divorce. The house she lived in wasn't in dispute, because it was paid in full and inherited from her mother in Glory's name only. Not that Sterling would have tried to lay claim. He seemed pretty determined back then to leave the house on Viator Drive to be with his new love, if that's what you'd call her. But Glory knew that he had invested a tiny bit of his money in a two-unit duplex in Jennings. He rented out both for a while, until he realized he could just rent one unit and keep the other apartment for himself, his friends, and lord knows what else. Glory was glad to let him have it, uncontested. She had no desire to be a landlord and chase down rent.

On the drive she tried her daughter on her phone for what must have been the tenth time, but got no answer. It was possible that she was transported down that nondescript corridor of I-10, with little more to it than competing Cracker Barrels and Waffle Houses, by pure anger and annoyance. Anger because against all good sense, she was being dragged into Sterling's funny business again. Annoyance because of that letter. She wasn't fully convinced that it was real. But if it was, it meant that Delphine and her father were in cahoots about something, and Delphine should know better by now.

Furthermore, it was clear that Glory had been specifically excluded, which was unacceptable. Not because she cared about whatever it was Sterling did with his time, but because she cared deeply about her daughter. If only she'd answer that damn phone.

The house itself was gray, dull, and lifeless, matching the sky above it. Glory parked her car along the curb and surveyed the duplex. It was never fancy, but at least it had been tidy. That wasn't the case anymore. Wind whipped a Whataburger bag around a tree, which stopped its graceful tumble on a lawn that was patchy and bald. She made her way through the double carport on the broken side of the house, in which no cars were parked, and noticed the side house door and shattered glass. Flies buzzed around trash cans that hadn't been emptied for days, judging by their sour smell.

Unsure what to do, she peered through the broken glass. She spotted a retro kitchen table with a Formica tabletop, its edges wrapped in chrome, like the kind found in diners. Its matching chairs were tossed to the ground.

For a brief second she contemplated calling the police, and under normal circumstances she would have. Except she couldn't escape the nagging feeling that Delphine might be implicated in this somehow, and without knowing the specifics, she wasn't about to go calling on the law unless she had no other choice.

"Sterling?" she called out quietly, at first, and then louder and clearer. If he was in that house, there was no way he would have slept through that. From her purse she pulled out a stun gun. Delphine had laughed at her when she bought it at Lafayette Shooters. She had explained to Glory that a stun gun only works at close range and that she couldn't envision her mother in hand-to-hand combat. Glory bought it anyway, not feeling quite ready for a gun, but wanting just a little something.

Glory entered the unlocked house, stun gun at the ready. The first thing she noticed was the odor. Upon entering she immediately stuck her head back out the side door and gagged. Her eyes teared at the stench. She gasped for fresh air and when she gained her composure, she covered her nose with a scarf she found in her purse. She told herself she'd do one quick tour of the house and then get the hell out of there.

But there was no need to tour the house. When she stepped into the kitchen, Sterling was right there. A black handled knife pierced his chest and a hook with feathers had snagged his eyelid. Blood smeared the floor. Maggots infested his lifeless body.

Glory froze. The only physical reaction she could manage was to clamp her thick hand down on the stun gun. It snapped and threw white sparks from its metallic teeth.